Praise for *Hemlock Lane*

"Marshall Fine's *Hemlock Lane* is a poignant, exquisitely drawn family drama told in Rashomon style. Nora's journey had me reflecting on my own perspective regarding my family's dynamics, and each new chapter served as a reminder of the subjectivity of truth. Bravo."

—Terence Winter, creator and executive producer, *Boardwalk Empire*

"Wonderful storytelling, human and incisively written. A truly suspenseful novel in which the reader is kept guessing whether a young woman will escape the yoke of a narcissistic, willful mother. Searing and utterly truthful. Marshall Fine's fine new novel of a fractured family has an unlikely heroine you will never forget."

—Robert Klein, author of *The Amorous Busboy of Decatur Avenue*

"Rich and compelling—this beautifully written novel took me on a journey of twists and turns through a family story that continually reveals new secrets, even as it is breaking your heart."

—Patricia Clarkson, Emmy and Golden Globe Award winner

"The novel is a time machine. Marshall Fine's prismatic fiction makes you feel as if you're right in the middle of these characters' lives, witnessing a tumultuous period of history."

—Matt Zoller Seitz, author of *The Sopranos Sessions* and *Mad Men Carousel: The Complete Critical Companion*

Praise for *The Autumn of Ruth Winters*

"Readers will enjoy cheering for Fine's late bloomer."

—*Publishers Weekly*

"This is a feel-good novel that should appeal to fans of Phaedra Patrick, Jojo Moyes, and Kirsten Miller. Utterly charming. Recommended."

—*Library Journal*

"A late-in-life coming-of-age tale, proving that reconnection and reconciliation don't have an age limit. Fans of Hazel Prior's *How the Penguins Saved Veronica* and Lee Smith's *Silver Alert* will find lots to like in Fine's heartwarming novel about unexpected connections at unexpected times."

—*Booklist*

"An utterly beautiful tale of familial love that cannot be extinguished through conflict and anger and the rewards of stepping out of one's comfort zone at any stage of life."

—Kyra Davis, *New York Times* bestselling author of *Just One Night*

"If it is possible to write a bildungsroman about a woman in her sixties, Marshall Fine has done it. Fine takes his reserved heroine, Ruth Winters, on a journey through buried resentments, stifled grief, and petty slights until she finally accepts the love and compassion that was within her all along. She blossomed on the page like Austen's Elinor Dashwood right before my eyes. Marshall Fine has created a beautiful and moving character, that if we open our hearts, we will see Ruth Winters everywhere."

—Griffin Dunne, author of *The Friday Afternoon Club*

"A delightfully shrewd and entertaining novel with an aging, quirky heroine who reminds us that some of life's most profound turns can be at the end of the roller coaster. I fell in love with Ruth Winters and think you will too."

—Julia Heaberlin, internationally bestselling author of *Night Will Find You*

"The moving story of a lonely, ordinary woman told with compassion, wit, and an incredible wealth of very human detail. Time, memory, family, and second chances, it deals with it all. I was rooting for Ruth Winters all the way to the end. Highly recommended."

—Paul Giamatti

"As a longtime film critic, Marshall Fine often showed a kinship for the gonzo wallop of Tarantino, Scorsese, and Bloody Sam Peckinpah. So Fine fans may be shocked that his funny, touching, and vital first novel, *The Autumn of Ruth Winters*, features a retired widow in her seventies going it alone in suburban Minnesota. Look deeper and Ruth and her creator, both from Minneapolis, prove a natural fit. Ruth has a gunslinger's mentality when it comes to keeping the world at bay, plus a sharp tongue for those who try her patience, and that includes Marvel movies and a call from her estranged sister. It's a family crisis that gives Ruth a second shot at life and even romance. Don't worry how Fine manages to persuasively enter the head and heart of a woman who's discovering her real self for the first time. Just let this book work its magic. It's an exuberant gift."

—Peter Travers, *ABC News* and *Good Morning America*

"In *The Autumn of Ruth Winters*, Marshall Fine unspools the complex threads of familial relationships and weaves them back into an affecting tapestry of life's biggest and smallest moments."

—Rob Burnett, writer-director, *The Fundamentals of Caring*

"What really hides behind the forced smiles of 'Minnesota nice'? Longtime critic Marshall Fine pushes past middle-aged, Midwestern politeness to reveal some surprising drama in *The Autumn of Ruth Winters*. Yet, filled as it is with sibling rivalries, bad marriages, and secret scandals, ultimately this is a novel about forgiveness, uncovering not only disappointments but opportunities—once missed, now reclaimed."

—Stephen Whitty, author of *The Alfred Hitchcock Encyclopedia*

"Only a really great writer can take a story about a somewhat difficult woman and make you care and keep reading till the end. But then, *The Autumn of Ruth Winters* is an absorbing novel for anyone who believes in love, in living life without comparison, and in the idea that, as George Eliot said, 'It's never too late to be what you might have been.'"

—Georgette Gouveia, author of The Games Men Play series

HEMLOCK LANE

ALSO BY MARSHALL FINE

The Autumn of Ruth Winters

HEMLOCK LANE

A Novel

MARSHALL FINE

This is a work of fiction. Names, characters, organizations, places, events, and incidents are either products of the author's imagination or are used fictitiously. Otherwise, any resemblance to actual persons, living or dead, is purely coincidental.

Published by Lake Union Publishing, Seattle
www.apub.com

EU product safety contact:
Amazon Media EU S. à r.l.
38, avenue John F. Kennedy, L-1855 Luxembourg
amazonpublishing-gpsr@amazon.com

ISBN-13: 9781662530487 (paperback)
ISBN-13: 9781662530494 (digital)

Cover design by Kimberly Glyder
Cover image: © Mark John, © Igor Ustynskyy / Getty; © YANUSHEVSKAYA VICTORI / Shutterstock

Quotation from the Allen Ginsberg poem "Mescaline" by written permission of the Allen Ginsberg Estate.

Printed in the United States of America

For my family

THURSDAY

Do the thing you fear most, and the death of fear is certain.
—Mark Twain

NORA

Nora Levitsky pulled off New York State Highway 17 into the parking lot of a diner in Roscoe, New York. From here it was only about one hundred miles south to the Tappan Zee Bridge in Tarrytown, less than two hours to her parents' house in the hills north of its eastern end.

No point in arriving any earlier than necessary, she thought. *I'd like to be able to breathe easy for a while longer.*

Plus, it *was* lunchtime, and she'd skipped breakfast to get an early start from Syracuse.

She parked her 1959 Ford Country Squire station wagon, formerly her father's work car, in the diner's half-full parking lot and went inside, where the hostess seated her in a booth. When the elderly waitress shuffled over with a menu, Nora said, "That's OK—can I just have a grilled cheese sandwich and a large Coke with ice? Thanks."

The waitress, whose name tag said **Sal**, blinked a couple of times behind oversize bifocals, then said, "Want french fries?"

"Absolutely. And some ketchup, please."

When she'd gone, Nora reached for her purse and dug out the note from Stephen. She'd found it in there at the gas station a few miles back, when she fished for her wallet to pay for gasoline.

The note provoked the same giddiness in her now that it did the first time she read it at the gas pump. Stephen's hand-scrawled message was playful and affectionate, talking about their future and joking about finishing law school "so I can become a public defender and start representing people who have no hope of paying me."

That first time she'd read it, Nora felt tears on her cheeks and, after noticing the woman at the next gas pump looking at her, brushed them away with a chagrined smile.

Their future. Together.

Right there, at that moment in June 1967, Nora Levitsky—who'd once vowed she would never, *ever* get married—realized she was thinking about sharing a future with a husband.

Nothing was set. They'd barely discussed the subject beyond the fact that both had confessed to not being repelled by the idea. For Nora, that in itself was a big step.

Nora had been conscious, from a young age, of the inherent unfairness in the larger world, vis-à-vis boys and girls and, when she got older, men and women. She was about to focus her entire career on that exact question. And yet here she was, thinking seriously about marrying Stephen Cantor, soon to be Stephen Cantor, Esq.

This, however, would not be a topic of conversation during the coming weekend at her parents' house. The trip home from Syracuse was meant to be a stealth mission to check on her father, without giving away any of her own imminent plans.

As slow as the waitress's pace was when she shuffled from the kitchen to Nora's booth with her order, Nora was still impressed by how fast the food arrived. She took a bite of the sandwich. The bread was perfectly toasted and buttery, the sandwich's center lush with the melted American cheese, which arrived in an optimal molten state: hot, but not so hot as to blister the roof of her mouth.

The sandwich was why she stopped at this diner, something she'd tried to do once on each round trip between Syracuse and Tarrytown.

She peeled a straw and inserted it in the fountain Coke. The first sip carried exactly the icy crackle of palate-cleansing crispness she craved. She wished she could share this place with Stephen: *He'd love their fries,* she thought, deciding he'd also be amused by this waitress.

Then she considered the possibility of introducing Stephen to her parents.

This was a nonstarter, a bad idea that made her lungs tighten with the earliest stirrings of asthma.

So why had she agreed when he suggested meeting them this weekend? Perhaps because he had been so sincere that it disarmed her.

When Stephen realized he would be in New York the same weekend she would be at her parents', he said, "I could come up to Tarrytown on Friday night. Would that work? It would mean so much to me to meet your folks. You make your mother sound so intimidating. I don't know what I'd do if she didn't like me."

"Well of course she'll like you," she'd lied.

Nora couldn't think of a plausible reason to say no. Now she needed to find an excuse to keep this meeting from occurring. Nora loved Stephen and thought he was almost too good to be true. Yet she knew that, to her mother, Stephen would never be good enough.

Full stop.

Nora didn't care what her mother thought. She never had. Her mother's opinion of Stephen would have no bearing on Nora's future with him, a fact she knew would set off fireworks when her mother figured it out. Nora wanted to avoid that confrontation this trip.

~

Nora had had the same boyfriend all the way through high school with her mother's tacit approval. His name was Charlie, and she dated him mostly for convenience's sake; they broke up after high school, when they went to different colleges. When she got to Syracuse for her undergraduate studies, she rose to become social chair of her sorority and dated regularly. But she never dated anyone steadily, because her focus was squarely on her studies.

Boys in her college classes would ask her out, and she would sometimes agree to go to a movie and for a beer after. But Nora had a cheerful diffidence that said "Yes, I'm here laughing at your jokes and drinking a beer. But, mentally, I'm a thousand miles away." She rarely had more than two or three dates with any would-be suitor before her obvious lack of interest caused them to give up pursuit.

In graduate school, she had different men in her program hovering—always—but remained goal oriented through those busy two and a half years. There was no one who made her think about getting serious about a relationship until she met Stephen Cantor during her final semester of graduate school.

They took the same literature class, Three Novels of Jane Austen, to satisfy elective requirements they'd both left for last. He wasn't the only man in the class—but he was the only one who had read Austen's work previously, without being required to do so. Nor was he the only man in the class to ask Nora for a date—but he was the only one to whom she said yes.

In part, it was because he invited her to a campus film society screening of the 1940 *Pride and Prejudice* with Greer Garson and Laurence Olivier, an attractively nerdy choice that happened to align with their classwork. In part, she did it because he seemed interesting when he talked in class. And in part, she realized, it was because he was good looking.

After the movie, they walked to a nearby café, where they both ordered pie. They sat there into the wee hours, through many coffee refills, until the place closed for the night, talking about the careers they saw for themselves.

Nora told Stephen that her goal was to quantify her long-running sense of gender disenfranchisement of women and use those figures to help women advance. Specifically, her doctoral thesis was inspired by Betty Friedan's *The Feminine Mystique*, connecting various economic and legal burdens women faced in everyday life to roles for women portrayed in popular media.

Nora effortlessly reeled off statistics, gaining speed and passion as she went: about the pay disparity between men and women, as well as the number of women at various levels of the workforce versus the number of female characters on TV shows or commercials shown doing a job more complicated than cashier or secretary. Once she got started on the topic, it was hard to stop her. The numbers seemed to roll out in an excited tumble.

When Nora paused to take a breath, Stephen smiled and said, "Your eyes got kind of fiery there for a moment."

She could tell he wasn't flirting, at least not consciously. As he spoke, his sincerity melted her. It always would; there was an essential decency to him that shone through, drawing her to him. Nora was thankful that he seemed incapable of recognizing that he could use this charm as a power over her. He was too sincere for that.

He went on: "It took me a while to find the thing that made me burn in that same way."

He told her that his father was the first in his immigrant family to finish college. He went on to law school, then built a practice in Chicago as an entertainment lawyer who worked within the arena of Chicago nightclubs and record labels of the 1940s, the 1950s, and now the 1960s, representing everyone from individual blues artists to record companies to the entire stagehands' union (as well as a few organized crime figures). He wanted Stephen to join his practice and, when the time came, take it over.

For the first two years of law school, he told her, that was what he thought he'd do. Then a high school friend asked him to help out for a couple of weeks at a free legal clinic on Chicago's South Side, one of its most blighted neighborhoods, while he was home the August before his third year. Dropped into the deep end, he found he was able to help one family avoid an eviction, then was unsuccessful in doing anything for a man who the police had beaten after an arrest for public drunkenness. In those few short days, he had an epiphany about the two-tiered nature of justice in a city he thought he knew. That forced him to reconsider his future.

"It helped me find a purpose—that's why I'm going to be a public defender," Stephen had told her, just before the waitress came to tell them the café was closing for the night.

~

As Nora got up to pay her bill at the Roscoe Diner, she knew that at that moment, Stephen was flying to Manhattan to attend a family wedding on Saturday. He'd suggested coming up to her parents' house for Friday dinner. In a moment of weakness, Nora said yes, figuring she would cancel later. And now it was later.

While her mother desperately wanted her to be married, she also wanted to dictate the terms, including selecting the perfect future professional to tame and domesticate her willful daughter. Even the hint that Nora was considering a future with an unknown young man would be enough to set her mother off.

The previous year, Nora had spent the summer living at home while doing field research toward her PhD at a marketing firm in Manhattan. Her mother began trying to arrange dates for her with several newly minted physicians, all of whom were either the son or nephew of someone in her mother's social circle.

Her mother's list of prospects was long; she even showed it to the horrified Nora. But after the first fix-up—a handsy dermatology resident from Yonkers—Nora put her foot down and told her mother, "Enough." When her mother mentioned that "my friend Betsy's son, Lewis, who is already a successful internist, is looking for a tennis partner this weekend," Nora responded by disappearing from the house.

"Gone to Gina's" read the note she'd left on the dining room table at the place where she normally sat at dinner. Gina Briganti was her childhood friend, a would-be actress working as a proofreader and living in Manhattan. Gina had a fourth-floor walk-up in the West Seventies, a short stroll from the American Museum of Natural History subway stop on Central Park West, and was happy to let Nora sleep on her couch.

The next day, the receptionist at the marketing firm where she was doing research tracked Nora down to the cubbyhole she'd been assigned, which had no telephone. Telephones were reserved for actual employees.

"You have a call," she said to Nora, looking annoyed. "You can take it in the conference room."

The receptionist was secretly known to the staff as Big Edna. A steely matron with a lacquered beehive, she peered at Nora over the top of the half glasses perched at the end of her nose. "Don't make a habit of this. I'm not your maid."

"No, ma'am," Nora said, scuttling around Big Edna and down the hall to the conference room. A cream-colored phone with multiple clear plastic buttons sat on one end of the table. Nora picked up the receiver and heard nothing, then pushed the blinking button on the phone and heard something.

"Hello?" she said.

"Nora?" It was her mother. "Nora? Where are you?"

"I'm at work, Mother—which you must already know because you dialed me here."

"I'll thank you not to get smart with me, young lady," her mother said sharply. "We were worried about you. Why did you go to Gina's?"

"Because you won't stop fixing me up on dates with men I'm not interested in." She paused to calm her respiration when she felt a familiar breathiness that was a precursor to tightening in her chest.

"What do you mean? That Daniel was very nice—"

"He was a drip."

"—and he's on track to be chief dermatology resident at Mount Sinai, his mother says. You should give him another chance."

"Mother, he spent the entire evening talking about how *Gunsmoke* hasn't been the same since Dennis Weaver stopped playing Chester."

"Your father loves *Gunsmoke*."

"Well, I don't. Plus, it's been three years since Dennis Weaver left that show."

"What is your point?"

"I don't have time for dating. I'm doing my doctoral research."

"Is it even safe where Gina is? Doesn't she live in Spanish Harlem?"

"It's not that bad. Sleeping here shortens my commute in the morning."

"You never discussed this with your father and me."

"There's nothing to discuss, Mother. This is my last summer before I finish grad school. I'm not going to spend it dating the synagogue sisterhood's Dork of the Week."

"What will you do for clothes?"

"I have enough for a few days, and Gina's about my size. I can borrow from her. Plus I brought my bathing suit to wear to the laundromat if I need to wash anything."

"Nora Jane!"

Nora sighed. There were slabs of marble with more whimsy than her mother.

"Sorry, Mother, but my mind is made up," she'd said and stayed away for the rest of the week. The blind dates ceased.

~

That was last summer. Now here was Nora, heading home for a mid-June weekend: *My last weekend there ever.* She chuckled at her own grandiosity. Yet that fact was becoming increasingly real to her.

"Today is the first day of the rest of your life." Wasn't that what the poster in the campus bookstore had said? Granted, that statement could be applied to every single day, ever—even your last one. But Nora was feeling the truism's power on this particular weekend.

She had her PhD and her future, both firmly in hand.

Her doctorate in the emerging discipline of marketing had earned her a teaching position that started in the fall.

A teaching position at Northwestern University near Chicago.

Where she would live.

And perhaps even get married.

Welcome to the future. Step right this way.

Was it wrong of her to avoid revealing any of this to her parents? She knew that every facet of her announcement—no matter how much or how little of it she decided to share with her mother—would land explosively. It felt like a premeditated emotional hit-and-run. The question was: Who would be the victim?

Encounters of this kind, involving what was sure to be her mother's vocal displeasure and disapproval, never bothered Nora emotionally, or so she believed. Yet they always provoked Nora's asthma. It might be one of her mother's belittling remarks or, more likely, one of the arguments her mother regularly picked by casually denying a reasonable request for no real reason.

"But I'm going to Gina's to do homework!"

"No, I think I need you here."

"Why?"

"To set the table for Clara."

"I can do it when I get home. It only takes five minutes."

"I'm sorry, I just don't think so. You can do homework here."

"Fine. I'll call Gina, and she can come over here."

"Now, I can't have all that disturbance in the house today. I just can't."

"But we're only doing homework!"

By the end of these arguments, Nora would find herself struggling for breath, though she masked this as much as possible. She had an intuition that her mother would use any sign of weakness, such as a diagnosis of stress-related asthma, as leverage against her. The last thing she wanted was her mother saying "Now, Nora, is your health worth a risk like that?" Because the answer to that question would always be no.

In her research about asthma at the local library, she found that treatments were limited. But she read about athletes with asthma who worked to increase their lung capacity by regularly swimming laps. She got her father to take a membership at the Tarrytown Y and became a habitué of its pool, building her lung capacity swimming laps. She'd also found a yoga book about how to control her breathing and learned to steadily relax her way through stressful moments that caused shortness of breath.

But it wasn't her own health she was worried about on this trip; it was her father's. Nora thought back to the previous year, when she'd been home for the naming ceremony for her sister's baby, Judy. In an offhand moment, Nora had watched her father reach down to pick up his grandson David. She looked away for a moment to respond to something her sister, Amelia, had said, and when she turned back, her father was bent over at the waist, gray faced and sweating, working to catch his breath while David sat on the ground crying in front of him.

"Daddy, are you OK?"

"I'm fine—just had to stop for a second to catch my breath. That boy's getting heavy."

Her father resisted any further fussing, wiping his face with a handkerchief and going back to the festivities. Later, Nora asked Clara, who had been the family's live-in housekeeper for Nora's entire life, "Is my dad OK? He seemed shaky this afternoon."

"I heard your mother say the doctor mentioned high blood pressure," Clara replied. "But you know how he is with things like that."

Nora knew. Her father always presented himself as the picture of health, no matter how he felt. Any indication otherwise sent her mother into a dither of anxiety, convinced that he could drop dead any minute, forcing her and the children into the poorhouse.

Now Nora was on her way home, summoned by a call from her father: "I need to see you this weekend," he said. "There's something I need to talk to you about." But he would say no more.

Nora, however, had secrets of her own: the job in Chicago and her imminent move there. And, of course, Stephen.

Even if this was not the weekend that her parents would learn of Stephen's existence and importance in her life, that day would come. When it did, she knew that through no fault of his own, Stephen would arrive with two strikes against him because, for her mother, it was a question of control.

First, her mother had never met Stephen. *How could Nora be considering a future with someone who was a complete stranger to her family?* Strike one.

More to the point, her mother had not had a voice in choosing Stephen. His pedigree was outside her sphere of influence—and her geographical frame of reference. *He was an unvetted stranger from who knows where.* Strike two.

Then there was Stephen's chosen career path. A lawyer, yes—but he was joining the Cook County public defender's office. He'd be doing intake work until he passed the Illinois bar, when he would start defending cases in court. He would be making an annual salary and not a big one, hardly the sort of breadwinner Nora's mother had in mind for her: someone with a Park Avenue practice and a house in Scarsdale.

She knew her parents assumed she'd move back and start her career closer to home. Even if she was living and working in Manhattan, she would be within easy distance for regular dinners at home and family gatherings for birthdays and holidays. They would, at a minimum, be disappointed about her decision to move to Chicago.

She would start her career at Northwestern's Medill School of Journalism, teaching in its nascent marketing program. She would also be leading a major research project, for which she'd received a sizable Ford Foundation grant just the week before.

When she had begun grad school at Syracuse, she made a passionate case for bypassing the master's degree program and creating her own doctoral curriculum. She had identified numerous ways the emerging science behind marketing helped to perpetuate stereotypes of women. Nora intended to provide a course correction, if not an entirely new message. She sought to shift the direction that marketing was heading by calling attention to the old images, in order to find a new paradigm that empowered and liberated women.

"It's your funeral," her doctoral thesis adviser told her when she described what she hoped to do. But by the start of Nora's second year of grad school, she had made a believer of the sour old gentleman, who warmed to Nora's persistent logic and intelligence. He'd pointed her toward an old colleague at Northwestern, then acted as her cheerleader until she landed the prestigious post.

~

As she drove toward Tarrytown, Nora took the entrance ramp to the New York Thruway near Monroe, New York, a straight shot of freeway through to the Tappan Zee. As she drove, she considered the most immediate bombshell she was withholding from her parents.

Move to Chicago? Her mother had been unhappy when Nora told her she was only going as far as Syracuse for college.

"Why so far away?" her mother complained. "We'll never see you."

That's the point, Nora thought.

After high school, she wanted a college experience that had freedom as its baseline. If her mother had her way, Nora would enroll at Sarah Lawrence in Bronxville or Vassar in Poughkeepsie, close enough to commute to college and live at home in North Tarrytown. Syracuse represented Nora's escape hatch.

Would she have been interested in teaching at Northwestern if she hadn't met Stephen? She had an offer to join the faculty at Syracuse and another to teach at NYU. There was also an offer to become a vice president at the Manhattan firm where she'd done some of her doctoral work. But the Medill School was giving her an opportunity to do research no one else had explored. Her project would have national scope. With luck, so would its impact.

If she moved back to New York, even if she lived and worked in Manhattan, she would be within too-easy reach of her mother. Nora wanted that factor excised from the equation of her life, the way it had been while she lived in Syracuse. Falling in love with Stephen made her happy—and moving to Chicago would remove her from her mother's daily orbit once and for all.

~

It was about 3:30 when Nora pulled into the driveway of her parents' two-story Tudor house on Hemlock Lane. The street snaked through a secluded suburban neighborhood called Sleepy Hollow Manor, a couple of miles north of hilly central Tarrytown. *Hemlock Lane—home of my poisonous mother,* Nora joked to herself. It had been her private jest since the day as a preteen when she'd come across the word *hemlock* while reading and looked it up.

The garage door was up, and her mother's cream-colored Pontiac Brougham sat there, next to the empty space where her father's equally massive Cadillac was usually parked.

Nora retrieved her small suitcase from the trunk of her car and walked in through the garage. The garage's interior door opened to a small vestibule, with coat hooks and a bench on one wall for boot and shoe removal. There was a door into the kitchen next to a staircase to the rooms above the garage.

Nora stuck her head in the kitchen, which was sunlit but deserted. She walked far enough into the house to determine that her mother was probably upstairs somewhere. *No point in stirring up a hornet's nest any earlier than I have to,* she thought, listening at the stairs and hearing no movement.

She left her suitcase at the foot of the stairs, then went back through the kitchen and up the stairs in the back vestibule, which led to what her mother once grandly referred to as "the servants' quarters" or, occasionally, "the carriage house."

To Nora, it was just Clara's room—that's how she thought of it now and forever. And that's where Nora found the family housekeeper, taking a break before returning to the kitchen to start the dinner she would cook, serve, and clean up.

"Knock, knock," Nora said as she stepped into the small living room. Clara, who was reading a magazine in an easy chair with a gooseneck lamp next to it, smiled and rose to hug her.

Clara had looked like a giant to Nora when she was a girl. But now, as they hugged, she noticed that the knotty woman had somehow become shorter than she was, though not by much. As wiry as Clara was, she still felt solid. There had never been much meat on her, but she still hugged with strength.

Nora also noticed Clara had a few more wrinkles and more gray hair. Nora had always thought of her as old because Clara had been an adult for Nora's entire life. Still, to Nora, Clara seemed youthful next to Nora's parents.

Their embrace warmed Nora in its accustomed, welcome way. But when it ended, Clara took her by both shoulders, held her at arm's length, and scrutinized her for a second. Then she cocked one eyebrow and said, "OK—what's the real story here?"

"I was hoping you could tell me," Nora said. "Is something going on with Daddy? He insisted I come down, but he wouldn't tell me why."

"Sorry, I don't know squat. I think he's had a few meetings with lawyers lately. I assume that's about selling the business. I guess there's been some kind of holdup, but he didn't say specifically."

"Is Mother feeling all right?"

"You know your mother. She's not happy unless she's complaining."

Clara walked to the door of her room, opened it, and looked down the stairs. Then she came back and said, "You heard from the Ford Foundation?"

Nora raised her eyebrows and gave Clara a smile. "I got it," she said. Clara started to let out a whoop, but Nora put a finger to her lips. "Shhh."

Clara made the motion of locking her lips with a key and throwing the key away, but lock or no, her smile was almost too big for her face.

"Oh, honey, I'm so proud of you."

They hugged again briefly, as though not wanting to be discovered.

"You're the only one who understands what this means," Nora said.

"That's because I've known you since you were born," Clara said. "You've always been my special girl."

Nora drew comfort from the thought. Clara had been her confidante for her whole life. Long before her father called summoning her for this weekend, she had told Clara of her news about Chicago and about Stephen. When she heard that Nora planned to wait until she was ready to move to Chicago before she told her parents, she tried to talk her out of it—"At least tell your father"—but when Nora proved unmovable on the idea, Clara had agreed to do whatever Nora needed for her to succeed.

But before she could bring Clara up to speed, there was a knock on Clara's door.

"Yes?" Clara said.

The door opened, and Nora's mother walked in.

"Here you are," she said to Nora, giving her a brief hug. "I saw that awful car of yours in the driveway, but then I couldn't find you anywhere. Of course, you're hiding from me up here."

"I wasn't hiding, Mother. I didn't see you when I came in, and then I found Clara up here."

"I was in my sewing room," her mother said. "To what do we owe the pleasure of this visit?"

"I told Daddy I was coming down to bring some stuff from my apartment. Didn't he tell you?" It was the untruth she and her father had settled on.

"I don't know why you're still living up there. You've finished your degree. When are you going to move back? Your father said you were looking for work in the city."

"My lease runs to the end of June. I'm wrapping up a few things before I move out."

Her mother gave her the kind of hard look that would send Nora's older sister, Amelia, spinning into a whirlwind of self-doubt. But her mother's disapproval had never been an effective goad for Nora.

Her mother shifted her gaze to Clara and said, "We'll eat at six, instead of six thirty, because I have mah-jongg at Reva's house tonight." Turning back to Nora, she said, "Your father wants to know if you want to go to the Mets game tomorrow evening."

Perfect, Nora thought. It gave her the excuse she needed to put Stephen off. She smiled as she said, "That sounds like fun, even if the Mets are playing like shit."

The look on her mother's face could have cracked an anvil. While Nora had cursed liberally from a young age, she tried to avoid doing so in front of her mother.

"I'll thank you to watch your language," her mother said. "As much as you're trying to disguise it with those dungarees, you're still a young woman. Please try to act like it."

She turned on her heel and walked out of the room. When they heard her footsteps recede down the stairs, Nora and Clara shared conspiratorial smiles.

Clara had always been the voice of reason in Nora's life. She turned to Clara for counsel, for succor, for love, for encouragement, and for hard truths. Clara had pushed her to excel, had taught her to see the bigger picture and aim higher. Clara was the reason Nora was a confident, poised young woman with a tantalizing future laid out before her. All she had to do was escape from her mother in North Tarrytown.

"You shouldn't provoke her like that," Clara said. "You know how she is about those things."

"Honestly, it just slipped out," Nora said. "We're a lot looser with that language at school." She thought a moment, then said, "Although I can't say I've ever heard my mother fart."

"Oh, I have," Clara said with a straight face—and her lack of further explanation drew a surprised laugh from Nora.

~

That night at dinner, Nora's father started the meal by recounting a story about the funeral he'd been to that afternoon, a service he had attended with his partner, Stan Schwartz, for the owner of a large copper-pipe factory. Apparently, an act of kindness that Stan had done some years earlier for the dead man's family resulted in the news from the son of the deceased that their company would be getting a lucrative scrap-hauling contract.

Stan—Uncle Stan to Nora—was her father's longtime best friend and business partner at the scrap-metal yard they owned. He was also literally her uncle, because he was married to her father's sister, Aunt Delia.

"It goes to show that being a mensch pays off in the long run, if you treat people the way you'd want them to treat you," her father said. Nora knew her father and uncle were in the midst of selling their business, a deal Nora only had the haziest awareness of. She wondered why landing new business would matter at this point, when her father was supposed to be on the verge of retiring.

"I'm glad your brother-in-law's glad-handing does some good every so often," her mother said.

"He's your brother-in-law too—and that 'glad-handing,' as you call it, built our business and helped create this life of ours. We wouldn't be where we are today without Stan."

"You've always sold yourself short," her mother said.

Nora winced at the unexpected assessment and could see her father slump a little. Hoping to shift the conversation's trajectory, she said, "You mentioned Wheeler Copper. Are you talking about Andy Wheeler?"

"Andrew, yes," her father said, his dark cloud dissipating.

"He's my age," she said. "I knew him a little in high school. Aren't they from Hartsdale?"

"Yes—but he looks older than you. Maybe because he's lost his hair."

"He's your age?" her mother said. "And look at that—*he's* already running a company."

"Because his father just died," Nora said. "I don't think he's celebrating his promotion this week."

"I'm just saying—he has a direction in life," her mother sniffed.

"I just finished a PhD in under three years," Nora said. "That feels pretty directed, if you ask me."

"In *marketing*," her mother said. "Somehow, it manages to sound nebulous and tawdry at the same time."

"You are such a snob, Mother." Nora could feel early stirrings in her lungs. She tried to calm her breathing.

"I have standards. For myself and for my children. Including you, young lady. At your age, your sister was already married, with a child."

"Yes, how embarrassing to have to tell the ladies in your mah-jongg group that your spinster daughter works in marketing. Oh, the *shame*. I should probably have become a streetwalker instead."

"Nora," her father said, his face reddening. Trying to change the subject, he said, "I think you said you have a job interview in the city tomorrow. Will you be back in time to go to the Mets game tomorrow night?"

"My meeting is at lunch, so I should be back early enough. What time do you want to leave for the stadium?"

"The game starts at seven thirty. So with traffic—"

They were interrupted by the three-note chime of the front doorbell. Clara appeared from the kitchen to answer the door.

"Who in the world would call at dinnertime uninvited?" Nora's mother said. She turned to Nora. "Are you expecting someone?"

"Not me," she said with a shrug.

After a moment, Clara reappeared.

"It's Charlie Grossman for Nora," Clara said, with a knowing look only Nora caught.

"Did you tell him we're eat—" her mother started to say.

But her father interrupted her, saying loudly, "Charlie, get in here, son." Then, turning to Nora, he said, "Why didn't you tell me you were seeing Charlie again?"

"Because I'm not," Nora said, trying to find the correct fixed smile for this encounter.

Then Charlie was upon them, all bluff bonhomie, the high school boyfriend her father had always liked and her mother had tolerated. The boyfriend she'd broken up with at the end of high school—more than six years ago.

"Hey, Levitsky family—how are you?" Charlie said. "Mrs. L., I swear you look even younger than the last time I saw you."

"Oh, please," her mother said, smiling as she blushed behind her napkin and looked down at her dinner.

Charlie went over to Nora's father to deliver a firm handshake. "Mr. Levitsky, how are you, sir?"

"Fine, Charlie. What have you been up to?"

"I just finished my second year at Rutgers Law. I'm working at my father's firm in White Plains this summer."

"Sounds exciting," Nora murmured, keeping any expression out of her voice.

"Oh, real exciting," Charlie said with a laugh, as though Nora had just fed him a straight line for a particularly funny joke. "If you call proofreading contracts for typos exciting."

He laughed again, and Nora's father joined him. Nora worked at not rolling her eyes.

"You'll make partner in no time," her father said.

"Well, I *am* on the nepotism track," Charlie said slyly, and the two men laughed again.

There was a momentary pause; then Nora's mother said, "You know, Charles, we were just eating dinner."

But Nora's father jumped past her: "Of course, where are my manners? Charlie, please pull up a chair and join us." Conspiratorially, he added, "You remember Clara's lamb chops."

At this, her mother did roll her eyes. But Charlie said, "Thank you, I can't. I'm meeting my parents at the country club for dinner in a little while—and it's prime-rib night! I just wanted to talk to Nora for a minute, if I could."

"What is it?" Nora said flatly, without moving from her seat at the dinner table.

"Could we talk outside? Just for a minute? Please?"

"I don't want my food to get cold."

"It will just take a minute—honestly," he said, and her father turned to Nora.

"Go ahead. I'll have Clara keep your plate warm."

Clara, who'd been watching the exchange, took Nora's plate to the kitchen. All her mother could think to say was "This *is* dinnertime."

"OK, I'll be right back," Nora said, rising and setting her napkin on her chair. But before she and Charlie could leave the room, her father stopped them.

"Wait a minute, Charlie—what are you doing tomorrow night?"

"Nothing I can think of," he said.

"Great. Why don't you come with us to the Mets game?"

"I'd love that—who are they playing?" Charlie said, throwing Nora a triumphant look that gave her a sinking feeling.

"Does it matter?" Nora said. "They'll get their a—they'll get their tails kicked, no matter who they play."

Ignoring her, her father said, "The Cubs. That Ferguson Jenkins is pitching."

"That sounds like fun," Charlie said.

"Good. Can you be here by five?"

"You bet. I'll have to get off work a little early, but I happen to know the boss." He and her father laughed at this as well.

"Now that that's settled," Nora said, "can we go talk so I can get back to my dinner, please?"

She led Charlie down the hall and out the door to the sunporch in the rear of the house. It was a short walk, but long enough for Nora to mentally catalog what Charlie might want. She had a good idea of where this conversation was headed.

~

Until she reached high school, Nora had avoided the hormonal infatuations that regularly seemed to afflict her best friend Gina and other girls in their circle from preteen days. While her friends flitted and flirted from crush to crush, Nora was clear-eyed about the boys in their grade. To her, they all seemed obsessed with either Elvis Presley, Mickey Mantle, Y. A. Tittle, or a new magazine she'd heard about but never seen, called *Playboy*.

Nora was an athletic girl, a competitor who worked past the limitations of asthma to excel at rough-and-tumble games like basketball, touch football, and baseball. She played baseball every day one summer in pickup games with the boys in her neighborhood in a local schoolyard. She could both hit and throw a fastball and was usually either a captain or among the first chosen when they picked sides for the day's contest. But when those same boys—many of whom weren't nearly as good as Nora—began to play for organized Little League teams, she was not allowed to join, because girls were not permitted.

Nora bristled at the limited opportunities for girls' sports. The rules for girls' basketball and field hockey emphasized courtesy over aggression, cooperation over competition. The other sports available, like tennis, golf, and track and field, interested her even less because she thought them too dainty.

The summer before ninth grade, Nora bloomed. A rangy beanpole who was a bit of a tomboy, she grew three inches and developed both breasts and hips—nothing as ample as her sister's, whose curves made her a boy magnet from a young age, but Nora's development was noticeable, nonetheless. As a junior counselor at a summer camp, she spent the months before high school hauling canoes in and out of a lake, rowing boats, swimming, hiking, and otherwise toning and tanning her blossoming physique.

By the first day of freshman year of high school, she looked like a sun goddess, even in bobby socks, saddle shoes, a Peter Pan collar blouse, and a pleated skirt: her auburn hair sun bleached, her skin a golden tan, her body lithe and firm. She found herself the object of unwanted attention from older boys, who Nora shooed away like so many gnats.

She may have looked different to the young men who circled her at school, but Nora still felt like her old self: focused on academics and extracurriculars. Even at fourteen, she had her eye set on college, when she would escape her mother's house.

Nora's friends talked almost exclusively about boys. Gina, Susan, and Andrea arrived at Sleepy Hollow High fully steeped in the drama of teenage romance, something Nora listened to them chatter about with amusement and a little disdain. These were her best friends, but still . . .

Based on her observations, boys demanded too much time for too little return. And boys always got preferential treatment over girls, she noticed at a young age. One particular incident shaped that observation.

Entering sixth grade, Nora had the highest grades and best behavior record of any child in her grade at her school. But when sixth graders were chosen to be crossing guards for the school safety patrols, the position of captain, always reserved for the class's top-ranked student, went to Todd Prunty, who was a distant number two in the class, "because the safety-patrol captain is always a boy." Nora was named Todd's lieutenant, even as her sense of injustice simmered.

Among her group of girls, Nora was always the instigator, the fun one, the smart one (though she and Gina jostled for that particular top rung), the one who took no guff from any boy. But if girls thought

Nora was fun, many boys didn't, because they couldn't handle her tart-tongued humor. That had been true since elementary school.

So it came as a complete surprise when Charlie Grossman asked her for a date. One day in October of freshman year, he walked up to Nora at lunch and said, "Hi, Nora. Would you like to go with me to the autumn dance a week from Saturday? My dad would drive us."

Just like that. No "Hi, I'm Charlie, we've never met or really talked, but we've been in the same synagogue Sunday school since fourth grade and now we're in the same earth science class." Nor did he say, "You may have heard that I'm the star receiver of the freshman football team and might be about to go up to the varsity."

Nora appreciated that. Charlie was confident without being cocky. He was handsome but not conceited. When he asked her out, he sounded hopeful, rather than entitled.

So she said yes. And as it turned out, Charlie was the perfect boyfriend for their four years at Sleepy Hollow.

Though she disapproved of the idea of boyfriends on principle, Nora understood why, as a social construct, a boyfriend was a necessary evil in high school. She was popular and active in student government, theater productions, and a handful of other activities. Living in that world meant a regular schedule of social obligations; having a steady boyfriend meant always having an answer to the question "Who's taking you?"

Charlie was as active and well liked as she was, and their various extracurriculars often dovetailed. So while Nora disdained the role of girlfriend as an adjunct position, she was able to direct the busy social life the two of them led, without seeming to step on his toes.

Charlie was thoughtful and kind, smart if not particularly witty. He remembered her birthday and was presentable to her parents. He was also undemanding sexually, settling for regular make-out sessions in the back seat of his car (which Nora had to admit she enjoyed), though she did have to keep his hands in check.

To Nora, *boyfriend* was a job description, almost like a business partner, a position that didn't need to come with romantic strings attached. A boyfriend merely needed to be someone she enjoyed spending time with and even kissing, but not someone to get goofily romantic over. Charlie was good company, and Nora wasn't looking for much more.

By the beginning of senior year, she knew she and Charlie had no future. But she rode it out the rest of the year for convenience's sake and because she didn't have the heart to break it off.

Though they never officially split up, the die was cast when Nora chose Syracuse after Charlie was accepted at Penn State. When she returned to Tarrytown for Thanksgiving weekend in the fall of freshman year, Charlie turned up at a gathering of high school friends with a girlfriend he'd brought home from college. That was that.

At Syracuse, Nora set two goals for herself: She wanted to finish her undergrad work in less than four years; she did it in three and a half. Then she planned to finish her PhD in two and a half years and did exactly that.

This required rigorous scheduling, to study for the overstuffed class lineup she enrolled for each semester, while maintaining an active social life. After earning a 4.0 average during her freshman year, she convinced her academic adviser to approve extra coursework each subsequent semester, letting her take one or two classes over the limit each term. Together with staying in Syracuse to take summer classes (while working as a bartender at night), she finished her undergraduate work at the end of senior year's fall term, a semester early.

She immediately dove into graduate school the next semester, which would have been the second half of her senior year. She stayed in Syracuse and took graduate classes during summer semester, then rolled straight through the next two academic years (including the following summer, which she spent doing research in Manhattan and living at home) to cross the finish line with her PhD.

Through it all, Nora maintained a wary attitude toward men and marriage. She had clear ideas about the future she wanted, built around a career that challenged and fulfilled her. If there was to be a spouse, he would have to be someone who also challenged and fulfilled her, in all the best ways.

"I'm going to be *somebody*, not just somebody's wife," she remembered telling Clara one night when Clara was visiting her at Syracuse. "Look at you, Clara—you've been happy being single. You don't need a man."

"Well, I can't say I ever had a chance to find out, because I've been working for your folks since I was nineteen. My schedule never allowed for much running around."

"I remember 'Sammy-day,'" Nora said.

"Yes, Sam Klay," Clara said. "I haven't thought of him in ages. I wonder whatever happened to him."

"Would you have liked to get married and have kids?"

"Married? I don't know—maybe. But kids? Hey, I have your sister and you."

After undergraduate school, a number of Nora's girlfriends began to get married, but Nora never got the impression that marriage would allow them to continue their own lives. Instead, they appeared to have signed on as supporting players in their husbands' careers, leaving their own dreams and aspirations behind.

That held no interest for Nora. What she was looking for was an equal partnership. Doing it any other way felt too much like being an employee, rather than a mate.

Stephen embraced her partnership idea, which made him different from any of the men she'd known before. He was enthusiastic about her work and bought her roses when she'd gotten the news about the Ford Foundation grant. He even joked that he hoped she would be so successful that he could stay home with their future imaginary children while she pursued a career.

And Charlie? Having barely lasted through high school with him, Nora couldn't imagine resuming any sort of involvement at this point, though she knew that's why he had turned up unannounced tonight. *Because of what happened last summer,* she thought.

It was late August, the week between the end of her summer doctoral work in Manhattan and her return to Syracuse for her final fall semester. Charlie called her out of the blue one evening, just after Nora had squabbled with her mother at dinner.

Eager to escape the house, Nora jumped at Charlie's invitation to meet at Tuffy's, the tavern near the Tarrytown GM plant that had been serving them alcohol since they were sixteen. Nora met Charlie there, then drank too many beers with whiskey chasers during a comfortable evening of talk that felt like old times.

When they got to their cars in the parking lot, the lights of the Tappan Zee were reflecting off the still surface of the Hudson River. The romantic backdrop and the whiff of hydrangea in the air inspired an affectionate parting hug, which turned into a brief, drunken make-out session. *Like old times indeed,* Nora thought, when she pulled away from the eager Charlie and, somehow, tipsily drove herself home.

Charlie called the next day. Nora asked Clara to tell him she wasn't home. When Charlie showed up at the Levitskys' front door, Clara told her, "I'm not lying to that boy again. If you don't want to see him, send him away yourself."

Nora would only speak to him through the screen door. She'd held up a hand to stop him before he could unwind what was obviously a well-practiced speech, then said, "Charlie, it was just kissing. Don't make a big thing out of it."

"But, Nora, if you'd just let me see you again, if we could just talk a little more—"

"No, Charlie. Now I'm going back to what I was doing. You should go. I think it would be better if you don't call again before I go back to school."

~

That was last August. She had not thought about Charlie Grossman again until he showed up at her parents' house and interrupted dinner this evening.

Nora closed the door to the sunporch behind Charlie. They were at least two rooms removed from the dining room, but Nora was taking no chances on being overheard by her mother's uncanny ears. Then she whirled on Charlie.

"What do you want?" she said. "I thought I was clear how I felt last summer."

Charlie held up both hands in a sign of surrender. "Sorry, sorry—I just wanted to talk to you."

"About what?"

"My father said he heard you'd be home. I was hoping to spend some time together, even if it's just as a friend."

"I'm not going to have any time while I'm home. And I resent you using my father as a way to butter me up."

"The Mets game? *He* invited *me*, if you recall."

"You didn't have to say yes."

"What am I supposed to do? I already said I'd go."

"Use your imagination. Find a reason *not* to go—and do it by the time we get back in there."

They gave each other a wide berth as they went back to the dining room, where Charlie resumed his bravura front: "Mr. and Mrs. Levitsky, such a pleasure to see you as always, but I have to go. And, Mr. Levitsky, I'm so sorry—I'm afraid I spoke too soon about going to the Mets game with you."

"Oh?" Nora's father said.

"I remembered this is the weekend we get new office furniture at my dad's law firm. I'm in charge of the changeover crew, and we start at close-of-business tomorrow."

"Oh, that's a shame," her father said. "Well, another time. I've got season tickets, and I'm always looking for someone to go to the games. God help me, the way they play."

"I need to run, or I'll be late," Charlie said. "Have a good dinner. Sorry to interrupt."

"I'll walk you to the door," Nora said.

When they got to the front porch, she said, "Thank you for that."

"Nora—" he began.

"Charlie, I've taken a job at Northwestern University. I'm moving to Chicago at the beginning of July."

"Chicago?" he said, blinking.

"And I've met someone."

Charlie looked as though he'd been slapped. "Who?"

"You don't know him. He's getting ready to take the Illinois bar exam. I met him last winter when we had a class together."

"Another lawyer?" Charlie said uncomprehendingly.

"That's not why I'm with him. Anyway, he's starting a job in Chicago, and I'll be teaching in the fall at Northwestern."

"Are you getting married?"

"We've talked about it, but nothing specific."

"What did your parents say?"

"I haven't told them yet. Or about Chicago and Northwestern. I'm going back to Syracuse to pack up my stuff, to get ready to move to Chicago at the end of the month. Then I'll tell them. So please don't say anything to your parents."

Charlie looked disconsolate, but Nora said, "Even if I wasn't going to Chicago, you and I were never going to get back together, Charlie. It just isn't going to happen. I'm sorry if you thought it was."

"Yeah," he muttered. "I know." He walked away, and Nora closed the front door behind him. She could feel tiny fingers tightening around her airways. She stopped, closed her eyes, and took three slow breaths: in through her nose, out slowly through her mouth.

When she returned to the dinner table, Clara brought her plate back from the kitchen as her mother clucked disapprovingly. "He's a nice enough young man, but . . ."

"It was good to see Charlie again," her father said. "I don't know why you two ever broke up."

"Why did you do that, Daddy?" Nora said. "You embarrassed Charlie, and you embarrassed me."

"How did I embarrass you? By inviting him to the game?"

"You put him on the spot. Charlie knows I don't have feelings for him anymore. When you invited him, it made him think maybe he and I still had a chance. Which we don't."

"But why not? You two were so close for so long."

"In high school! That was six years ago."

"Well, he's not going to the game, and that's an end to it," her mother snapped. "Can we please find another topic of discussion besides Charlie Grossman?"

Nora and her father both focused on their plates. In the moment of silence, Clara stuck her head in from the kitchen and said, "Who's ready for pie?"

"Cherry?" Nora said, with childlike eagerness. "I haven't had your cherry pie in ages."

"What else would I make when I knew you were coming home? If I didn't make a cherry pie, you'd bellyache until I did."

That made Nora and her father laugh. Even her mother smiled, though her expression also showed her disapproval of Clara's wisecrack.

After dinner, Clara drove her mother to her mah-jongg group because her mother was afraid to drive after dark. Nora and her father retired to the den to watch *Daniel Boone* on their color TV. They'd had a color set since Nora's last year of high school. It was a novelty, the only one in their neighborhood. There had been so few shows broadcast in color at that point that her parents insisted on watching them all, at first. Now her family was blasé about it.

Nora sat through *Daniel Boone*, during which her father pointed out (not for the first time) that the actor playing Daniel's faithful Native American companion was, in fact, a Jewish singer named Ed Ames.

When that show ended, he changed the channel to *Bewitched*, a comedy about a beautiful modern witch who uses magic to make herself into a subservient suburban housewife. Nora found it insulting but didn't say so to her father. Instead, she simply excused herself to go upstairs, saying, "I want to get an early start in the morning."

"What time are you catching your train?" her father asked. "Maybe I can drive you to the station."

"My lunch is at noon, but I want to be on a nine thirty train so I can do a little shopping first."

"Sorry—you know me. Out the door by six to beat the traffic to the scrapyard. The road construction in the Bronx just gets worse and worse. They'll never finish building that farkakte Cross Bronx Expressway."

"I thought you and Uncle Stan were selling the business. Why are you still killing yourself at that time of day?"

"Hey, someone has to show the new guys how it's done," her father said.

Nora knew she couldn't ask her mother for a ride at that time of morning. Her mother never left the house, even to make the five-minute drive to the Philipse Manor train station and back, without being perfectly coiffed, with a full face of makeup. Her mother's morning beauty regimen consumed a solid seventy-five minutes, more if false eyelashes were involved. She certainly wasn't going through all that just to drive Nora to the train. Nora knew better than to ask.

"It's OK—I'll walk to the station. It's supposed to be a nice day."

At that moment, the telephone rang.

"Who would be calling at this hour?" her father said.

"I told Gina I was going to be here. I'll go take it in the kitchen so you can watch your show."

Once there, she picked up the wall phone and said, "Levitsky residence." She cringed; old habits died hard. She assumed Gina would razz her, but she heard a different voice instead.

"You sound so official," Stephen said with a chuckle.

"I am always surprised when I turn out to be my mother's daughter after all. How are you? Where are you?" Nora said, thankful she was the one who'd answered the phone.

"We're staying at the Plaza. It's as grand as you've heard."

"Stephen, I've *been* to the Plaza."

"Of course you have. I'm the bumpkin who gushes about being in a fancy New York hotel." She could almost hear him smile. "So how are you?"

"Dealing with my mother, as usual."

"I can't wait to meet her, the way you talk about her. You should listen to yourself sometime. So anyway—I was able to get a train schedule from the hotel concierge. Tell me what time dinner is tomorrow night, and I'll figure out which train to catch."

"Stephen, I'm sorry—my father made plans for us for Friday night. He just told me tonight—sort of a father-daughter evening. I'm sorry, I couldn't say no."

"Of course you couldn't. I understand completely." His sincerity always touched her.

"I know we're having family brunch around noon on Saturday with my sister and her family. Maybe you could come up then."

"I don't think so. I'm not completely clear on the wedding details, but my mother was adamant about not planning anything for Saturday until we know the schedule. So far we don't have it."

"Oh, I'm sorry," Nora said, trying not to oversell her feigned disappointment.

"I was so hoping to meet your parents."

"There'll be other occasions," she said. "Go enjoy the time with your own family. I know you said you don't see your East Coast cousins very often."

That seemed to settle the matter, and after a couple of hushed *I miss yous*, they hung up and Nora went to her room. She knew it would be a while until Clara brought her mother back from mah-jongg.

She changed into pajamas, then looked around the bedroom, which seemed trapped in amber as her high school refuge. She knew that Stephen was her future, and this bedroom was her past. She was ready to move on; this weekend would bring a close to one phase of her life as she moved into the next.

But she would still need luck to make a clean getaway.

~

Nora had long ago internalized her mother's lifelong indifference, which always seemed at odds with her need to monitor Nora's behavior. When Nora decided to go to Syracuse, she felt her mother's separation anxiety had more to do with control than concern.

For a long time, Nora associated any tense maternal interaction with the shortness of breath that took hold of her lungs. She felt relieved when, at the age of ten, she was diagnosed with hay fever and allergies, which could lead to asthma symptoms. The asthma could also be triggered by stress, the doctor said. *So I'm not only allergic to my mother,* she thought with relief.

Nora went through the limited series of allergy immunotherapy shots available and found that it did mitigate her allergic reaction to pollen and cats. But she knew there was no way to inoculate herself against her mother, except with distance.

So she did her best to stay out of her mother's vicinity. There were times her mother made that easier than others. Beginning the summer after each girl finished first grade, her mother sent both Nora and Amelia to sleepaway camp for the two months of summer vacation. Nora understood now that this freed her parents to—do what? She had never asked, and her parents had never offered.

While Amelia was homesick and hated camp, Nora reveled in being removed from the house in North Tarrytown to a cabin in the Adirondacks, twenty miles west of Saratoga Springs. Summer gave her a taste for freedom, something she wanted more of. She hoped she would find it again when she left for college.

Yet, when Nora started looking at universities outside the New York metropolitan area, her mother seemed shocked at the notion of her daughter going "away" to school.

"What's wrong with City College?" she demanded. "Your sister went to City College—and lived at home. Or, if City College doesn't suit you, you obviously have the grades to apply to Barnard, or Vassar, or Sarah Lawrence."

"I'm not going to be one of those stuck-up twats that goes to Sarah Lawrence," Nora blurted out. Both her parents' eyes widened, and her mother gasped.

"Sorry, sorry," Nora said. Her mother gave an unhappy "Harrumph," while her father blushed and looked at his dinner plate. Nora knew she'd embarrassed him: Young women, in what passed for polite society in the late fall of 1960, didn't use that language.

"Anyway," she went on, "Syracuse sent me early acceptance. And that's where I'm going." She hoped they didn't notice her struggle to breathe smoothly.

"What if we won't pay for this little adventure?" her mother said.

"Lillian!" her father said, then turned to Nora. "If that's where you want to go, of course we'll make sure you can, sweetie."

"They offered me a full academic scholarship if you won't," she said to her mother, as though playing a high hole card. This Syracuse-induced bout of separation anxiety on her mother's part seemed uncharacteristic, until Nora realized Lillian would no longer have anyone to order around except her father and Clara.

In the end, her mother gritted her teeth and acted excited for Nora when they drove her up to Syracuse to move into a dormitory for freshman year in the fall of 1961. Nora even overheard her father saying, "Lillian, it's Syracuse, not the North Pole. We can drive there in less than a day." But they never visited her again after that.

Her parents made it clear that when she finished in Syracuse, they expected her to return to New York City to begin her career: "You'll graduate, and then you'll move back here," her mother said, more than once. Nora had no intention of doing that but knew better than to say so.

When Nora finished her undergraduate degree at the end of the fall 1964 semester, her parents made their second trip to Syracuse, this time to attend commencement.

They watched Nora go through the ceremony in a crowded auditorium. Her mother even joined her father in a brief outburst of applause when Nora's name was announced and she marched across the stage to accept magna cum laude honors.

After the ceremony, her parents threaded their way through the crowd of new graduates and their families to where Nora stood near the stage talking to a group of classmates. Her father took her in a bear hug that almost knocked off her mortarboard.

"Honey, we are so proud of you," he said, and she saw tears in his eyes.

Her mother kissed Nora's cheek. "Yes, you made us proud. This is quite an achievement." As her mother never failed to mention, they'd paid for almost three years of textbooks and train fare while Amelia went to City College, only to have her drop out short of a degree.

Before Nora had a chance to absorb her mother's rare compliment, they were joined by a bespectacled older man with a full gray beard and brightly colored academic robes.

"Nora, are these your parents?" the man said.

"Yes, of course, Professor Bruce Goodrich—this is my mother and father, Lillian and Solomon Levitsky. Dean Goodrich is head of the School of Communications."

"Oh?" her father said, shaking the dean's hand vigorously. "It's an honor to meet you, sir."

"Believe me, Mr. Levitsky, the honor is mine. Your daughter is a remarkable young woman. To do what she did in the time she did it? Quite remarkable. It's been a pleasure to watch her growth."

Her mother seemed dazzled at having this scholar, whose academic robes fairly shrieked his position of authority, sing the praises of her daughter. She said, "Yes, we're both quite pleased."

"Not as pleased as we are that Nora will be staying on for graduate school," Dean Goodrich said.

"What?" her parents said in unison.

"I'm sure it's no surprise to you what a go-getter she is," the dean continued. "The spring semester starts in less than a month, and I believe Nora is already a *semester* ahead in her coursework."

"That's an exaggeration, Professor," Nora said with a smile. She turned to her parents, both of whom were struggling to find words. "I was going to tell you at lunch, as a surprise," she said to them, still smiling, fighting back the tendrils that were tightening around her lungs.

"Yes, this is quite a surprise," her mother said.

"Well, I'll leave you to celebrate," Dean Goodrich said. "Congratulations, again."

As he walked away, her mother turned to Nora and said, "Celebrate? What are we celebrating? The fact that we don't know what our own daughter is doing with her life? Or that you would go behind our backs like this?"

"Mother, I told you last summer I was looking at graduate schools."

"*Looking*," her father said. "And you mentioned NYU, if I recall."

"But I decided to stay here—jump right back in. I've got a plan, Daddy. I'm going to get my PhD in less than three years."

"Your PhD? In what?" her mother asked.

"Marketing."

"Oh, please," her mother said with a hand wave. "A PhD in nonsense is more like it." She turned to Nora's father, who said nothing.

"I've already started my research about the way marketing and media keep women from a greater place in the world."

"Oy," her mother said, rolling her eyes. "What are you talking about?"

"I read this book by Betty Friedan, called *The Feminine Mystique*—"

"My friend Estelle read that book," her mother snapped. "She said it's nothing but the ravings of a crazy person. Just trash. You're going to study trash now? For this you graduated magna cum laude?"

"It's not trash, Mother," Nora said, trying to steady her breathing without betraying the effort. "If you can't be happy for me, maybe I'll just stay up here and work until grad school starts next month, instead of coming home for the holidays."

"Now that's not what she meant," her anxious father had said. "It's just that this is all taking us by surprise. Why don't we all go have lunch and celebrate this happy day?" Nora had seen her father give her mother a look, and her mother had sighed her assent.

~

Nora wondered if it was obvious to her parents how badly she wanted to get away from her mother. If it was, had it always been?

She'd been eager to leave long before she finished high school. She made a point not to spend the entirety of any college break at home in North Tarrytown, through her six-plus years in Syracuse. There were always exams to be studied for, papers to be written, or a research project that needed extra attention, requiring her to cut her break short in order to get back upstate.

Playing tennis on a breezy spring day when the pollen count was up could still bring on shortness of breath; so could spending time in an enclosed space with a cat. But, in her years at Syracuse, Nora had never had the kind of stress-related asthmatic episodes her mother could provoke. She began to associate clear lungs with breathing easily on a metaphoric level.

Her urge to break free of her mother's grasp on her life (and her lungs) always trumped her mother's ability to control her. She refused to be ruled by her mother. At a young age, she'd realized there was no punishment that her parents were willing to mete out that she could not withstand and then rise above, though she might have to take a couple puffs of Primatene to get through.

But, as she got older, she began to notice that when her mother's anger didn't have the desired effect on Nora, she would turn the same ire on her father. Nora could see him shrink under her cutting words; he rarely fought back. Nora's first impulse was to flee the scene, in the hope that her mother would let up if the real object of her anger disappeared.

She finally asked Clara, who had confirmed it for her: After Nora left for college, her mother's verbal assaults on her father all but stopped.

Nora knew her mother would explode when she found out that she was moving to Chicago instead of back home; she shuddered to think how her mother might take it out on her father. But she knew that she had to keep this plan to herself until it was a fait accompli. There should be no suggestion that her parents' opinion—her mother's opinion—would factor into the final decision in any way. This was a done deal, and she was just passing along the news.

Her life was no longer a democracy in which her mother got to vote.

The challenge would be getting through the weekend without having to answer any pointed questions about her future plans, because she was never comfortable lying. Her father had asked her to come down; staying out of her mother's sight shouldn't be that difficult, given the constant churn of her social calendar with the synagogue, bridge, and mah-jongg.

Still, lying to her mother, if it came to that, was challenging. Her radar was acute, so the degree of difficulty was high. It reminded Nora of a trick she'd seen in a movie, in which someone yanked a tablecloth out from under a fully set table of crystal, china, and silver. The act was performed with such speed and finesse that nary a piece of tableware seemed to move. In the movie, someone else then attempted the same stunt on a different table, bringing the contents crashing to the floor.

There was only one person she could trust with her plans, the one person who had pushed her to achieve from the time she was a little girl. And she had heard her drive into the garage a little while ago, chauffeuring Nora's mother home from her mah-jongg game.

So, as she had done on so many nights since she'd been a tot, Nora put on her robe and slippers and quietly made her way down through the kitchen and up the back stairs to Clara's rooms over the garage.

~

From a young age, Nora remembered listening to her sister, who was five and a half years older, argue with their mother about her bedtime. There was always something Amelia didn't want to miss: a radio show she "had" to hear ("You're too young to be listening to that idiocy," her mother said of *The Jack Benny Program*, even after it moved from radio to TV) or a book she "just couldn't put down" ("Lights out, young lady—you have school in the morning," her mother would scold).

Early on, Nora noticed that the more Amelia pressed her mother, the deeper her mother dug in her heels. Bedtimes were enforced with military discipline, under penalty of punishment severe enough to make arguing foolhardy.

Their mother exploited Amelia's insecurities to control her behavior. While Amelia was born eager to please, Nora realized that her mother would never be satisfied, a lesson she knew Amelia never absorbed.

Nora's habit of sneaking out of her room to explore the house after her parents had gone to bed started one evening when she awoke needing to use the bathroom. To her, it felt like the middle of the night, though it was only 11:45 p.m. Wide awake after she'd finished with the toilet and realizing she was the only one up and about in the whole house, she felt a strange flash of power from this sensation of solitude within a house that was fully populated but completely silent. Rather than return to bed, she went downstairs and wandered around the living room in the semidarkness, which was illuminated by a streetlamp on the corner.

She examined the breakable keepsakes and objets d'art her mother kept as decorative touches and which she expressly forbade her daughters from touching: the Hummel figurine of a mantilla-wearing old lady holding a bunch of multicolored balloons; the baroque-looking candy dish bearing jelly-filled hard candies her mother prohibited the girls from eating ("They're for company," she'd say, or, "You'll get cavities").

With her mother safely asleep upstairs, Nora popped one of the forbidden candies into her mouth. When it landed on her tongue, she thought, *Raspberry? Ick!* and spit the moistened candy back into her hand, then replaced it in the dish.

She only explored the house on nights when she woke up and couldn't fall back to sleep. There was a feeling of accidental magic, as though she might still be dreaming as she wandered through quiet rooms.

Then one night, her father sat down at the dinner table with an elaborate brochure for the latest craze in home appliances: a black-and-white television. He showed it to her mother, who browsed through it skeptically.

"Stan and Delia are getting one," he told her.

"That figures" was all her mother said.

From her position at the dinner table, all Nora could see was the brochure's sepia-tinted cover illustration: a drawing of a happy family gathered around a large box with what appeared to be a porthole on the front. But the porthole seemed to emit glowing rays of light. Nora's curiosity was piqued.

That night at bedtime, Nora dozed off while Amelia read in bed. When Amelia snapped off the light, it woke Nora, who looked at the radium-illuminated dial on their nightstand clock. Just 10:00 p.m. Mandatory lights out in the Levitsky house, by order of her mother. And that included in her parents' bedroom.

She lay in the dark, listening to her sister's breathing as it evened out into a steady rhythm. When Nora could hear her father's snores through the wall, she crept out of the bedroom and headed downstairs to her father's office, where she'd seen him take the brochure after dinner.

She turned on the desk lamp, but the brochure wasn't on the desktop. All the desk drawers were locked, except the center one, which held paper clips, a few postage stamps, and some documents.

But there was a letter opener lying on the desk blotter. Nora had seen people jimmy open desk drawers with letter openers in the movies, and it always looked simple enough to her seven-year-old eyes. When she reached for the potential tool, she accidentally knocked a paperweight—a large wooden *L*—onto the floor with a clunk.

Good thing the door is closed, she thought as she retrieved the paperweight under the desk. Then the door to the office opened and the overhead light blazed to life.

"Nora Jane—what on earth?"

It was Clara.

"I couldn't sleep," Nora lied, popping out from under the desk.

"Get out of your father's office right now!"

"But I'm not tired."

"Well, then come to my room before your mother finds you're out of bed. And snooping in your father's office? I don't know which she would think was worse—but I know you don't want to find out."

While everyone else went to sleep at 10:00 p.m., Clara sat up reading novels she got at the local library, usually until midnight, sometimes later. Or she read *Time* and *Reader's Digest,* to which Nora's father subscribed, or her mother's copies of *Ladies' Home Journal* and *Redbook.*

Clara shooed Nora up to her room. It was cozy: a bedroom with a single bed, a bathroom, a small kitchen and dining area, and a sitting room with a couch and an easy chair with a reading light. Nora was too young to recognize most of the furniture as castoffs from an earlier life on the main floor of the house.

Nora curled up on the couch, and Clara covered her with a quilt. Then Clara read to her from *Reader's Digest* ("My Most Unforgettable Character: Jimmy Durante") until Nora dozed off. When she awoke the next morning, she was back in her own bed. It became a regular thing, two or three times a week, their little secret, Nora and Clara, until Nora was too big to be carried.

There were several years, before Nora started kindergarten, when her father kiddingly referred to her as "Clara's shadow." From the time Nora could crawl, she followed Clara from room to room, morning to night, as Clara took care of the house. While Nora's first word was "Daddy," her first sentence was a question: "Help Clara?"

Eventually, her parents gave her toy appliances—a small vacuum cleaner, a toy stove—so she could "help" without getting in the way. After Nora started school, she still made a point of coming home and helping Clara make dinner, once she'd finished her homework.

Clara had long been her most trusted adviser. Oh, she had Gina and other school friends. But as Nora began to realize that she *must* get out of Tarrytown and away from her mother to breathe free, Clara was the one whispering in her ear about the bigger world outside. She was the one who would listen when Nora's mother wouldn't. She was the one who encouraged her, which her mother never did.

And Clara was the one who insisted that Nora take as many advanced classes as possible when she got to high school. Clara counseled her through the various stages of teen social drama and romantic angst. She provided comfort as she anguished over social standing in middle school and gloried in it through high school. She listened as Nora underwent her first uncertain infatuation with Charlie, through the relationship's end.

Most important, Clara never judged, something of which Nora's mother seemed incapable. Clara never criticized and listened more than she spoke. When she did speak, she would say something like, "You might want to think about that again." Nora learned to heed that advice, as well as to hear what she wasn't saying.

Why did her mother never offer this kind of comfort? It wasn't that she was reluctant to exercise control over Nora's life. Far from it.

But her mother's motto, which Nora heard all through her childhood, was "Children should be seen and not heard." In practical terms, this meant that unless Nora had something to say that affected the nuts-and-bolts details of her mother's daily life, her mother didn't want to hear from her.

Nora knew it hadn't been like that for attention-starved Amelia. Over and over, Nora saw the pattern repeated: her mother ignoring Amelia, who would then find a way to end up at odds with her mother, which brought her attention, for better or worse. This dynamic continued unabated into Amelia's marriage. Amelia inevitably would plead and apologize until she'd restored uneasy equilibrium with her mother.

Nora avoided those kinds of run-ins. For a while, this convinced her mother that Nora was a more compliant child than the emotionally demanding Amelia. Her mother assumed Nora was toeing her various lines.

Nora was both intelligent and canny. She was a single-minded, competitive student from a young age, who never obviously flouted her mother's wishes. But when she did break a rule, she knew enough to hide it from her mother, who didn't search out bad behavior so much as punish blatant noncompliance. She was discreet enough that she never needed to lie. Her mother didn't suspect when she started smoking cigarettes in high school, or when she and her friends would drink. Her mother never checked up on her without having an obvious cause, so Nora made a point of not giving it to her.

Early on, Nora found that it was a mistake to take personal problems to her. She'd learned this lesson when an elementary school friend hurt her feelings by not inviting her to the chum's birthday party.

When she went tearfully to her mother to complain, her mother sighed deeply, and Nora felt her chest tighten. Then her mother looked at her and said, "What's the problem?"

She listened as Nora explained the situation. But, when Nora finished, her mother said, "Never expect anything from other people. Then you won't be disappointed."

Nora learned to take her problems to Clara. Clara would listen and ask questions, sometimes gently challenging her by saying, "But you just said . . ." Inevitably, Nora worked her way to a practical solution because Clara was a practical person. She was not afraid to preface a question to Nora with "Well, if you'd come down off your high horse, you might be able to figure this out for yourself." She knew Clara cared enough to offer real help.

~

Now, in her pajamas and robe, Nora climbed the stairs to Clara's room and knocked on the door—their old knock, shave and a haircut—and heard Clara say, "Door's always open."

Nora quietly closed the door behind her. Clara was wearing a flannel bathrobe in Black Watch plaid over her pajamas. When Nora said, "Whatcha reading?" she held up a volume of Reader's Digest Condensed Books, showing the title page for *A Thousand Days: John F. Kennedy in the White House*, by Arthur Schlesinger Jr. Like Nora, Clara claimed the late president as one of her favorites.

Nora said, "I thought you read that already."

"I wanted to read it again—just not the whole thing. But these condensed books leave a lot out."

"Why do you think they're called *condensed*?" Nora said with a laugh.

"All right, you," Clara said, then surveyed her. "What was that scene at dinner with Charlie about?"

"He showed up out of the blue. Apparently, Mother told Mrs. Grossman that I was going to be in town. I never understood why she and his mother were friends."

"Your mother likes to look down on people. Do you think she ever let Mrs. Grossman forget she didn't think Charlie was good enough for you? Especially when he decided to go to New Jersey for law school. Can't you just hear her? She runs roughshod over that women's group of hers." She gave Nora a level look: "So what did he want?"

Nora rolled her eyes. "Do you remember I told you we had beers together at the end of last summer and wound up making out in the parking lot at Tuffy's? Well, he thought it meant more than it did. Not one of my proudest moments."

"Nora Jane," Clara said. "Just leave that poor boy alone."

"I told him tonight we had no future because I had met someone I thought I was serious about."

"How did he take it?"

"The first thing he said was, 'Another lawyer?' As though one attorney was as good as the next, so why not him?"

Clara smiled and shook her head.

Nora sat down next to Clara, who sipped from her teacup, then looked up at her. "So tell me about Stephen Cantor."

"Oh, Clara," Nora said, in a tone so dreamy that it made Clara smile.

"That good, huh?" Clara said. "Where'd you meet him?"

"It was in a literature class. He loves Jane Austen. He just *gets* things, Clara—about why the war is wrong, about the civil rights movement and how discrimination and poverty are all interconnected. I mean, he loves Shakespeare! He showed me how everything in politics—everything in all of human relations!—it's in Shakespeare!"

"I was never able to make much sense of Shakespeare when I had to read one of his plays back in high school," Clara said.

Nora beamed. "Stephen wants to help people. That's why he's going to work in the public defender's office in Chicago. He wants to make a difference."

"How well does making a difference pay?"

"Not as much as Charlie Grossman will make working for his father. But, if we *did* get married, between Stephen's salary and mine, we would be OK."

"You're going to have to introduce him to your parents sometime."

"Oh, it's way too early for that," Nora said. She looked at Clara for a moment. Feeling tension gather as she breathed, she willed herself to relax. Then she said, "Any idea what my father wanted me to come down for?"

"I didn't know you were coming until he mentioned it at breakfast yesterday."

Nora thought for a moment as she looked at Clara, rocking quietly in her chair. She pointed at the drawer in the reading stand next to her aging nanny and said, "Do you still keep a box of Jujubes hidden away there?"

"Want one?" Clara pulled the drawer open, extracting a half-empty candy box. She handed it to Nora with a rattle. Nora shook a couple of the tiny candies into her hand and tossed them into her mouth. They proved unyielding when she tried to bite into one.

"How old are these? They're like rocks."

"Ever hear that saying about how beggars can't be choosers?"

Nora laughed as she grabbed a tissue and spit the candy into it, saying, "Next time I'll bring you a fresh box."

"Those aren't much softer."

They both laughed, before Nora turned somber.

"I wish I knew what Daddy wanted. Has he been feeling OK?"

"I think so. He fainted a month or so back while he was working in the garden."

"No one told me that."

"Well, it was a hot day. Luckily, Frank was here, mowing the lawn, and saw him go down." Amelia's husband had performed the chore since he'd joined the family, in a vain effort to win his mother-in-law's approval.

"What did the doctor say?"

"Oh, your father wouldn't go to the doctor. You know him. He said it was the heat and the sun and the fact that he hadn't drunk enough water."

"What did Mother say?"

"That this was why he needed to hire someone to do the rest of the gardening. Well, he won't have a yard to worry about when they move to the co-op in the fall."

Nora had been surprised by the phone call from her father earlier in the spring, announcing major impending changes. He and Uncle Stan were selling their business and retiring. Her parents were going to sell the house in North Tarrytown and had found a co-op near the Bronx River Parkway in White Plains ("It's got a Scarsdale postal code," her father said). The impending loss of her childhood home had unsettled her a little, but only until she realized that the move could hardly have been better timed: The inevitable upheaval surrounding it was certain to provide a welcome distraction when she revealed her plan to move to Chicago.

"How have things been otherwise?"

"I would have said about like they always are. But then last week, your mother answered the phone after lunch one day. It was a lawyer looking for your father; something the lawyer told her must have been upsetting because she lit into your father that night at dinner."

Nora thought about the odd note struck by her father when he'd called: insistent that he needed to talk to her in person, equally insistent that it was nothing to be concerned about. "Can you just indulge me with a visit?" he said.

She felt bad about keeping her plans a secret from her father. But she had no interest in having *that* scene with her mother on a face-to-face basis. She already knew how it would go and had decided to break the news in a phone call and deal with the fallout later. Once she told them, there was no rule saying she had to endure subsequent angry phone calls from her mother. If she decided to give Nora the silent treatment, so much the better.

Clara had been her first phone call when she was offered a job interview at Northwestern. Clara was the one who said, "Of course you should take it," when the job offer came. And Clara was the one who said, "I'd think hard about when you want to break this news to your mother," after she accepted the job, sealing her move to Chicago.

Now, as she told Clara her plan—to wait until she was practically in Chicago before informing her parents—Clara objected: "It seems sneaky. I raised you better than that."

But Nora was insistent: "It's my life. Let me do it my way."

Clara's slate-colored eyes took on a steely cast, and she looked away for a moment, shaking her head. Then she turned back, took Nora's hand, and said, "I will always be on your side."

As eager as she was to break away, Nora was also unsteady at the thought of losing Clara from her life. In the same call where her father had told her about selling the business and moving, her first response had been "Moving? What about Clara?"

Her father had said, "Actually, we're going to lose her anyway. Her sister in Scranton is sick, so she's going back to take care of her. But she's going to stay until we get moved. After that, there really wouldn't be room in the new place."

~

Now Clara told her, "The co-op is a nice little place with an extra bedroom for you or the grandkids, if they stay over."

"Meanwhile," Nora said, "Mother will get to move close enough to Scarsdale for bragging rights." She sighed. "How will the Levitsky family survive without you, Clara?" She doubted her light tone did much to conceal the sharp pang she felt at the idea.

"Oh, you'll be just fine," Clara said. "Now it's time for me to get some sleep."

Nora stood and started for the door, then turned back around and said, "Did Daddy really get me to drive down here just to go to a Mets game with him?"

Nora shared her father's long-suffering passion for the expansion-team Mets, now in their fifth season in the National League. Like him, she'd become a fan after her family's fortunes had unexpectedly improved when the team came into being a few years earlier.

"I guess you'll find out tomorrow night. I'm just glad for the chance to see you before you move to Chicago. Now, scoot. You may not need your beauty sleep, but I do. Didn't I hear you say you have to be up early for a job interview?"

Nora scoffed. "I'm having lunch with a professor at NYU who's interested in my research project. Though it's true, she did want me to teach at NYU."

"Don't mention that little fact to your mother."

Nora moved back to Clara and gave her a hug. "I miss talking to you," she said, holding Clara at arm's length. "I assumed you would always be here whenever I came home. Now there's not even going to be a 'here.' Or at least not this one. When will I ever see you?"

"Well, when you decide to tie the knot, I hope you'll invite me to your wedding. I've never been to Chicago."

"Invited? You're going to be a bridesmaid."

"At my age? Honestly, Nora Jane."

"I mean it. I've already decided that the bridesmaids' dresses will have big puffy sleeves and those empire waistlines."

"I don't have the figure for that."

"Does anyone?"

Clara laughed. "Just try putting me in a getup like that and see how far you get."

"We'll see."

"Or you could come visit me in Scranton," Clara said.

"Don't think I won't." She hugged Clara again and kissed her good night on her cheek, as she had since she was a little girl, then went back to her room.

As Nora lay on her bed, her bedroom felt as small as a closet. She was almost twenty-five. This room belonged to a high school girl from what seemed like another century, instead of earlier in this decade.

On one wall was a cardboard **KENNEDY/JOHNSON** lawn sign. A member of the Young Democrats in high school, Nora had volunteered for JFK's 1960 presidential campaign the fall of her senior year. She graduated from high school the following spring, aglow with the promise of the newly inaugurated young president. Looking at the sign now, she remembered how unhappy her mother was when Nora used her father's industrial stapler from his workbench to pin the posterboard to the wall, its thin wooden stake still dangling from the bottom.

"You said no pins or thumbtacks—you never said anything about staples," Nora said, an argument that was true technically, if not in spirit. Rather than repaint the entire room, her mother let it stay—and there it remained.

Beyond that, there was only a single bulletin board allowed on Nora's walls: "Otherwise, it makes the room too messy," her mother said. That lone vessel was festooned with photos of her favorite singers and movie stars from her younger days. She'd cut them from the covers and inside pages of movie fan magazines: Tab Hunter, Rock Hudson, Ricky Nelson—and, of course, Elvis Presley.

When was the last time she'd even heard about Elvis? She looked at the cavalcade of teen idols and felt a twinge at realizing how much these figures once meant to her.

As museum-like as it all seemed to her now, the exhibits in this institution were comfortingly familiar. She'd lived her whole life in this house, although she spent her teen years breathlessly plotting her escape. She felt a sudden and unexpected sense of loss at the idea that someone else would soon be living in this house—in this room. And in Clara's room.

Her family had lived in the house for her entire life, and Clara had worked and lived in the house since before she was born. The two—the house and Clara—were inextricably linked in Nora's mind. Now that both were about to disappear, she felt irrational anger that her personal history was being sold away so unceremoniously.

Face facts, she thought. Her plan for her future did not include living under her parents' roof ever again. Still, she felt a twinge because she assumed this house would always be here. Just in case she needed a refuge.

Grow up. Her parents were both in their sixties, living alone in this big suburban dwelling. Even if they never sold it, she knew her parents would die someday. Then she and Amelia would have to sell the house anyway. Or Amelia would decide she wanted it and move in. In any case, it would no longer be Nora's.

As she thought about the house, however, Nora was struck by how many of her memories had to do with battles with her mother. These skirmishes often left her wheezing, though she tried to keep her parents from discovering her ragged breathing. The arguments generally focused on the same kinds of things: how Nora wore her hair; whether she should be allowed out on school nights; what her curfew should be when she was out on dates with Charlie; and when she was allowed to use a family car. She and her mother argued about trivialities and otherwise talked about little of significance. The important conversations in Nora's life happened with Clara.

Nora knew from Clara that she had been a surprise baby, born when Amelia was five, at a point when her mother thought she was past such a threat. The pregnancy was difficult, and her mother struggled after the birth, battling pain and exhaustion. When she withdrew daily to her sewing room after breakfast, Nora became, in essence, Clara's baby. Clara gave Nora the kind of maternal attention a child needs from the time Nora's mother was hit with crippling postpartum depression.

As Nora got older, though she couldn't have put it into words, she came to regard her mother less as her parent and more as her boss. Her mother treated her as someone who had to be kept in line, rather than as a child to nurture.

Still, while Nora was quietly resistant to her mother's will, she was never overtly rebellious, out of respect and love for her father. Like so many daughters, Nora was a daddy's girl. As little as she cared about her mother's opinion, she relied on her father's affection. She knew that when her mother was unhappy with Nora, she took it out on Nora's father. Life seemed harder for everyone in the household when her mother's dudgeon was elevated.

So Nora quietly did what she wanted, without calling attention to herself. This wasn't much of a challenge, given how little interest her mother had in engaging with her daughter.

Nora had earned the right to operate on autopilot because she brought home honor roll report cards starting in elementary school. From that point on, her mother withdrew even further, if that's possible, from her life. Nora saw her at meals and occasionally after school, but she never offered details about her day-to-day existence, and her mother never asked. It was Clara with whom Nora shared her inner life.

Nora seemed to elude her mother's grasp at every turn. Now Nora was going to cut the string for good.

As Nora drifted off to sleep, she thought once more about what her father wanted to talk about. Maybe he just needed company for the baseball game.

Then she slid into a dream in which she strode across the Syracuse campus in vaulting giant steps that felt like flying.

FRIDAY

I know too much, and not enough.
—Allen Ginsberg

SOL

Solomon Levitsky seldom used foul language in what he thought of as real life—which was anywhere outside his office at All-American Scrap Metal in Queens.

At work, it was another story. He could curse like a sailor when bargaining over a load of scrap and be even saltier when chewing out an inept worker. His longtime employees knew his basic sweet nature and understood that his anger flashed only briefly. He would utter a string of curses in English and Yiddish before he calmed down and continued.

The cursing in Yiddish was fluent, though Sol was American born and Bronx reared. He was the second generation to emerge after his forebears, Jews from a small Romanian shtetl, had immigrated to the United States after the American Civil War.

Away from the office, however, Sol wouldn't dream of slipping into that kind of colorful language. He didn't even think it. It was not the way he had been brought up. More to the point, his wife, Lillian, reacted angrily on those occasions when he slipped.

When his older daughter, Amelia, had brought profanity to the dinner table after discovering it as an adolescent, Sol was the one who washed her mouth out with soap, telling her, "Only people with poor vocabularies use language like that. I'm not raising ignorant children."

Sitting in his first base box seat with his daughter Nora in a half-full Shea Stadium on a warm Friday night in mid-June, however, all that Sol Levitsky could think was *I am so fucked.*

The Mets were winning, for a change. Oh, they were a terrible team, of that there was no doubt. Yet to Sol's astonishment, they were beating the Chicago Cubs. Early in the game, the Mets got to the formidable Ferguson Jenkins, one of the few Black pitchers in the major leagues (though the number was growing, which Sol thought of as social progress).

Jenkins had already hit two batters with pitches when he surrendered a two-run homer to the Mets' Tommy Davis in the fourth inning. Now Jenkins stood on the mound, looking angry and impatient as he waited for manager Leo Durocher to trudge out from the dugout and remove him from the game. Durocher, who had his own colorful history with both of New York's erstwhile teams, the Dodgers and the Giants, drew a smattering of jeers and cheers as he walked back to the bench after bringing in Bill Stoneman in relief.

Having sat through what seemed like an endless string of losses in the Mets' first five seasons, the die-hard Sol should have been thrilled to see these signs of life from the Mets' bats. His loyalty to the team had been cemented the day the Mets bought the property Sol and his brother-in-law, Stan Schwartz, owned. The original site of their successful scrap-iron business had been part of a huge parcel of Queens commercial wasteland that became Shea Stadium, which opened in 1964.

Part of the purchase price for All-American's property, which Sol negotiated himself, was a box behind the first base dugout with four seats, which he and Stan received in perpetuity (along with a perennial parking pass). The tickets usually fell to Sol because Stan was more interested in betting on baseball games with his brother, who was a bookmaker, than watching them.

Yet Sol couldn't enjoy this momentary surge in the fortunes of his favorite team. *Because of this fucking mess we're in,* he thought again.

He looked at Nora, who sat next to him in the otherwise empty box—a lovely young woman who, at that moment, happened to be loudly jeering Cubs shortstop Ernie Banks as he struck out to Tom Seaver.

My beautiful daughter with the big brain, Sol thought. It had only recently occurred to him that the soon-to-be-added PhD after her name meant she could use the title "Dr." in front of it.

"This is my daughter, Dr. Levitsky," he imagined himself saying and had to fight back tears of pride at the thought.

Sol loved both his daughters but found himself perplexed by Nora, who seemed to know exactly what she did and didn't want, almost from the moment she was born. And she was never afraid to make her preference known. Sol remembered the anguish in his wife's expression the time baby Nora finally accepted the bottle from her, after resisting it for several minutes, only to throw it on the floor.

Nora was the child who surprised her parents—not just with her arrival but with her thoughts and actions. Sol knew his wife found Nora exasperating in her tendency to string together one question after another. No matter the answer to the last question, it always seemed to trigger another one.

Sol's conversations with the young Nora had fascinated him in their ability to cover subjects as wide ranging as Jackie Robinson and Negroes in baseball, President Truman and the atom bomb, and who was funnier: Abbott and Costello or Dean Martin and Jerry Lewis? (He preferred Abbott and Costello's quick-witted patter; she liked Jerry Lewis's uninhibited slapstick.)

But Sol also knew that his wife had much less patience than he did, particularly for the questions "Why?" and "Why not?"

~

Sol was still working up the courage to talk to Nora about this "thing" that seemed to circle his fevered brain like a vulture eyeing carrion. It had been costing him sleep. He was counting on her to solve at least part of his problem.

For the past week, as he lay in bed at night, it felt as if someone had placed a barbell across his chest, and the feeling didn't leave him when he was upright. He couldn't seem to catch his breath. His heart felt as though it struggled to catch up with his breathing—or maybe it was the other way around.

And it had started with the phone call from the lawyer ten days earlier, telling him there was an unexpected obstacle blocking the sale of his business.

"You have a liability issue," Peter Cooperman, his longtime attorney, said in his gravelly monotone. "The appeals court reversed the ruling on the wrongful death–negligence case. You're either going to have to settle or go back to court. Everything else is on hold."

The case itself seemed straightforward. A driver for All-American, a private contractor with his own truck, had been crushed when the eighteen-wheel trailer he'd been pulling overturned on an interstate cloverleaf entrance, an accident ascribed at the scene to traveling at excessive speeds. The driver had a spotty driving record and a history of reprimands for loads that were poorly distributed, which had resulted in a couple of tipping near misses. In the end, the accident was officially attributed to both driver error and poor equipment maintenance (bad brakes).

The driver's wife, however, found a lawyer willing to argue that the negligence was on the part of All-American: This was obviously a driver who proved he required supervision, if he was, in fact, competent to remain employed. By retaining him as a driver despite his record, the company assumed the risk and could be found liable for negligence.

When Sol pointed out to the lawyer that he and Stan were removed from those day-to-day decisions at the point the accident happened, Cooperman said, "Doesn't matter."

A postaccident report said the truck's brakes had failed, contributing to the rollover—and the driver had a counterfeit safety-inspection sticker on his truck. When the case was decided in All-American's favor, Sol assumed that was that.

Then the driver's family lawyer appealed, on the basis of uncovering a new document: a form Sol had signed, presented to him by Stan as needing a quick signature, no doubt among a stack of papers he wanted to clear from his inbox. In its fine print, in a section neither partner bothered to read, the form said that All-American vouched for the driver's qualifications, which included his inspection sticker.

Based on that form and Sol's signature, the appeals court reversed the ruling and All-American was back in the crosshairs. As a result, all funds involved in the sale of All-American had been temporarily frozen.

"We're liable for not knowing we were being lied to?" Sol said.

"For the moment."

"But we're moving to a co-op after Labor Day. I'm about to put my house up for sale."

"That's going to have to wait, I'm afraid," Cooperman told him.

The phone call left Sol with both sinking spirits and the anxious need to keep this information from his wife. Then, a day or so later, Cooperman's office rang back to ask Sol a question on an unrelated matter. But the lawyer had a new secretary, who mistakenly called Sol's residence, instead of his office. Lillian had taken the call, then leaped at Sol when he got home to find out what legal catastrophe was bearing down on them: "Why would your attorney be calling you?"

Sol waved it off as nothing to worry about. His secretary called the house by mistake, that was all.

"But why? Why does he need to speak to you? Is something wrong?"

He repeated his assertion that it was a simple mistake, that he talked to Cooperman several times a week about a variety of mundane matters, none of which were potential catastrophes. Then he successfully redirected the conversation to her current work as treasurer of her synagogue women's group. She treated members who were behind in their monthly dues like common scofflaws, whose fiscal inconstancy provoked her ire ("That Inez Greenstein hasn't paid into the coffee fund since March!").

But even as she launched into a recounting of her pursuit of missing payments, Sol could tell that she wasn't distracted from the issue of the lawyer. Her antennae for upset—whether in him or the girls—were highly sensitive. She seemed to have an ability to detect unhappiness in him, no matter how scrupulously Sol masked his roiling emotions with a placid exterior.

But Sol also knew that at least for the moment, her curiosity was outweighed by her need for nothing to be wrong. Lillian was a nosy, anxious woman but one who, when it came down to it, believed ignorance could be bliss, if the news was bad.

Sol could give himself vertigo with the uncertainty of his legal situation. On the one hand, Cooperman said, a court had already decided in All-American's favor one time, which was a mark in their favor. On the other hand, he said, you just never knew: "I mean, one of the judges who ruled against you on the appeal is so old, he was appointed by Coolidge."

There was no predicting how things would go a second time, he said, because it was a whole new trial: "I mean, technically, this time they could take everything you have."

When Sol blanched, Cooperman added, "But that seems unlikely."

Sol had been in a churn ever since, struggling for breath, with a burning in his stomach that felt like a small volcano.

~

At the inning changeover, Sol said, "Honey, I need to ask for help with your mother."

Eyes widening, Nora said, "What is it? Is something wrong? Is she sick?"

"No, no, nothing's wrong with her. I'm the one with the problem."

"Are you OK? Clara told me you fainted."

"That was just too much sun. I'm fine."

"Then what's wrong?"

"There's a legal issue that's come up that's stalled us selling the business."

"You're not in any trouble, are you?"

"We don't really know at this point. We just don't know how it will go."

"And Mother's not taking it well?"

"I haven't told her yet."

He saw comprehension blossom in her eyes. They both understood Lillian's tendency to overreact. To Lillian, there was no uncertainty: The news would always be bad. Not knowing would scare her to death, and that would color their life together from then on until the case was resolved. Unless . . .

"I was hoping you'd help me tell her," he said.

Sol couldn't read Nora's expression. She paused, then said, "Is that why you wanted me to come home this weekend? To tell her?"

"What? No, no, honey—not this weekend. Good God, no. I'm not ready to tell her yet."

The color, which had drained from Nora's face, began to return. Then Sol continued, "I want to wait until you move back here at the beginning of the month and tell her then. Having you nearby will make this all easier for her."

"What?" was all she could manage to say in response.

Nora's face took on an expression that resembled panic, but that made no sense to Sol: Nora didn't panic.

"Well, I know your lease in Syracuse is up, because I pay your rent," he said with a smile. "I just assumed you would come back home to work. Oh, I know—not *home* home. You'll want an apartment in the city—maybe you and Gina can find a place together. But you know what I mean. I know your mother would love to have you closer."

Just then, the Mets' Ed Kranepool hit a home run that brought the crowd to its feet, leaving Nora and Sol the only ones still seated.

Sol scarcely registered the action on the field. His daughter's beautiful face had turned to a mask of anguish.

"Honey, what is it?"

"Daddy," she began, as though struggling for what to say next, "I have to tell you something."

"Yes, Punkin?" he said. His mind immediately roiled with worst-case scenarios: Was she involved with drugs? In trouble with the law? In some sort of financial trouble? No, Nora was too smart for anything like that, he knew.

Is she pregnant? Oh God no!

He didn't want to think about his little girl having sex, let alone producing a baby. He'd already gone through that with Amelia. The memory still unsettled him—and she was married. But an accidental pregnancy also seemed unlikely, for the same reason: Nora had too good a head on her shoulders.

She looked him in the eye and said, "I'm moving to Chicago."

Not a pregnancy, but it still delivered a punch to his solar plexus.

"Chicago? In Illinois?" It was all he could say. He sat, stunned for a moment, then said, "When?"

"At the beginning of the month." She hesitated, then said, "I have a job teaching that starts in the fall and a grant to do research that's already begun."

"In Chicago? Illinois?" He realized he sounded like a fool, repeating this. "But we assumed you'd come back here when you finished school. I even remember you mentioning something about teaching at NYU."

"Daddy, this is such a great opportunity. I'll be an assistant professor at Northwestern in Evanston. It's just north of Chicago."

The crowd whooped again, but when he looked at the field, all he saw was the team mascot, Mr. Met, mugging with a fan near the third base dugout. He turned back to his daughter.

"The first of July is in two weeks. And you're moving to Chicago? When were you going to deliver this bit of news to your mother and me?"

Nora looked shamefaced: "I'm sorry, Daddy. I knew that no matter what I said, Mother would never approve. So I wanted to avoid that argument altogether. Or at least as long as possible. I was going to call in a week or so."

Sol couldn't keep the note of hurt out of his voice: "What about me? Don't you care how I feel about this?"

"Oh, Daddy," she said, crying as she hugged him. "I love you. But I need to get out on my own and start my life. Not here. Not with her looking over my shoulder."

Sol had always marveled at Nora's determination. He knew he couldn't change her mind about her mother. She'd told him as much when they had one of their few real arguments, after Nora had told them that she'd applied—and been accepted—at Syracuse without telling them first. He and Nora had always been able to talk, in a way he knew she couldn't with her mother. But their argument forced him to concede that he had been in denial over the true nature of her relationship with her mother.

"I have to get away from here—from her," she'd told him when he went into her room to get her to reconsider Syracuse.

"Don't talk that way. She's your mother. She wants what's best for you."

Nora snorted, then said, "Sorry, I don't believe that. She treats me like an employee."

The clanging dissonance rattled his head: The daughter he adored, speaking a truth that clawed at his soul about his wife, the woman he'd tied himself to until death. Sol couldn't bear to hear it and said, "Don't ever talk that way about your mother. I will not listen to that kind of talk." From that point, he knew, he and Nora would never agree about Lillian and could no longer discuss her.

Nora never brought it up again, but now, Sol could no longer ignore it when he saw it flash in her eyes. *She thinks we can't talk,* Sol thought, understanding that she was about to start a life that had nothing to do with them.

And, though he knew he was an exceptionally fortunate man, in that moment Sol felt genuinely cursed, burdened now with not one but two secrets he someday would have to reveal to his wife.

~

As the game continued, Sol realized he was juggling too many things in his life to absorb Nora's news. Things had ground to a halt on finalizing the deal to sell All-American to a Japanese concern. The more demanding element was the postponed sale of the house he and Lillian had been living in for thirty years. He'd put enough money down on the co-op they would move to in September, so that was not an issue for the rest of the year. It was a smaller place—but it would only be the two of them. And it was adjacent to Scarsdale; he knew the location had helped persuade Lillian, after she'd initially resisted the idea of moving at all.

When they did move at the end of the summer, Sol knew she would take time to adjust. Not just because of the new surroundings but because Clara was leaving her. That, unfortunately, was one fact of which he *was* certain.

Clara's announced departure to care for her ailing sister in Scranton had presented an unappetizing prospect for Sol and Lillian's future: keeping up their large suburban house without Clara for the first time since they'd moved in.

"Do *you* want to train someone to replace Clara?" Sol asked Lillian. "Only so they can cook and clean for us in this big house, where we'll be living all by ourselves? I wouldn't expect you to do any of that. Why don't we find someplace smaller?"

Given the confluence of events, it had proven easier to convince Lillian to move than he expected. Sol found them the co-op near Scarsdale, but they had not yet listed their house for sale. Clara would stay on until the end of August. At that point, Sol was supposed to retire—but that was in a universe in which he and Stan finalized the sale of their business and stepped away. Sol now was haunted by a new fear: *What if I can't retire?* It made his chest hurt again.

The approach of all these events also reminded Sol that it had been a long time—almost as long as he'd been married—since he'd had to deal with Lillian without Clara as a buffer or an ally. It didn't seem possible, but Clara had been there, in the rooms over the garage, for *thirty* years now.

Sol thought of Clara as part of the family, and a crucial one at that. He had never forgotten the way she had stepped in at a critical moment and become an indispensable part of the household. No matter how early he rose over the years to leave for work, Clara was up before him, the coffee made, his bagel waiting to be toasted. She was his window into Lillian and the girls during those years when work kept him out past the girls' bedtime; she filled him in about their lives as he gobbled his breakfast and gulped his coffee before facing morning traffic.

When Clara told him she had to leave, Sol tried to convince her to stay until the end of the year. There were two bedrooms in the new place, he pointed out, and the housework would be greatly reduced because the co-op was so much smaller.

Clara, however, felt an understandable obligation to go back to care for her widowed younger sister. Sol had been to Scranton on business and found it a depressing little city. But you didn't get to choose where you came from.

Lillian had not taken the news of Clara leaving well. For the two weeks after Clara gave her notice, there would come a point at least once every evening during dinner when Lillian would put down her fork and say, "I don't know what we'll do without Clara."

Sol would have to spend the rest of the meal (if not the evening) trying to calm her anxiety and change the subject. After a couple of months, she'd stopped bringing up the topic and instead started saying to Sol, "Well, we'll just see."

Sol knew Lillian thought she could change Clara's mind. Sol also knew that would not be the case, because Clara had told him so after they had all visited the co-op and Lillian had decided she liked it.

"Sol, things work now with just me and Lillian at home because it's a big house," Clara said. "She has her parts of the house, and I have mine. If I'm not in the kitchen or doing the laundry or the housework, I always have my place upstairs."

"But you're so important to all of us," Sol said. "You're part of the family."

"I appreciate that, Sol, but I've seen your new place. There won't be anything for me to do there that takes more than an hour a day. How am I supposed to fill the rest of my time? And again, Lillian and I have always gotten along because we could give each other room. In the new place, either we'd be in each other's apron pocket all the time—"

"Now, it's not *that* small."

"—or I'd feel like I was hiding from her in my own room."

"That room does have its own bathroom."

"So do prison cells," Clara said flatly. She sighed and said, "Sorry, I don't mean to sound unappreciative."

The prospect of being alone in a small apartment with Lillian all day, every day, did sound a little like a life sentence to Sol. He reminded himself that he loved his wife, to whom he'd been married more than three decades.

Like so much in Sol's life up to that point, the co-op had fallen into his lap, as though summoned by a wish from a genie. At the end of his synagogue men's group's monthly lunch, Sol mentioned in passing that they'd made the decision to sell their house and find somewhere smaller, in case anyone heard of anything that might be right.

Sid Kramer, who owned a jewelry store in White Plains, said, "My wife's aunt just went into the hospital this week, probably for the last time. She has a co-op that they're going to have to get rid of. Want to look at it before it goes on the market?"

It was that simple. Sid took him to see it after lunch, and to Sol, it seemed perfect. Spacious, without being too big for the two of them.

"Yes, I think we're definitely interested," Sol told him. "Let me bring my wife to see it. How's next weekend?"

Sol knew Lillian was still reeling from the idea of selling the house. While she told him she was ready for the change, he could feel her heels dragging anytime the topic came up.

His wife hated complication in any aspect of her life. She valued order and familiarity. They gave her a sense of comfort, he knew—whereas complications (which included looking at a series of properties and having to choose among them) set her on edge.

But if Sol could keep things simple—find the right place on his first try so the entire move would feel seamless—maybe they could glide through the transition with as little friction as possible. That strategy, he decided, would require Clara's help.

"If you could come with us when she sees it the first time, it might . . ." Sol began, before finding himself at a loss for words.

"It might help her see it through my eyes, instead of just her own," Clara said.

"Yes, thank you."

That night at dinner, Sol said, in passing, "I heard about a co-op that sounded like it might be right for us. But it isn't on the market yet."

"Then what good would it do *us*?" Lillian said.

"Well, it will be on the market—in a week or so," he said. "But I think we might be able to get an early look at it this weekend."

"If you want."

Two nights later, at dinner, Sol said, "I didn't hear from Sid today about the co-op. I'll call him tomorrow."

The next evening at dinner—it was now Wednesday—Lillian said, "Did you hear anything about that co-op?"

"*That* co-op." A hopeful sign: not just "a" co-op, in the general sense, but this specific co-op that had taken her interest.

The next afternoon, when Lillian answered the phone, it was Sol asking, "Are we free to look at the co-op on Saturday morning?" to which she said, "Of course."

At breakfast on Saturday, Sol said, as though he'd just thought of it, "What if Clara comes with us? I bet she could help you when it comes to being able to see what will fit and what won't. In case we like it."

"I suppose that would be all right." It was as close to agreeable as she got.

When Clara came in to clear the breakfast dishes, Sol stopped her. "Clara, would you like to come with us to look at a co-op that's about to come on the market? We'd value your perspective on how much of this"—he gestured at the house furnishings around him—"how much of this might fit into someplace that's more manageable for the two of us."

Sol worried that it sounded like a memorized speech, which it was. But then, to his surprise, Lillian said, "Yes, Clara, please come."

An hour or so later, the three of them stood in the co-op's dark living room while Sid pulled back a pair of thick blackout drapes of wine-colored velvet. Sunlight from a southern exposure poured in, revealing a spacious room with a fireplace and built-in bookshelves. A pair of French doors that had been hidden by the drapes opened onto a spacious balcony, overlooking a swath of greensward and a short stretch of the Bronx River.

Clara opened the door, stepped onto the balcony, and then turned back to Lillian and said, "You could put your plants out here in the summer and still have room for some furniture—it gets a lot of sun."

Lillian just said, "Hmm," but Sol saw a flicker of interest from her. As Sid showed them through the apartment, Clara and Lillian fell behind. Sol could hear their conversation take on a tone Sol seldom heard from his wife: chitchatty girl talk between friends—almost lighthearted, like a younger Lillian that Sol barely remembered.

"Your dining room table might fit in here and still have room for the china cabinet," Clara said.

"What about the sideboard?"

"What's in the sideboard?"

"Extra dishes, extra linens."

"I don't remember us ever needing extra. So what do you need them for?"

"But what would I do with them?"

"That's the kind of thing that people pass on to their kids, isn't it?" Clara said.

"You're right," Lillian said, as though the thought had never occurred to her. "We *could* give them to the girls."

To Sol's eye, she seemed to engage with both Clara and the apartment from that point on. The two of them worked their way through the rest of the rooms, making lists out loud of what would fit, what wouldn't, what should be put into storage, and so on.

Two days later, as it happened, the old lady with the co-op expired. Sol hung up the phone after speaking with Sid and went to Lillian.

"The co-op is ours if we want it," he told her. "No bidding or anything. The price is right and so is the timing. Should we do it?"

"Well, of course—why are you even wasting time asking me?" she'd said. "Call him back before he decides to sell it to someone else."

It was theirs, as of September 1. It was possible, he realized, that he might wind up owning both places at once, which might strain finances, but not too badly. With luck, before long, it would just be him and Lillian and the co-op.

At that point, Sol knew he would have to find a new approach to his marriage and his life.

~

For most of his years with Lillian, the secret to the success of his marriage was limiting his and Lillian's exposure to each other. Sol was a firm believer in the maxim "Absence makes the heart grow fonder."

Sol left the house every morning no later than 6:30 a.m.—and often earlier—to avoid the traffic between Tarrytown and Queens. It was the same in the evening. He would wait until after 6:00 p.m., often much after, to avoid the evening rush hour, before heading home. Lillian had Clara serve dinner to her and the girls every evening at 6:30 p.m., and Sol did not often make it home in time to join them. For years, this was a point of contention between him and Lillian, one of the few on which he wouldn't yield because the work demanded his attention.

But he also knew they couldn't squabble if he wasn't home. And when he was home, well, it was a large house, and most of his limited time was spent on the yard or with his daughters.

Now Sol faced a future living in close quarters with his wife by himself, for the first time since Amelia was born and Clara came to live with them.

The prospect unnerved him. While he loved his wife, Sol was also intimidated by her. He was not an unconfident man in business, but Sol was afraid of his wife and her sharp tongue. And there was an even greater fear as well: that she might repeat what happened a few years before Nora was born.

Clara had called him at the office, something that was out of the ordinary. She told him that, after putting Amelia down for her nap, Clara had gone looking for Lillian to ask her about lunch—and found her unconscious on the bathroom floor. Clara had roused her enough to get Lillian to the bedroom, then called the doctor.

Lillian was still sleeping when Sol got home, but the doctor had gone. As Sol walked in the door, however, the phone rang with the physician's call.

"What do you think is wrong?" Sol asked.

"She may have accidentally taken too many pills. When I got her to wake up enough to answer questions, she mentioned having a bad headache—"

"Yes, she gets those."

"—and said she took several pills for the pain. She couldn't remember how many. She may have done it out of impatience or confusion." He paused. "Or she may have done it on purpose."

"On purpose? My wife? She wouldn't . . . do that."

"At one point, when she was conscious, she became distraught and said things that force me to consider that possibility. Has your wife been unhappy lately?"

The thought shook Sol on multiple levels. Yes, Lillian had been unhappy after Amelia was born; that was why he'd hired Clara. But was she still so unhappy? So much so that she would take her own life? How had he not seen it?

He knew she'd been exhausted by Amelia's birth; she'd talked of nothing else. But to the point of suicide?

The next day, Lillian was awake, alert, active—and acting as if nothing had happened. When Sol asked her about the day before, she said, "I took a nap. Is that a crime? I lay down because I was getting a migraine. The next thing I know, the doctor was in my bedroom. You're all making a commotion out of nothing. I've been telling you how tired I am since the baby was born."

But Sol couldn't forget what the doctor had said. *What if she is unhappy enough to do something like that—again? What would I do with two little girls and a house in the suburbs, if I don't have a wife?*

His fears gradually subsided, and Lillian returned to her old self—until Nora's birth. When she began retreating to her sewing room, isolating herself for hours at a time, Sol would fret about whether something serious was wrong, but worried that she would snap at him if he checked on her. The one time he knocked at the sewing room door and offered a timid "Are you all right?" she responded angrily, saying, "Please stop spying on me."

But the thought never left him: *What if Lillian does kill herself?* What would that do to the girls? His constant vigilance during that year was wearing. For his concern, he received only the cutting edge of his wife's tongue, when she complained about him trying to control her.

Sol hadn't always been afraid of his wife. There was a time when her sharp wit had been applied without a coating of acid. He remembered her being genuinely funny when they were first married, someone who could unleash a laugh that tickled his soul. Lillian could do impressions of radio stars like Fanny Brice and Gracie Allen, though only when the two of them were alone; she was too self-conscious to ever be a performer.

Something had changed in her after Amelia was born, he believed, though she had returned to her old self—mostly—after Clara arrived to help with the housework and childcare. But after Nora was born, the old Lillian disappeared for good, replaced by a sour, angrier version. In that iteration, the threat of self-destruction seemed to lurk just beneath the surface, at least in Sol's mind.

He couldn't confide those fears about his wife to anyone—not even Stan, his closest friend, because Stan would tell Delia, who would inevitably say something to Lillian. Sol knew what a betrayal that would be in Lillian's eyes.

No matter how he felt about his wife at that point, he couldn't even think about divorce. In Sol's world, divorce was a word whispered in shame, almost as shameful as marrying out of the faith. It was a nonstarter, not even to be considered. "Till death do us part." No other options were available. It didn't matter how unhappy you were; your only escape from a miserable marriage was death—yours or your spouse's. No one cared if you wanted to stab each other in the neck with butcher knives. There simply was no way out.

But after her "accidental" overdose, Lillian became moodier in every way. That included sharp-edged comments—not just to him but to the girls and Clara. At those moments, he tried to focus on the things about her that had first attracted him: her humor, but also her insecurity, which always seemed so close to the surface, and her vulnerability, which she tried to mask with an all-encompassing sense of authority. Though they seldom made an appearance, Sol knew that her vulnerable qualities were there, deeply hidden beneath the haughty surface.

In recent years, since the girls had moved out, Sol wondered if he'd only fooled himself into believing that vulnerability was there. And at those moments, he cursed himself as a coward, for his reluctance to get between the girls and Lillian's vitriol.

He simply couldn't bear the idea of his wife focusing her ill temper on him. His fear shamed him as much as his failure to shield his daughters when Lillian blew up at them. Yet her needling remarks prickled—her contention that he let Stan take advantage of him; her complaint, despite the growth and success of his business, that he had never aimed high enough. This, from a woman who, at least in Sol's recollection, had been impressed by someone his age owning his own business when they first met.

His own behavior left him feeling defeated and unhappy, two sensations he had gone out of his way to avoid for most of his life. When Lillian unleashed her beam of rage and disappointment on the girls, Sol would sit quietly, offering only a half-hearted "Now, Lil," from time to time. Then he would slip into the kitchen and tell Clara under his breath, "Give the girls a little extra ice cream for dessert," as though this made up for his unwillingness to stand in Lillian's line of fire.

And now his approaching retirement meant being home more, in a smaller space, in greater proximity for more of the time, an easy target for his wife's complaints. Clara was leaving, and now so was Nora, so he'd be on his own with his wife.

Each of the elements in play at the moment—Sol's retirement, selling the house, moving to a co-op, Clara's departure—had been enough on its own to pitch Lillian into a multiday tizzy. The legal threat seemed certain to provoke something worse, and Sol knew he would have to tell Lillian at some point.

But not now.

Everything in him resisted letting her in on the situation. But Nora's revelation about her future had him scrambling.

He didn't want to tell Lillian by himself. But he wasn't going to have Nora around to help him after this weekend, the way things stood. Unless he could talk her out of it, she would be in Chicago.

So maybe he needed to tell Lillian while Nora was still here.

~

As the crowd rose for the seventh-inning stretch, Sol remembered something Nora had told him earlier. When the crowd sat after singing "Take Me Out to the Ball Game," Sol turned to her and said, "When you were talking about Chicago before, you said *we*."

Nora looked at him, smiled shyly, and said, "I met someone." Then she launched into the tale of Stephen Cantor, which was more of a short story.

Since she was a teen, Nora had alarmed Sol with her outspoken opinions against marriage. Even now, as she spoke glowingly of Stephen, she told Sol she was still struggling with the concept of a wedding: "I don't *just* want to be someone's wife," she said.

Sol wasn't sure what she meant by that but tried to look Nora in the eye as he said, "Just tell me he makes you happy."

"Oh, Daddy, he does," she gushed.

"That's all that matters. We can't wait to meet him," Sol said, even as he thought, *Another goddamn secret.*

"Actually, I had to find an excuse to keep him from coming up to meet you two this weekend."

"Wait," Sol said, "he's in New York? Now *I'd* like to meet him."

"I'm not letting him within a mile of Mother. Focus, Daddy."

"Yes, of course."

They drove home, listening to the postgame wrap-up show on WJRZ radio. The Mets' manager, Wes Westrum, talked about the game with announcer Ralph Kiner, who kept calling him "Skip."

As he listened and drove, Sol's chest felt like it was encased in cement. He couldn't focus on one problem because two others kept intruding. He was afraid Lillian would read the aggravation of every fact he was keeping from her just from the tension in his shoulders. He needed Nora's help but had no idea how they would tell her, while protecting Nora's secret.

When the postgame show was over, Nora switched the station to WABC, which was playing "Windy," by the Association.

"That Tom Seaver looks like he has some promise," Nora said.

"You always had a good eye for talent."

"About time they found some decent pitching."

"Maybe this was the game that will turn things around," Sol offered hopefully.

"At least until tomorrow's game," Nora cracked, earning a laugh from her father.

He turned to Nora and said, "I'm sorry. I am going to need your help telling your mother before you leave. But I have no idea how to do it."

Nora sighed and looked straight ahead, where glimpses of the dark Hutchinson River Parkway flashed by in the headlights. "When? What do you want me to do?"

"Probably after brunch tomorrow. Let me see."

"Just tell me what you need."

"I don't know yet. Let me sleep on it, and we can talk tomorrow."

He tried to sound carefree when he said it. Then he glimpsed his reflection in the rearview mirror.

Sol Levitsky, portrait of the doomed.

I am so fucked.

~

It was almost 11:00 p.m. by the time they finished the drive from Queens to North Tarrytown. Sol noticed there was a light on in Clara's rooms over the garage. The house was dark, except for a light bulb over the sink in the kitchen and night-lights in the hallways. Sol and Nora said their goodbyes in the kitchen.

"It looks like we both have secrets from your mother," Sol said.

"I'll keep yours if you keep mine," Nora replied with a rueful smile.

For a moment, Sol felt as though he were about to be discovered by Lillian. His confusion must have shown on his face, because Nora hugged him, then said, "Get some sleep, Daddy. You look tired."

"You too, honey," he said and kissed the top of her head.

"Yes, sir," she said and kissed his cheek. She waved a fist and offered a sotto voce version of a cheer: "Let's go, Mets!" then disappeared up the stairs.

Instead of finding his own way to bed, Sol retired to his office in the back of the house. It was a small den off the laundry room, with a window onto the backyard. He pulled the string on the desk lamp with the green glass shade, bathing his messy desktop in light.

He pushed aside the pile of paperwork for the sale of All-American—critical at the point they could move forward; worthless, for the moment. Then he took a small key out of the center drawer and used it to unlock the lower right-hand drawer of the old wooden desk. He extracted a pint of Specht slivovitz, a shot glass, and an ashtray and set them all on the desk in front of him.

He reached back into the drawer and found a pack of Tareytons and a book of matches. He had switched to the mild-tasting filtered cigarettes after years of smoking unfiltered Pall Malls, when he saw a TV commercial in which a doctor explained the health benefits of Tareyton's "patented Micronite filter."

Sol pulled the door to his office closed, then pushed the window up and lit a cigarette, exhaling smoke into the still night air outside.

He poured a shot of slivovitz and downed it in a swallow. Then he took a thoughtful drag on his cigarette while he waited for the fire ignited by the liquor to hit bottom. He poured a second shot, which he sipped while he sat and smoked. He only smoked when he had a problem he needed to puzzle through.

~

Until the uncertainty about the lawsuit arose, Sol had considered himself a lucky man. He had never faced serious tragedy in his life. While his parents were now dead, that was a loss everyone suffered at some point. His older brother, Louis, had been killed at twenty as a doughboy in the Argonne Forest. Again, sad—dead too young. But it was no more than hundreds of thousands of American families had to bear during the Great War.

In most respects, Sol knew himself to be extremely fortunate. Too young for the Great War, exempted from service for World War II because his company was crucial to the war effort, he had been blessed with life's bounty: a beautiful family and a successful business that supported them through the Depression into what, until recently, had looked like a future of unimagined comfort. Before the lawsuit's revival, there had been little serious or important for him to complain about.

Yet Sol often felt his nerves were frayed and taut, unable to withstand even the slightest twang or plink. When he thought about what made him feel that way, the answer was always the same: Lillian.

Sol loved his wife, but trying to make her happy left him perpetually depleted. Happiness seemed like an ambitious target; if he could keep her from being actively unhappy, that would at least give him breathing room.

But, too often, even that seemed beyond his reach. In a college philosophy class, a professor painted the mythic figure of Sisyphus as a metaphor for resilience. Sisyphus had been a wicked king, whose punishment from the gods for his wickedness was to spend eternity pushing a boulder up a hill, only to see it roll back down again, forcing him to repeat the task, again and again, day after day, forever.

But the professor said that even though Sisyphus is doomed to fail in his daily chore, he is a figure to admire and even emulate because he still has the inner fortitude to start at the beginning and tackle this insurmountable obstacle yet again, over and over. Anyone who brings that kind of doggedness to most tasks we face in daily life, the professor had claimed, was bound to succeed.

Now Sol saw how wrong that interpretation was, because now Sol knew: Sisyphus pushed that boulder because he didn't have a choice. It was punishment—and the only reason he continued to do it was the knowledge that if he refused, the gods had something even worse in store for him.

Lillian—or, rather, Lillian's unhappiness—was Sol's boulder, one from which it felt as if he'd never be free. She had always been demanding—of him, of the girls—but, in the past few years, she had become increasingly fearful, particularly about financial matters. That made her more demanding still.

She had always been nervous about their money, though Sol was already successful when they married. He found that Lillian was frugal to the point of parsimony, because she was sure they could run out of money at any minute.

He knew he had to be careful how he broke the news about the legal trouble for exactly that reason. He had to avoid triggering her sense of alarm, because she treated every crisis as an emotional five-alarm fire, escalating to full-blown panic. That fear brought Sol back to his concern about how many pills of various sorts she might have stored in the medicine cabinet or elsewhere.

~

At rest, Lillian's face wore an expression most people would interpret as haughty. Often, the expression masked how she really felt, a fact Sol wasn't aware of the first time he met her.

When Sol had been introduced to Lillian on a spring evening in 1934, the look on her face seemed to say "It will take a lot more than you to impress me, Buster." Sol took that expression as a romantic challenge because he was drawn to the young woman whose face it adorned.

They met when they were seated across from each other at a Passover seder at the home of Sol's Aunt Mildred, his late father's sister, whose husband, Jim Sanderson, came from a wealthy Pennsylvania family that owned a steel mill.

Uncle Jimmy was not Jewish when he married Aunt Millie, which technically made the marriage a shanda, a shame on the family. But his willingness to convert to Judaism made up for a lot. So did the fact that Uncle Jimmy came from money and wasn't afraid to use it to help his wife's large family, including ones trying to escape from Europe at this fraught moment in history.

Also in his favor: the fact that he insisted on hosting the family for holiday meals, whether for Passover, Hanukkah, the High Holidays, or the occasional Shabbas dinner. It was always an event for the far-flung members of Sol's family to travel from the Bronx, Queens, the Lower East Side, New Jersey, and wherever else they came from to visit Millie and Jimmy in their Park Avenue digs.

By 1934, Sol and Stan had turned their small scrapyard into a successful scrap-metal business that seemed to grow and expand annually. But that took twelve-hour days and more, which kept Sol too busy to think about dating, let alone marriage.

At the age of thirty, he was that unique Jewish bachelor who had fled his parents' nest without first being married. He had a small apartment in the South Bronx just off the Grand Concourse and owned his own car, which he drove to his scrapyard near Willets Point every day.

The Great Depression was in full swing, but Sol and Stan's business found ways to not only survive but thrive. In those parlous economic times, Sol never took success for granted and worked hard to make sure it was always foremost in his thoughts. His mother and sister tried to fix him up with eligible young women from their synagogue, to little avail.

At the seder at Aunt Millie's, Sol was introduced to Lillian before the meal began, then found himself seated across from her and his cousin Bernice, who was Aunt Millie's daughter and a few years younger than Sol. Bernice worked in the secretarial pool at a large insurance company in Manhattan. So did Lillian; the two had hit it off on a coffee break on Bernice's first day and become work friends. Finding that the older woman had no Passover plans, Bernice invited her to the seder.

Sol, who was seated next to his mother, gazed at the dark-eyed young woman as she and Bernice chatted about work before the seder began. Lillian kept making remarks that made Bernice giggle, though she kept her voice low enough that Sol couldn't hear what she was saying.

He snuck glances at her whenever they looked up from the prayer books during the seder to take a sip of wine or a bite of one of the ritual foods on the seder plate.

Lillian wasn't traditionally pretty. Her eyes had sleepy lids that made her look sad, and the eyes themselves seemed to bulge ever so slightly. Yet she was attractive in a way he couldn't put a finger on. Perhaps it was her hauteur, as though she were looking down her nose at everything and everyone around her.

Lillian smiled at Sol across the table, even as she turned and said something under her breath that made Bernice burst out laughing. He felt an urge to know what she was saying and to make this woman look at him again and smile. But Sol sensed something else, a helplessness he couldn't put his finger on. It made him want to protect her, to rescue her from whatever it was that was frightening her.

After seder prayers were concluded and the meal began, the conversation grew spirited about Franklin Delano Roosevelt, who was about a year into his first term.

"What has he done, after all the campaign promises?" Uncle Jimmy said.

"Done?" Bernice shot back at her father. "Give the man a chance. He's barely had time to learn his way around the White House. And he's got Republicans yapping at his heels like a pack of hyenas."

"Some of his proposals sound very innovative," Lillian put in, and Sol saw his opening.

"Yes," he said, "look what he's already done to put people back to work with that Civilian Conservation Corps."

Lillian had smiled at that, a smile that he now recalled, taking a drag from his Tareyton, because it had made him feel as though he couldn't catch his breath for a second—but in a good way, not the way he'd been feeling lately. Whenever Sol had glanced in her direction the rest of the evening, she was looking at him.

When the meal was over and the help was clearing the table for dessert, Bernice came over to him and said, "Can you spare a cigarette?"

"Make that two, if you don't mind," Lillian said.

"My pleasure," Sol said, pulling out a beat-up pack of Camels and offering them to the two young women, before taking one himself.

"Let's go out on the terrace to smoke," Bernice said. "It's such a warm night."

"Lead the way," Lillian said.

Sol followed them down a hall to a pair of doors that led to a balcony. There was enough room for a chaise longue and matching chairs with ottomans, as well as end tables for drinks. Bernice and Lillian sat down in the chairs to smoke and chat, while Sol leaned on the railing, which faced west on Park Avenue, between Seventieth and Seventy-First Streets.

It was balmy for a late-March night, and he took a moment to unbutton his shirt collar under his tie. The sky in the west was dark purple with lingering hints of pink and red. He could see the lights of the George Washington Bridge, still only a couple of years old, to the north. As he looked down from the twelfth story, the cars inching their way down Park looked toy size.

"Do you live in the city?" Sol asked Lillian.

She gave him a look that surprised him with its interest, then said, "I do. My family, or what's left of it, is in Brooklyn."

"I'm sorry—how do you mean, what's left of it?"

"She's being dramatic," Bernice said. "We were just talking about the trouble in Germany. Lillian has cousins in Berlin."

"I'm sorry to hear that," he said, shaking his head. He had read stories in the liberal *New York Post* about the increasingly draconian laws in Germany, prohibiting Jews from working in certain jobs or owning businesses. "That Hitler and his followers? Animals. The Jews ought to just leave."

"And go where?" Bernice asked. "It's not like Jews are so popular anywhere else."

"You say that so casually: 'They ought to just leave,'" Lillian said. "Have you ever had to leave your home to start over in a strange place?"

"No, ma'am, I'm Bronx born and bred," he said with a smile, which curdled a bit under Lillian's cool look.

"Well, I have," she said, as though this ended the discussion.

It would have, but Bernice piped up, "You said you were three when your family immigrated, Lillian. How much do you even remember?"

Lillian blushed with embarrassment, and in that moment, Sol felt all the insecurity and fear that seemed to percolate just under her haughty exterior. Just for a second.

But Lillian recovered her composure, saying, "That's not too young to share the sense of loss that your elders are feeling. I never want to feel that again."

"Well, the point is this Hitler is a sonuvabitch—you should pardon my language," Sol said. "Someone ought to get rid of him."

They all smoked their cigarettes a moment, before Sol said to Lillian, "I would never have known English wasn't your first language."

Lillian softened at the compliment as Sol said, "Do you still speak German?"

"Only a little," she said, "when provoked."

"Well, I only speak English, so you're ahead of me," Sol said. "Although I do know some Yiddish—which is sort of the same, isn't it?"

Bernice said, "Let's hear it."

Sol struck the pose of an orator—one hand clutching his lapel, the other held upward, index finger pointed skyward for emphasis—then said, "Gey cacken affen yam."

Lillian's eyes widened, and she let out a hoot of laughter. Her hand flew to her mouth in an attempt to disguise her amusement at the fact that he'd just said "Go shit in the ocean" in Yiddish. Her expression cycled from humor to reproval as she said, with a small smile, "That's extremely vulgar."

Sol smiled roguishly. He'd seen it—the look in her eyes when he made her laugh. It was as if she saw him differently and let him know it. Just for a second. But he had seen it. More important, he had felt it. When she laughed, it was as if an innate tension within Lillian released, like a balloon suddenly deflating. She could smile and relax, if only for the moment. When he felt her laugh, it lifted him. He wanted to feel that again.

"Where did you grow up?" he said.

"Williamsburg."

"Does your family still live there?"

"Yes, my parents and my younger sisters. My parents own a tailor shop, and my sisters work for them."

"Do you remember what it was like to travel on a ship?" Sol asked, and the two of them were still talking an hour later when Sol's aunt came to tell them they were the last guests remaining. Other cousins had driven Sol's mother home when she wanted to leave early.

"Sorry, Aunt Millie, we lost track of time," Sol said.

His aunt and cousin saw them to the door, where Bernice and Lillian said they'd see each other at work the next day. They joked about what their coworkers would say if they brought matzo for lunch.

When they reached the elevator, Sol said, "Where in Williamsburg does your family live? I do some business over there."

"Between the Brooklyn entrance to the bridge and the river."

The elevator came, and Sol tried to continue the conversation as they rode down.

"You know," he said, "I wait all year for the seder, just to be able to eat my Aunt Millie's carrot ring."

"Yes, that *was* unusual," Lillian said. "Tasty but a strange texture—not quite bread, not quite cake."

"Exactly. My mother has the recipe, but she can never get it right. She was sitting next to me tonight, eating it and muttering to herself. Aunt Millie only makes it for Passover. Something about the matzo flour, I guess."

When they got to the lobby, Sol said, "I have my car. I can drive you home, if you'd like."

She gave him a look he couldn't interpret, then said, "I don't think so. But I suppose you could walk me to the subway."

He not only walked her to the subway—he rode it with her to her stop at Twenty-Third and Park Avenue, talking as they rode, then walked her home to a brownstone on East Twenty-Second Street near Third Avenue. At the door to her rooming house, he said, "Would you like to go out sometime?"

Lillian gave him a head-to-toe once-over, smiled a small smile, and said, "I guess we'll have to see, won't we?"

Encouraged by the smile, Sol moved in for a kiss. Her smile turned icy as Lillian held up a hand to stop him, saying, "Don't be presumptuous."

Sol laughed, then surprised her by taking her upturned hand in his and kissing it. He took a step back and tipped his hat with a smile.

"Good night, Lillian," he said, then practically floated back to the subway stop. He barely remembered the rest of his trip back to the Bronx.

At work the next day, as he bargained with his regular peddlers and made deals with foundries seeking scrap, Sol couldn't stop thinking about the sloe-eyed young woman from the seder.

They had made each other laugh on the subway ride. Sol mentioned seeing photos in the newspaper of Mount Rushmore, where sculptors were currently chiseling the faces of four presidents into a South Dakota mountainside, to create a national monument.

"Their faces will be big enough that people will be able to see them from miles away," Sol said.

"Why?" Lillian asked.

When he replied, “Why not?” she laughed lightly. Thinking a moment, she said, “Will mountain climbers be able to scale the presidents’ noses?” and that had made Sol laugh.

The next day, when he called his cousin Bernice to ask if she could get him Lillian’s phone number, Bernice teased him: “Yes, she may have mentioned you took her home—I forget,” she said, not hiding her glee at his discomfort. But Bernice called him back the following day to give him the phone number and tell him, “She said she’s usually home after six thirty. And her boardinghouse doesn’t allow phone calls after nine p.m.”

When he called the number at 7:15 p.m., a harsh female voice answered the phone on the second ring: “Pickwick Arms.”

Sol asked for Lillian, and the woman said, “Just a sec.” Sol heard her say to someone, “Tell Miss Pikorny that she has a phone call.”

There was a minute or so of silence before Sol heard the gruff voice say to someone, “Remember: The time limit is three minutes. Leave your dime in the cup next to the phone when you’re done.”

There was a rustling sound as the phone changed hands; then Lillian said, “Hello?”

“Hello, Lillian, this is Sol Levitsky, Bernice’s cousin. We met at the seder at my aunt and uncle’s?”

“Yes, I remember you. How are you?”

Her tone was friendly but cool. Why did her diffidence excite him? He couldn’t say, but Sol found that it did. Maybe it was because he knew that the warmth of her laugh lurked beneath her frosty front. He ached to make her laugh again. He did break through her tough shell enough to get her to agree to go to a movie the following Sunday afternoon.

He picked her up in his car and immediately ran into trouble when she seemed to balk at getting in: “I’ve read about what happens to single women when they ride unchaperoned with strange men in cars,” she said.

"Fortunately, for us, we've been introduced and we're not strangers, so you don't have to worry," he said with a smile, opening her door for her.

"You have all the answers, don't you?" she said, but her look was one of amusement.

When she asked what they were seeing, Sol said, "Everyone is talking about this movie at the Little Carnegie, *The Lost Patrol*."

Lillian made a face. "You're taking me to a war movie?"

"Or we could go to Radio City. There's that Clark Gable picture, *It Happened One Night*. And there would also be the Rockettes."

They wound up at Radio City, in time for both the Rockettes and the Mighty Wurlitzer organ, which filled the massive theater with a cascade of rich, bone-rattling chords. Once the film started, Sol was less interested in Clark Gable and Claudette Colbert than in sneaking glances at this unexpected young woman, who took in the comically romantic antics with what seemed like rapt attention and even the occasional chuckle.

After the movie, Sol said, "Would you like to get some coffee?" pointing to the nearby Automat.

"I guess so," she said, looking at her watch.

Once inside the shiny silver cafeteria, they found the distinctive dolphin-shaped spigots on the coffee machine, and Lillian said, "Thanks, I'll pay for my own."

But Sol saw that Lillian was unhappily surprised to find herself without the requisite five cents. He watched her dig through her handbag, her jawline becoming tenser by the moment with the fruitless search. Before the situation could get more awkward, Sol dipped into his pocket and came up with a nickel. "Here you go—my treat."

Lillian turned a bright crimson beneath her linen-pale complexion.

"It's all right—don't worry about it," Sol said, touching her elbow, and she gave him a grateful look.

Money, Sol discovered, was a touchy subject for Lillian. Her job in the secretarial pool had allowed her to move into Manhattan to work. But, he later learned, her salary barely covered the essentials: rent and meals at the dingy Pickwick Arms, subway fare to work, an occasional new frock or hat. Otherwise, she lived what he thought of as a penny-pinching existence, in which, she told him, her entertainment needs were amply met by library books and long walks around Manhattan on her weekends off. He knew it had been like that for her for a few years, but he wasn't sure exactly how long.

It took a while before she opened up about her family in Brooklyn. But it was obvious to Sol early on that the poverty of her early years had made her fearful about finances, as well as angry at being afraid about money. Her crippling cheapness seemed at odds, in Sol's mind, with her strict, discerning standards for the way they went about their lives. After a while, he learned that there would always be that moment when she would turn up her nose and ask, "Isn't there anything else?"

Still, she didn't do that when Sol proposed, a few months into their spring-summer relationship. The courtship featured Sunday drives north from the city on the lush Saw Mill River Parkway in his Model A roadster. Their excursions took them to sleepy rural villages like Pleasantville in Westchester County north of the Bronx, or river towns along the Hudson River, such as Ossining and Croton-on-Harmon. These were communities with thriving commercial centers and commuter railroad stops, surrounded by farmland, forest, and the rest of the Hudson River Valley.

On one such drive, Sol canted west from Greenburgh and drove to Tarrytown. They drove past the train station, which was near a busy ferry terminal, where a regular boat brought rail commuters across the Hudson from Nyack. He then drove north up Albany Post Road, winding past a Revolutionary War–era cemetery on a hill and a sign that said **WELCOME TO SLEEPY HOLLOW**.

Sol pointed out the sign, and Lillian said, "Sleepy Hollow? Like in the ghost story?"

"You know Washington Irving?" Sol said, impressed.

"Do you think I don't know how to read?"

"No, no, of course not," he said, defensive until he saw her smile.

"The way they treat that Ichabod Crane," she said, "and the way the writer describes him, I always wondered: Do you think Ichabod Crane was Jewish?"

That made Sol laugh. "An idea I have never in my life even considered," he said, still chuckling. "But it makes sense."

They crested a ridge, and Sol turned left down a street lined with a mix of completed homes, houses under construction, and empty lots, all separated by the roads, which were freshly paved, with new curbs and gutters.

It was a housing development with homes in a variety of architectural styles. They all had front lawns, or dirt where those lawns would be, with more land marked out for backyards. Some of the completed homes had attached garages and driveways. Down the hill they could see the sun sparkle off the Hudson River.

"What is this place?" Lillian asked as they drove the streets lined with newly planted trees.

"It's called Sleepy Hollow Manor, part of Philipse Manor. Philipse was a big shot back before the American Revolution who owned all this land. I looked it up."

"Well, it's certainly lovely," Lillian said, as though it couldn't possibly have anything to do with her.

Sol pulled to the curb in front of a Tudor-style house whose mansard roof was still to be installed. The framing of an attached two-car garage appeared to include a second-floor apartment.

"Don't you think this would be a good place to raise a family?" he asked her.

Lillian said, "Do you mean this neighborhood—or this specific house?"

"Both."

Lillian gazed at the house, where twine strung between sticks marked off its freshly seeded front yard. Then she turned and looked Sol in the eye. "What are you saying?"

"That I want you to marry me. And that if you do, someday, I'll buy you this house."

Lillian could only smile; then she'd nodded and said, "All right." Sol had taken her in his arms and, for only the fourth or fifth time, kissed her deeply.

~

They had been married in the spring of 1935, shortly after Sol turned thirty-one, when Lillian was twenty-nine. After their honeymoon, she moved into his Bronx apartment—at which point Sol insisted that Lillian quit her job, because he was making more than enough money to support the two of them. Later, he would think of it as one of the most significant mistakes of his married life, because it left Lillian to her own resources, which proved limited.

In the first months of their marriage, Lillian complained that she felt like a prisoner trapped in a Bronx neighborhood where she had never lived and where she knew no one. Used to the routine of going to a job and the social setting it provided, she was bored by endless days with nothing to do but clean the apartment, do the laundry and the shopping, and then put dinner on the table.

But once she joined a women's group at the synagogue where Sol's family belonged, she gradually developed a routine that encompassed the apartment's upkeep and an expanding social calendar. Then the complaining lessened because Lillian's time was filled.

By 1937, Sol's business was on firm enough footing that Sol was able to buy the house in Sleepy Hollow Manor in a foreclosure sale and move himself and Lillian from the Bronx. The move came when Lillian was six months pregnant with Amelia. Sol brought Lillian and Amelia home from the hospital to a house with a nursery freshly painted pink by the excited Sol.

But he quickly discovered that Lillian was physically and emotionally unequipped to add infant care to an already full schedule. If anything, Sol noticed, childcare overwhelmed her.

Sol didn't realize just how unhappy Lillian was until the night she burst into tears at dinner, a few months after Amelia was born. When he hired Clara to run the household for her, her mood improved and her humor returned. The pressure on Sol to do something about how Lillian was feeling was relieved by this young woman from Scranton. It felt like a dislocated shoulder that had been snapped back into place.

Clara became the indispensable cog, keeping Lillian afloat and the household on track, mostly by anticipating Lillian's and the girls' moods and needs. Clara had run all their lives, in ways both big and small, doing it without complaint, providing the lubrication that kept friction from developing whenever possible.

And now Clara was leaving too.

~

Sol finished the slivovitz he'd been sipping and poured one more finger into the glass. One more cigarette? Certainly. He hadn't figured this out, so why not?

Lillian initially had taken the news of Clara's departure so calmly that it surprised him. But Sol had seen the cracks in Lillian's facade as summer inched closer and Lillian's ability to deny Clara's impending departure began to crumble.

She became snappish about small things with Sol and Clara. It might be something Sol said or Clara cooked or someone did at the hair salon—it was usually just a pretext for Lillian to overreact and erupt in anger.

Sol, who never shied away from heated debate at work, learned there was no arguing with Lillian. All he could do was explain himself calmly, then weather her doubts and dissatisfaction.

When they'd gotten married, Sol knew that he wanted children and assumed that Lillian wanted them as well. He also made assumptions about how motherhood would soften Lillian. Weren't all women instinctively maternal?

How many other incorrect assumptions had he made about Lillian?

Even after Clara arrived, Sol was surprised at how Lillian treated their daughter. She seemed critical of Amelia as a toddler and tended to scold rather than correct her. Sol saw Amelia struggle for Lillian's approval.

If he was surprised at her treatment of Amelia, Sol didn't know what to make of Lillian's behavior after Nora was born a little over five years later. After Clara arrived, Lillian had rallied to be an occasional hands-on mother when Amelia was a baby. But after Nora was born, Sol watched with concern as Lillian seemed to withdraw—not just from the baby but from the family.

He heard from Clara when Lillian started sleeping late and took long naps on the couch in her sewing room. He saw that when one of the children started to cry, it would send Lillian into a meltdown of her own, until Clara took charge and calmed both mother and child.

Sol was relieved to have Clara to take care of the girls. She was already managing Amelia's care for Lillian; when the time came, she took charge of Nora as well.

He had no idea what to do with Lillian, who seemed to wander the house in a fog. Sol worried that her silent stare was the result of too many of the barbiturates the doctor had given her. What if she forgot how many she'd taken? He worried about a repeat incident and secretly kept count of all the pills in each of her prescription bottles in the medicine cabinet. But he never saw an unexplained dip in the supply.

Nonetheless, out of concern about her continued listlessness, Sol convinced Lillian to go see a doctor who had been recommended to him, who diagnosed iron-poor blood and prescribed multivitamins. Then he gave her a shot—"B_{12} and some other vitamins, for pep," he said—which seemed to revive Lillian to the point that she cleaned the entire house by herself and didn't nap the rest of the day.

An iron supplement and daily multivitamins also seemed to ease her symptoms. But not, Sol feared, her actual problem: She had never wanted a second child. No infusion of vitamins would change that.

Lillian could go days at a time without holding or talking to the new baby. Sol excused it in his mind: "She's exhausted by the childbirth and overwhelmed having two children. This will pass."

Lillian's funk—what Sol began to think of as her "fugue state"—lasted six months. By the time she did come around, Nora was so firmly bonded to Clara that the baby would sometimes howl if Lillian tried to soothe her when she was unhappy or attempted to change her diaper or put her down for a nap. A week of that and Sol could see Lillian surrender and relinquish Nora's care to Clara completely.

Sol tried to console Lillian as she attempted unsuccessfully to win back her baby's affections.

"She doesn't want me—she only wants Clara," she wailed to him one night. He spent a number of nights listening to her crying in the single bed that was a twin to his. When she stopped talking about it, Sol realized, she had given up on being Nora's mother.

Even thinking that made him feel disloyal to his wife. It made him feel ashamed: Of her? For her? Was there a difference? He preferred not to think about those feelings but, rather, simply move past them.

Then Sol could no longer deny the facts, because Lillian said them out loud. Nora was barely two when, one Saturday, she stumbled while playing in the sunroom and cut her forehead on the corner of an end table. It wasn't a serious gash, but it was deep enough that blood flowed freely down Nora's face and into her eyes.

Clara was off that day; Amelia was playing at a friend's house, and Lillian was upstairs in her sewing room. Sol, who had been in the side yard weeding his vegetable garden, heard Nora crying through the open window and went into the house to investigate. He found his tiny daughter, blood in her eyes, feeling her way along the dining room wall, leaving a trail of small bloody handprints on the wallpaper.

Sol said, "Oh my God!" then turned around and shouted, "Lillian!" Then he picked up the crying child and carried her to the kitchen sink, where he sat her on the counter. He grabbed a dish towel, the only thing at hand, wet it under the faucet, and then applied it to Nora's face to stanch the bleeding and wash the blood away.

"Dear God, what happened to my wallpaper?" he heard Lillian say in the dining room, before she burst through the swinging door into the kitchen. When she saw Nora's blood-drenched face, she shrieked.

Sol tried to remain calm as he said, "Get my car keys. I think she needs to go to the emergency room."

When Lillian hesitated, Sol spoke again, insistent without sounding angry.

"One of us is going to have to hold her down when they stitch her up. And I don't imagine you want her to bleed all over the upholstery of your car—or your lap. I've already got blood all over me. So you drive my car and I'll hold her. Now—go."

Lillian drove in silence and sat quietly until it was time for Nora to get stitches, when she averted her eyes. Sol held the trembling child gently but tightly in his lap, cooing to her to try to comfort and control her. But he, too, had to look away as the doctor used a hypodermic needle to inject anesthetic near the wound, before closing the cut with three neat stitches.

Having remained quiet during the emergency room visit, Lillian showed no such restraint as she drove home, while Nora slept on Sol's lap.

"Did you see the wallpaper in the dining room? Blood doesn't come out, not without leaving a stain. I'll never be able to match that."

"Wallpaper?" Sol said. "You're worried about the wallpaper? What about our daughter?"

"I never wanted that child, and you know it," Lillian blurted out.

Sol stared at her in disbelief, then turned his eyes forward and sat silently the rest of the way. He cradled his sleeping daughter against the bumps of the road.

That night, he and Lillian silently went about their bedtime rituals in their bathroom. Sol climbed into bed and picked up the Rex Stout mystery he'd been reading to see if he could finish a chapter before it was time for lights out.

Normally, once Lillian was ready for bed, she climbed in, turned off her bedside light, and waited for him to follow suit. Once his light was out, he'd hear her say, "Good night, dear," followed by the sound of blankets rustling and bedsprings quietly commenting as she rolled over on to one side, facing away from him.

But this night, she left her light on after climbing into her bed. When he looked over, she was lying on her back, staring at the ceiling.

"Lil? Are you all right?"

She turned her head to look at him, then looked back at the ceiling and said, "I shouldn't have said what I did about Nora, and I'm sorry I did. I'm a terrible mother."

"Stop talking like that," he said. "That's not true. It was an upsetting situation for all of us."

Lillian, however, was clear-eyed. "No, I can feel it. There's some connection she and I didn't make because I didn't spend enough time with her. It's my own fault she doesn't like me."

It gave Sol a pang to realize Nora probably felt closer to Clara than to Lillian. But that seemed to be the way Lillian wanted it, or at least it was something she was now used to. Clara spelled the difference between regular routine and household chaos in all their lives.

Sol loved his wife. Of course he did. He felt protective of her and hated to see her unhappy. He spent his life trying to appease her.

But there seemed to be a simmering sense of resentment that Lillian kept on a low boil at all times—over what, he could not say. It often felt directed at him for the simple reason that he was there at that moment—although God knows he wasn't perfect.

Yet, even at moments when he felt desperate about his marriage, Sol would never consider cheating on Lillian. It wasn't that he didn't look at other women in a lustful way. But Sol was not a cheater. He had been raised to be a mensch. As simple as that. It would have gone against his nature to dishonor his marriage.

~

Sol had doted on both daughters and tried to provide a buffer between them and Lillian when he could. But it was Amelia who needed his attention, more than Nora.

Sol loved Amelia for who she was: a bright, good-natured girl with a big heart. But, to Sol, Lillian's love for Amelia seemed to be based on Amelia meeting some invisible standard that Lillian set. Amelia needed to be who Lillian thought she should be, Sol understood. And Lillian was quick to point out when Amelia fell short.

Still, Sol was unhappy when Amelia began dating Alan Gilbert while attending City College, because Alan was ten years older than Amelia. He was a Korean War veteran attending college on the GI Bill who, when Sol met him, seemed personable and serious. Sol could tell Alan didn't seem as infatuated with Amelia as she was with him. But Sol sensed that his daughter hadn't noticed that. He worried that she would be hurt when it became apparent.

Sol was surprised when Lillian intervened in the relationship by sending Amelia to California to break it up. What could he have done? He agreed with Lillian that Alan was too old for Amelia. But he hadn't counted on his wife's sense of urgency to put an end to the couple. Absent that, he would have counseled patience, to let the relationship dwindle from what Sol saw as its lack of mutual spark, until it died a natural death.

Instead, Lillian made the arrangements with her sister Lucille without telling Sol first. They would send Amelia to spend the summer in Los Angeles, where she would work in the office at the furniture store of Lucille's husband, Ned, while staying with Ned and Lucille.

When Lillian revealed what she'd done, Sol objected: "How could you do this without telling me? What if I don't want her to go to California?"

"So now you want to make me look like a fool in front of Lucille?" Lillian countered. "After she and Ned have gone out of their way to help us?" Sol convinced himself there was no point in arguing with her.

Sol had a similar struggle getting Lillian to accept their son-in-law, Frank Goldfarb, after Amelia married him. The fact that Frank suffered an embarrassing business setback that landed him in bankruptcy court two years after the wedding only strengthened Lillian's conviction that Amelia should have married better.

Sol, however, came to like the jocular Frank. Frank had always treated Sol and Lillian with respect. When his business suffered its failure after he married Amelia, Sol didn't give a second thought to offering Frank a job at the scrapyard.

Lillian adamantly opposed the decision "because Amelia should never have married that man in the first place."

"Will you listen to yourself? Do you hear how you sound?" Sol said. "I'm putting Frank to work at the scrapyard—end of discussion." At work, at least, he still made the decisions.

Sol started Frank on the menial tasks around the yard, which the brawny Frank took to without complaint. He learned the scrap-metal trade, impressing Sol and Stan with his ability to juggle the complex schedule of purchases and shipments, arrivals and departures, sorting and haggling with the peddlers, who were still a major part of their business. When the scrapyard foreman left for another job a few months later, they promoted Frank to the position.

~

Sol stubbed out his cigarette and polished off the last of his slivovitz. He looked at the clock on the wall above his desk: midnight. He loved baseball, but going to a night game in Queens was a serious shlep. When the Mets inaugurated play in 1962, he had gone to as many of the home games as he could—first at the Polo Grounds, then at Shea Stadium when it was completed. He loved to take clients and his family to the sparkling new stadium, even though it housed the legendarily terrible expansion team. It sounded strange, but he felt proprietary about the massive structure, given his longtime connection to the land on which it sat.

Though he no longer attended every home game, Sol tried to go at least once every series when the Mets were in town. He watched many more games on TV, though this often felt like an exercise in masochism. He tended to go to day games on the weekend because the night games ended so late.

Thankfully, the next day was Saturday, so he could sleep in before his men's group meeting, if Lillian let him. Then he noticed the stack of paperwork about the sale of his business, sitting there in the middle of his desk, like a desert island from which there was no escape.

A pile of paper. Not a lot to show for the lifetime of work it represented, not to mention the incipient upheaval to his life. For the moment, that's all it was: a pile of paper, worthless while his future was so unsettled, legally speaking. Sol could feel the wave of momentous changes and crippling uncertainty bearing down on him. Would he survive, or drown in unexpected consequences?

Sol was sixty-three—young to retire, he thought. The idea of retirement had beckoned, though. The thought of having nothing he was required to do struck him as delicious, a release from the work ethic that had whipped him through the decades.

Now it seemed that retirement had been nothing more than a fleeting dream, so close and now suddenly out of reach.

Sol was particularly unhappy about postponing the sale of the house. While he relished the free time when he could get his hands dirty working in his garden or doing household repairs, his back and knees now complained bitterly after a weekend raking the leaves, though Frank had taken over most chores. He had looked forward to an existence in which he was no longer the one responsible for changing storm windows or shoveling the snow out of the driveway. Now, even after they moved, he would still be responsible for the upkeep of the house for the foreseeable future, even if that meant hiring someone to get things done. He had looked forward to not working; the idea of continuing enervated him.

He knew he shouldn't complain. He had made a handsome living out of scrap metal. As he looked back, his business life had been a series of fortunate leaps forward, fueled by Stan's chutzpah and Sol's business sense.

~

Sol had been taking business classes at City College when he first met Stan Schwartz. They were both in a class called The Law and Society, and a classroom debate grew heated one day between Stan and a classmate.

They were discussing Prohibition, which was newly enacted. The classmate, Victor Hodges, was taking prelaw courses and argued that the law was the law. If the Volstead Act was enacted in a legal way, then it was incumbent on the people to follow the law or there would be chaos.

Stan was having none of it: "What if the law is wrong?"

"Who's to make that determination?" their professor asked.

"Exactly," Hodges said.

"Well, obviously, either the Supreme Court—or Congress, if it can pull its head out of its collective keister and rescind Volstead."

"A civil tongue please, Mr. Schwartz," the professor chided.

"But until then," Stan continued, "it's incumbent on us as Americans to protest this egregious law through civil disobedience."

"By drinking alcohol illegally, I suppose," Hodges said.

"Exactly!" Stan said. "Who knows what they will try to ban next? Soda pop? Milk? Water?"

He got a good laugh from the class on that. Afterward, Sol sought out Stan, saying, "I liked what you had to say about Prohibition."

"Wanna get a beer and talk about it?" Stan said.

"A beer? Did you forget it's illegal?"

"Civil disobedience, brother. Time to begin your life of crime."

Stan took him to a speakeasy a few blocks from City College, on a side street in Harlem. All the employees were Black, and all the customers were white. As they drank the bitter bootleg beer, Stan and Sol found they shared a quick wit, a creative mind for business—and a strong interest in being their own bosses. Stan seemed awash in ideas, while Sol had the ability to analyze the pros and cons of Stan's brainstorms.

Sol worked part-time during college as a clerk in his father's office-supply store. His father talked about Sol taking over the day-to-day management of the store when he got out of college.

"To build a business that succeeds—and then to be able to pass it on to my children—that's my dream," his father told him.

But Sol had other plans. His goal was to find work as a bookkeeper while he studied to be a certified public accountant. Then he planned to open his own accounting practice, which he knew would provide a steady income. When he outlined his future goals to his father, the older man smiled and said, "It's a serious plan. That's good. I just want you to be happy." But Sol could see the disappointment behind the smile.

After college, he took a job in the business office of a large shipping company, where he processed forms and kept records all day: sales, payouts, losses. It all flowed past his eyes, these endless pieces of paper documenting cargo and commerce.

Then, one day at their weekly Friday lunch to plan the weekend, Stan sat down and said, "This is it. If we can come up with a thousand dollars between us, I can put us in a business where we can call our own shots."

Sol knew enough about human nature—and about Stan's numerous enthusiasms—to be wary of promises of easy success. Still, he said politely to his best friend, "What do you have?"

For a change, Stan's idea was not a get rich quick scheme. Oh, it was definitely a scheme, but one in which the profits would come slowly and steadily, never losing, always gaining, as long as they were willing to keep at it.

As Stan explained it, there was a scrapyard in Queens. Stan's father, who owned a service station in Queens, had a regular customer who was a junk peddler. The peddler worked in the neighborhood and would buy gas for his truck from Stan's father.

"But this guy was complaining because the yard where he sells the scrap metal he collects is getting ready to close. And none of the other yards in the borough are as convenient or pay as well as this guy does. The owner of the scrapyard is old and wants to retire. He wanted to pass his business on to his son. But his son—get this—is a tenor with the Metropolitan Opera and doesn't even speak to the old man."

"Is this story going somewhere?" Sol said.

"I'm getting there. Apparently, the scrapyard guy told this peddler, 'If I could find someone to pay me a thousand dollars to take this place off my hands, I'd sell it all tomorrow.'"

"What's your point?"

"My point," Stan said excitedly, "is let's buy this place and be in business for ourselves."

"The junk business?" Sol said. "No thanks. I'd rather stay at the shipping company, pushing paper. I think I can make vice president in a couple of years."

"Not junk—scrap metal. Huge difference. In the junk business, you're picking through other people's garbage. But scrap metal is like mining for gold or, in this case, iron or copper. There's always a supply—and there's always a demand. Basic business. This scrapyard is already a going concern; the owner wants out because he's old. If we can come up with the cash, then all he has to do is take the money and give us the keys. Like a captain handing the rudder to his first mate. Smooth sailing all the way."

"I don't know anything about scrap metal," Sol pointed out. "Neither do you."

"How hard can it be? You buy low and sell high, just like any other commodity. They already have a list of peddlers who regularly dump their scrap there. And a list of foundries that buy the scrap they collect. We just take over as the middlemen."

Sol was skeptical, but Stan wouldn't be dissuaded.

"C'mon, Solly—let's face it. You're never going to be vice president of that company, no matter how much you work. Do you know why?"

"Why?"

"Because you're a Yid—and those goyim will never promote one of us to a position of authority, no matter how smart you are. Even if those antisemitic ganefs did promote you, it would only ever be to something like head bookkeeper. You'd die of boredom."

This stopped Sol. He was only a couple of years into his current job and had to admit that, yes, he was bored, contemplating an escape route.

"How much money do you have saved?" Stan asked.

"I can't say, exactly. I'd have to sit down and—"

"Sorry, pal, that's crap and you know it. You always know exactly how much you have in your pocket, to the penny. Why would I believe you don't know how much you have in the bank?"

"I'd rather not say, then."

"Now you're being honest. I'll ask anyway: Is it more than the five hundred dollars you'd need to be a partner in this deal?"

Sol hesitated, then said, "Yes."

"Honest, Solly—I have a real feeling here. I know a scrapyard doesn't sound like much, but this feels like a huge gift is being dropped in our laps, if we only recognize it. You know what they say about opportunity knocking? They're banging on a brass gong this time, Solly. I've never been so sure of anything in my life."

Sol decided to believe in Stan's hunch. He'd held his breath and taken the plunge, taking five hundred dollars out of his savings account (half of what he had in the world) to buy the scrapyard.

~

Stan, as it turned out, had been right. They bought the business, and the first year, they broke even, while paying themselves just enough salary to stay afloat. By the end of the second year, they were turning a profit, and they kept it up—a little more each year, some years better than others, but there was never a year where they didn't end at least a little better off than the year before.

And, in a business dominated by organized crime, they were allowed to exist unscathed because of something Sol had done in elementary school.

During his school days in the Bronx, Sol was pals with Anthony Peccarino Jr., a boy he befriended in kindergarten, who shared Sol's love of cowboy movies and tales of the days of boots and saddles. By sixth grade, between the two of them, they'd read all the books by Zane Grey and Clarence Mulford in their neighborhood library. Together, they frequented their neighborhood movie theater, particularly for the films of Tom Mix and William S. Hart. Their passion for the Old West connected them through elementary school, when they were often in the same class.

Tony Peccarino was on the small side—certainly smaller than Sol, whose growth spurt put him a full head above his classmates in fifth grade. It made him feel protective of the diminutive Tony, who sat near him in class and made Sol laugh with smart-aleck cracks.

One day during recess on the playground, a pair of larger boys from another class started pushing Tony around. Sol stepped in, getting between him and his main antagonist, Ronnie Gennaro, a boy twice Tony's size. When Ronnie told Sol to mind his own business and gave him a shove, the eleven-year-old Sol responded by punching Ronnie in the stomach—hard.

Ronnie doubled over, then collapsed to the ground, rolled over on his side, and threw up, causing everyone in the circle around them to jump backward.

After that, no one bothered Tony, or Sol.

Tony soon got his own growth spurt, enough so that he was all-conference as an offensive lineman on his high school football team. As they got older, he and Sol drifted into different social circles, and the friendship moved to a kind of "inactive" status. They would nod to each other in the hallway at school, but that was the extent of it. After graduation, Sol headed for City College. Tony went his own way.

Shortly after Sol and Stan took over the scrapyard, which they christened All-American Scrap Metal, they had a visit from a member of the Guzzi crime family, alerting them to a business detail the scrapyard's previous owner had neglected to mention.

The man who delivered the news was roughly the same width as Sol and Stan combined, though not quite as tall. He wore a dark wool coat over a black suit with a black tie, and had black hair veined with gray, slicked back under a small hat. When he walked into the little shack that originally comprised their office, Sol thought the man was an undertaker who was lost and looking for directions in the tangled backwater of Willets Point. Then he got a look at the man's face and realized his mistake.

He had deep-set black eyes from which no light seemed to escape. What Sol mistook for a deep wrinkle turned out to be a scar that ran down his cheek from his hairline to his jaw.

In a cement mixer voice, polite but thick with the sound of Brooklyn, the man informed them that in order to operate at this or any other location in the immediate vicinity (meaning New York, New Jersey, and certain territories in Connecticut), All-American would need to tithe 10 percent of their weekly profits to the Guzzi family. They would also be required to contract all their hauling through trucking companies that the Guzzi family operated, which charged more than the going rate.

In delivering the message to Sol and Stan, the hoodlum said, "Do the right thing. You wouldn't want to get on the wrong side of Big Tony Jr."

A few days later, Sol found Anthony Peccarino Jr. in a coffee-and-pastry shop on Arthur Avenue in the Bronx. As the new head of the Guzzi family (after the death of his father, Big Tony), Big Tony Jr., as he now preferred to be known, held court there each morning with a handful of associates and underlings, before heading to his "office" at a social club a few blocks away.

When Sol tried to approach Big Tony Jr.'s table, a burly individual with no visible neck and a gun bulging through the front of his suit stood to block his way and pat him down. Before Sol could say anything, he heard Tony say, "Is that Solly? Rootin' Tootin' Ride 'em Cowboy Solly Levitsky?"

He shooed the henchman away from the frisk as he rose to take Sol in an affectionate embrace.

They spent the next few minutes catching up after not seeing each other since high school. They talked about life—marriage, children—and their favorite recent westerns, before Tony said, "So, Solly, what brings you here after all these years?"

"Well, my partner and I just bought a scrapyard in Queens."

"A scrapyard? Old Billingsley's place?"

"Yes, that's the one. We've renamed it All-American Scrap."

"That's you? Why didn't you say so?"

And, just like that, All-American's problems with the Guzzi family had disappeared, permanently: "Two words," Big Tony Jr. had told Sol: "Ronnie fuckin' Gennaro. I will never forget that. Now—try the cannolis here. The best!"

~

After a few years, business had built to the point that All-American Scrap was able to start buying out some of the smaller scrap operations in the area. Their yard in Queens expanded in the industrial-waste corridor of Willets Point. After America got into World War II, their business grew exponentially, with the US government as their best customer and All-American cited with a service medal for helping further America's war effort.

By the time the war ground to a close in 1945, All-American's Queens yard had grown to be the largest scrap operation in the region, with satellite operations elsewhere in Queens, as well as in the Bronx, Connecticut, and New Jersey. Sol and Lillian were settled in the house in North Tarrytown with two little girls and a housekeeper. Sol left early in the morning and came home after dinner most nights. It was the postwar suburban dream.

At the end of the 1950s, Sol had a plan to move All-American into the brokerage business, selling off their various properties in the tristate area in favor of managing the purchasing and sales on an industrial level for other people. They would become the middlemen who got a piece of both ends of any deal.

Sol knew what he wanted to do and how to do it, but he was still trying to figure out the best way to sell the main yard in Queens. The answer fell into his lap, as though ordained by God or, in this case, Robert Moses.

At the close of the 1950s, the massive industrial district in the marshes east of LaGuardia Airport, where All-American was entrenched, was chosen as the site for a stadium for New York's newest baseball team, the Mets. In the name of urban renewal and civic pride, Stan and Sol were offered a small fortune for their land, and they sold off the last of their scrap. They'd moved their offices to a satellite scrapyard they owned in Astoria.

That was 1959. Then, while Stan was at an industry conference earlier this year, someone made an offer out of the blue to purchase All-American.

Stan told Sol that the question had caught him by surprise, as did the follow-up: a tentative purchase figure that was an astronomical sum for 1967. Stan's impulse, he told Sol, was to say, "Where do I sign?"

Instead, he had the presence of mind to say "That's an extremely flattering offer. Can you give me a business card? I obviously need to discuss this with my partner. But I promise we'll be back in touch."

After listening to the details of the deal, Sol agreed that it was too good to pass up, and with a stroke of a pen, All-American seemed to be on its way to becoming the wholly owned subsidiary of a Japanese multinational corporation. Now, as with everything about the deal, they were "awaiting further developments."

Sol had been thrilled at the prospect of retiring, because Sol was eager to travel. But when he'd mentioned travel to Lillian, she'd dismissed the idea out of hand: "Well, you won't get me on any airplane. And I'm not getting on an ocean liner either. Do you think I've forgotten what happened to the *Andrea Doria*?"

~

Changing his wife's attitude toward travel would have to wait. So would travel itself. Everything was on hold because of the lawsuit, except their move to the co-op.

Sol needed to find a way to tell Lillian the bad news. Then Nora's secret popped back into his head, dealing him a small shock of alarm. Something else to keep hidden from Lillian.

As he thought about Nora, Sol realized how much he would miss her. A career, a job—his little girl, gone to live her life in Chicago. Not that he hadn't missed her when she left for college, but at least he knew he'd see her at holidays and school breaks, including summer. He could drive to Syracuse, if it came to that. But Chicago? When would he ever see her after she moved there?

He turned off the light in his office and walked down the hall, past photos on the walls of his daughters as little girls. Amelia, with blond ringlets that reminded Sol of Shirley Temple (though, naturally, he thought his daughter was prettier). Nora, her dark eyes giving her an air of mystery, even as a youngster in a sailor suit.

The Shea Stadium money had secured his family's future; he had assumed that selling the business would secure his children's and grandchildren's. Would he have to recalculate that equation? The thought made his chest hurt.

With a little luck, they might quickly steer clear of the lawsuit; then they would sell the house, and that would cover future expenses for the co-op. That was another reason to keep this from Lillian: She was worried about how they would be able to make the maintenance payments on their co-op when Sol stopped working.

He explained what a huge windfall selling the business would bring them, that they would never have to worry about money. But no figure he told her could assuage the fiscal panic that had branded Lillian as a child sleeping four to a bed in Williamsburg.

Sol knew his wife's early life made her want to take control of every minute of her own life and the lives adjoining hers. She was hardheaded and hard-shelled.

Yet, for all her haughty posturing, he knew there was a vulnerable woman inside who needed the security he represented. It had made him want to rescue her when they were young and kept him at her side all these years later.

But rescue her from what? She was out of Williamsburg—and he had moved them from the city to a suburban retreat she couldn't have imagined as a young woman. Why couldn't she simply enjoy what she had, instead of obsessing over the possibility of losing it?

He had hoped to rescue her from whatever it was that was holding her back from being the woman he believed she could be. But, in fact, the only thing holding her back was herself. And there was nothing he could do about that.

~

Sol had had little romantic experience before he met Lillian. Unlike most men his age, he did not enter puberty inflamed with hormonal urges to mate and marry. He was always more driven by business than by sex, seeking profit over enjoyment. He understood from an early age that physical pleasure was transitory, but a solid bank account was not.

Ironically, the woman who lit the fuse on Sol's long-dormant impulses had limited libido herself, which was the reason it took them some time to conceive Amelia. Given how infrequently Lillian let Sol make the journey from his twin bed to hers after Amelia was born, it was little wonder that Nora was a surprise when she was born five and a half years later.

Sol had never had a steady girlfriend before her. He had lost his virginity at a bordello in Greenwich Village one drunken night in college with Stan. But, given the eager participation of the prostitute from that night (and a few others after that, before he was married), Sol had certain expectations of marital sex, of which Lillian soon disabused him.

While she understood her role in the procreative act, and though she tried to appear willing, Sol always felt as if she was gritting her teeth when, after brief foreplay, he climbed on top of her.

On their one-month wedding anniversary, Sol took Lillian out for a celebratory evening and they both drank a little too much champagne with dinner. The alcohol lowered her inhibitions enough for them to pursue intercourse to completion (his, not hers). For the first time, she was an active participant, if only briefly.

He awoke the next morning, awash in warm feelings for his bride. But when he reached for her under the covers, she started, then moved away from him to get out of bed, saying, "What are you doing? It's daytime."

From then on, Sol made a point, once a month, of taking Lillian to a nice dinner that included a bottle of champagne. Those evenings inevitably ended in sex, bordering on passion.

One night, a year into their marriage, after dinner, champagne, and sex, Sol rolled off Lillian to go to sleep. Then he was startled to hear Lillian whisper in his ear, "I'm on to your trick."

Sol, who'd been dozing, tried to sit up, unsure if he'd dreamed this. But he couldn't because he realized Lillian was hovering over him in the dim light, still inebriated.

"What?" he said.

"You give me champagne so I can have sex with you," she said. "It's OK. It's the only time I like it." Then she rolled over and was asleep in seconds.

She never mentioned the champagne again, but she rarely refused the once-a-month offer at dinner. Nine months after one such evening, Amelia was born. Though it took almost five years, the same sequence of events produced Nora.

Then, a few months after Nora was born, the first time in a while that Sol had ordered champagne, Lillian spoke up.

"No champagne for me, thanks," she told the waiter when he brought the bottle.

"What? Why not?" Sol asked as the waiter removed Lillian's flute from the table.

"I'm not in the mood."

"For champagne?" Sol said with a direct look.

Lillian avoided his eye, picking at the salad with her fork. "Yes," she said. "For champagne. None for me, please."

Sol was surprised at the way his anger welled up, though he couldn't have said why. He only knew that at that moment, something had shifted in his wife. She had been withdrawing from him and the girls since Nora's birth. Though never an emotionally generous woman, Lillian's inward turn made her even chillier, and he had no idea how to get past this new barrier. He could see a lonely future with her stretching out before him and felt like its hapless victim.

Uncomfortable with how this epiphany made him feel, Sol methodically emptied the champagne bottle himself at dinner, drinking much more than he normally did. Then he made Lillian take the wheel for the trip home because he was too intoxicated to drive.

A timid driver by day, Lillian was all but immobilized driving at night and, despite a lack of traffic, took a half hour to make the ten-minute drive home. At one point, Sol angrily ordered Lillian to pull over and, when she did, leaped out of the car to be sick in the gutter.

When he got back into the car and Lillian pulled away from the curb, she said, "I don't know why you're angry at me. I'm not the one who told you to drink an entire bottle of champagne by yourself at dinner."

Sol had rested his cheek against the cool car window and said nothing. The evening was never mentioned again.

~

Sol spent the first years after he'd married Lillian working twelve-hour days with Stan, building their business through relentless hustle. Having rescued his wife from her poverty-stricken background, Sol assumed that she was self-sufficient enough to learn to enjoy her new life in the Bronx.

On the weekend, they socialized with other couples, most often with Stan and Delia. Stan and Delia, in turn, introduced them to other couples in their neighborhood of the Bronx. They ate at restaurants, went dancing, went to dinner parties.

She became active at the synagogue, but before that, Lillian had complained about being left alone while he went to work in Queens. Sol said to his sister Delia, "She's lonely. Could you maybe stop by once in a while?"

But when Delia began to visit, Lillian complained to Sol, "Why is she always bothering me?" Sol was mortified.

If there was a real issue in one of Lillian's complaints, Sol would try to find a way to resolve it to Lillian's satisfaction. More often, he was able to "Yes, dear" and "You don't say" his way through her dinnertime recitation of that day's assaults on her probity by Delia and leave it at that.

~

Why was his wife like this? Though he worked to coax softness from her stiff demeanor, her sense of humor became increasingly recessed the older she got. He'd once been able to make her laugh—and she had returned the favor. That seemed like a long time ago.

Still, he remembered that she had risen to a position of responsibility in her synagogue women's group because she was assured in her opinions and, once she got to know the women, happy to share them. Yet her relationship with Delia always seemed to put Sol in the middle between his wife and his sister. When they spent time with Stan and Delia, Lillian complained that "Delia makes me nervous. She's always making fun of me. I never know when she's being serious."

Delia had always been a kidder, someone who was expert in finding an unexpected bit of humor in almost any exchange. She also loved putting people off-balance for her own amusement, something Sol knew aggravated Lillian.

Sometimes Delia would pretend to angrily misunderstand something Lillian said, then laugh at the expression on Lillian's face when Lillian realized she was kidding. Or she'd say something purposely, ridiculously outrageous because she knew she'd get the desired response from Lillian.

Delia didn't tease Lillian to be mean, Sol knew. It was just how Delia was. But Lillian always took the ribbing as a personal attack, something designed to mock or denigrate her.

"She's always picking on me," she complained.

"She's not picking on you. She's trying to include you," he would counter, to no avail.

Clara spoke up one night when Sol wondered aloud to her why Lillian was always so tense during their evenings with Delia and Stan. The pair had just left, after their game of bridge disintegrated because Lillian felt the onset of a migraine headache. Sol was clearing coffee cups and dessert plates as Clara washed the last dishes.

"Why can't she and Delia get along?" Sol said in exasperation.

"That's easy," Clara said.

Sol looked at her in disbelief: "It is?"

"Sure. Delia thinks everything about Lillian is funny. And Lillian doesn't have a sense of humor about herself. Oil and water."

~

As Sol clicked on the light in the bathroom, he glanced at his watch again. 12:15 a.m. Had he remembered to turn off the sprinkler when he got home from the Mets game? He couldn't recall doing so. He took out his partial dental plate, brushed his teeth, put on pajamas, and donned a robe and slippers. His knees ached as he made his way downstairs.

Sure enough, the streetlights reflected the wet grass, dampened by his sprinkler. The full moon illuminated the faucet on the side of the house, as though shining a spotlight, as he turned it off. When he went back into the house, he could see the light still showing from Clara's window over the garage.

How does she do it? he wondered. He would be exhausted the next day, while Clara never seemed to tire.

Sol turned the lights off on the house's main floor and made his way back upstairs. Night-lights cast eerie shadows as he found his way to his bedroom and closed the door behind him.

In the dim light, he could make out Lillian's sleeping form on the other bed. She snored in a pattern that built over the course of a half-dozen breaths from a soft rumble to a full-blown crescendo of snorts, then receded again to the lower decibels, before beginning its next climb up the ladder of volume. Sol could sleep through it but not fall asleep to it. When it got bad, an abruptly barked "Lil!" usually broke the pattern long enough for him to doze off.

In the recent years of their marriage, Sol had resigned himself to a set of facts:

Lillian was unhappy if she was not in control.

But she was not happy when she was in control.

And there were too many things over which she had no control at all, which upset her further.

There was no pleasing her on some nerve-racking days. That was why keeping the truth from her had been the only possible course until the moment he couldn't keep it from her any longer.

Telling her his news would be like pulling the pin on a grenade, with only seconds to decide which course of action would save the most lives. Sol felt guilty likening his wife to an explosive device. But he also knew how true the analogy was.

The thought of telling Lillian the next day brought on the same crushing feeling in his chest: like someone was stacking cinder blocks directly atop his breastbone. Sol rolled over on his side, and the pressure eased a little.

By September, Clara would be back in Scranton and Sol would be sharing a co-op in Scarsdale with his wife. As he considered that prospect, words bobbed to the surface in Sol's mind like the answer in one of those Magic 8 Ball toys, before Sol could stop himself from thinking them: *And then what?*

He hated the question because he didn't have the answer. Or maybe he did know the answer and just didn't like it.

After all these years, was he so desperate to avoid being alone with his wife?

Unfortunately, he knew, he was.

Because, in the end, that was his fate.

Sol rolled over to sleep, thinking, *I am just fucked. Period.*

SATURDAY MORNING

Love is a serious mental disease.
—Plato

STEPHEN

Stephen Cantor could not believe the chaotic interior of his cousin's car.

He'd nearly sat upon a half-eaten Hostess Twinkie. He also noticed that the floor in front of the passenger seat was covered by used wrappers for hamburgers from McDonald's.

"Do you take actual women on dates in this heap?" he said as he disposed of the refuse, while trying not to soil his white oxford shirt and his only pair of clean khakis.

"I never drive in the city—that's why the car is up here at my folks' house," Arnie said. "Besides, you're the one who wanted a ride to see some girl. Next time, order a limo."

"Yeah, I'll make a great impression showing up in this rust bucket," Stephen said, indicating Arnie's 1959 Chevy Biscayne.

"Do you want a ride or not? I'm happy to just raid my mother's refrigerator and go back to the city. That's why I usually come up to the folks'. I never have food in my apartment."

"No, let's go before it gets any later. We have to be at the Plaza and dressed by three, so we need to leave Nora's no later than noon."

After laying a section of newspaper on the passenger seat as a precaution, Stephen got in and they set out from Larchmont, headed for the Hutchinson River Parkway and North Tarrytown.

~

Stephen had been disappointed when Nora canceled out on Friday dinner. But, after he'd declined Nora's invitation to come up for Saturday brunch with her parents, his mother revealed that his presence was not required for wedding-related events until 3:00 p.m. Saturday. *Plenty of time to surprise her Saturday morning,* he thought.

When Stephen met her less than six months ago, Nora certainly had been a surprise: intimidatingly bright and curious, witty with a sharp edge, with strong, well-reasoned opinions that occasionally clashed with his—not that it bothered her.

Unlike many of the women he'd dated while attending Syracuse Law (there hadn't been *that* many, because who had time?), Nora had no interest in marriage. In fact, on one of their first dates, she'd offered a ten-point list of reasons why marriage was unfair to women.

No, Stephen thought, not *unfair*. He remembered that the word she'd used was *inequitable*. He'd never heard it expressed that way. And as an attorney-to-be, he had to admit she made a good case.

She was the most vocally antimarriage woman he'd ever encountered. Whether in the literature class where they met or out with friends, she greeted the introduction of the topic into any conversation with an eye roll and a loud cluck of her tongue.

He remembered an early classroom discussion of *Sense and Sensibility*, when the professor, a tweedy woman of his mother's age, had asked why marriage was so critical for young women like the Dashwood sisters, in Austen's time.

Stephen recalled Nora's hand shooting up. It was only the second week of class, but he'd noticed Nora the first day. She had a regal posture and a sunny expression: tall, slender, carrying herself with an ease that seemed to inform her smile and laugh. When she raised her hand, Stephen thought afterward, the professor must have expected an answer about societal norms, as well as family fiscal concerns of the historical period.

Instead, when she was called on, Nora said, "Because, just like now, women were considered to be little more than property, chattel to be controlled by men."

The professor's eyes widened, and she adjusted a pair of silver-rimmed spectacles on her nose. "I hardly think that was what Austen had in mind," she said, one eyebrow raised in disapproval.

"Really?" Nora replied. "I think Austen saw that inequity with clear eyes. But she couldn't come out and say it, not in her world. I think if she'd lived in another era, one of Austen's characters might have walked out the door and gone her own way, like the heroine of Ibsen's *A Doll's House*."

Whose name, Stephen knew, was Nora.

After that, Stephen noticed, the professor seemed warier when calling on Nora in class.

It wasn't long afterward that he asked her out. He couldn't believe his luck when she said yes. Or when their date stretched late into the night at a local café because they found so much to talk about.

Once they'd been seeing each other regularly for six weeks or so, he found he was thinking about marriage, even if she was philosophically opposed to it. As their connection began to deepen and become more physical, Stephen found himself considering the idea of being paired on a permanent basis with this young woman with the effervescent intellect.

They both lived the highly scheduled lives of achievers yet found themselves spending increasing amounts of unscheduled time together, even while both were finishing demanding graduate programs. Still, her outspoken ideas about what marriage meant for women intimidated him too much to raise the subject, even after the two of them began sleeping together.

The issue of marriage finally arose one Sunday morning in early April, when they were lazing uncharacteristically late in bed at his apartment near campus. Stephen promised breakfast in bed, then disappeared for fifteen minutes.

When he returned, he carried a tray bearing coffee, bagels, and cream cheese. He proffered a copy of the *New York Times* (because Nora loved the Sunday crossword), which he'd trekked through an inch of new snow to purchase at a corner bodega. He got into bed in his red plaid pajamas and socks, still wearing the flap-eared fur crown that was his sole fashion quirk.

"I could get used to this," Nora purred, sipping her coffee, which she took black.

"What, breakfast in bed? Or doing this together on a more official basis?"

"Mmm, both probably," Nora said.

"I mean, I've thought about a more permanent thing sometimes, but it scares me a little. *You* scare me a little. More than a little."

Nora's smile was affectionate. "Good. I *should* scare you," she said with a laugh that always lifted his heart. Then she added, "I've thought about marrying you—and I didn't break out in a rash. So that's something."

Stephen hoped the handsprings he was executing in his imagination didn't show on his face as he said, "Really?"

"Yes, really," she said, smoothing his hair with her fingers. She stopped. "But there's no rush. Let's get ourselves set up and working in Chicago, then see how things go."

In the months they'd been dating, Stephen had listened t tales of growing up with—and plotting her escape from—an ir controlling mother in North Tarrytown. He'd been a party Northwestern job offer and her decision to keep the news f parents until the last possible minute: She would only reveal about her move in a late-breaking phone call, as the move w to happen.

He couldn't imagine hiding something like that from hi But when he said as much, Nora said, "You don't know m This is the only way."

Stephen was eager to meet the family housekeeper, Clara, described once as "my real mother." Yet it was the mother w she was so eager to shed whom Stephen most wanted to e He wondered how anyone could tame someone with a mir and sure as Nora's.

"Honestly—how bad can your mother be?" Stephen asked, to which Nora replied, "Ever read the myth of Mede it at that.

~

"So who is this chick? Somebody serious?" Arnie asked, son New Rochelle. Arnie zipped past traffic and maneuvered from the Hutch to the Cross County Parkway.

"I hope so," Stephen said. "We'll see." Wanting t subject, he turned to Arnie and said, "So how is it, your dad?"

Arnie was employed at his father's Mercedes dealershi Avenue in the West Fifties. Knowing Arnie's propensity fo father kept him busy delivering new cars or giving rides whose cars came in for service. It filled his time and ke trouble, the perfect job for ne'er-do-well Arnie, who w than Stephen.

Arnie wanted to move up to selling cars on the showroom floor (so he could make some real money—and meet women). His father had said, "You're not ready." The unspoken message was *And you never will be.*

Arnie had flunked out of several of the better prep schools on the East Coast before barely graduating from neighboring Mamaroneck High. He then put in an undistinguished couple of years at the State Jniversity of New York–Oswego. If he hadn't been expelled for running n illicit business buying liquor for underage townies (for a handsome ee), his unimpressive academic record would have done him in.

So Arnie had been conscripted to work at his father's dealership, here his father could keep tabs on him.

"You know my old man," Arnie said. "Everything is a lesson—or, orse, a test. Luckily, I don't see him much. Say, is this girl going to ve us anything to eat when we get there? I'm starvin' like Lee Marvin."

Arnie sailed down the ramp from the Cross County to the rthbound Bronx River Parkway. Within a mile, the BRP flowed into e northbound Sprain Brook Parkway.

It was a sunny summer Saturday in June, and the Sprain was gged with traffic racing north from the Bronx toward new suburban alls and spacious state parks in Westchester County. Their car ran into vall of stopped traffic from which there was neither retreat nor escape.

"Oh, man, look at this fustercluck," Arnie cracked.

Stephen groaned. "We definitely won't have time to eat if this traffic esn't ease up."

He looked out the window at the landscape, most of which seemed consist of rolling hills, forests, or a combination of the two. *So much en,* he thought, picturing the barren flatness of the prairies that tched west from Chicago.

~

hen wondered whether it was his imagination that made it seem as ora was trying to keep him from meeting her parents. She'd been so

blithe about canceling their Friday date. Stephen had to remind himself that not everyone got along with their parents as well as he did.

Take Arnie, as an obvious example. For years, Stephen's mother used Arnie as a negative role model for him. Arnie, whose mother was sisters with Stephen's mother, was the family black sheep, in trouble as a kid for everything from playing with matches to shoplifting. Truancy, underage smoking, and drinking—Arnie cut a wide swath as a would-be juvenile delinquent. Or so it seemed to Stephen, who only heard of Arnie's escapades after the fact from his mother (the versions Arnie spun for him were always spicier).

Every time Arnie misbehaved, Stephen had to endure a lecture from his mother about what would happen "if any son of mine got caught doing something like that." Not that Stephen ever would.

At the various East Coast boarding schools he'd attended, Arnie had displayed an entrepreneurial flair that left the straight-arrow Stephen dizzy, imagining doing anything remotely similar himself. Such as the time Arnie got caught in middle school selling pictures of nude women, which he'd cut out of an issue of *Playboy* with a pair of scissors, to his classmates for a dollar each.

So the irony was not lost on Stephen: Here was Arnie, working for his father like the dutiful son (even while resenting it), while Stephen was suffering guilt about his decision *not* to work for his father.

"The public defender's office?" his father had said. "I thought you had more sense than that."

But the weeks he'd spent at the legal aid clinic on Chicago's South Side the previous summer had opened Stephen's eyes to how ruthlessly racist and transactional Chicago law enforcement could be. Most lawyers, including his father, shrugged and said, "That's just the way it is." They'd learned to navigate the shoals and shallows of that particular environment, to their clients' best advantage.

But Stephen wanted more for the people he represented, a population he'd never encountered while growing up in the Lake View East neighborhood of Chicago near Lake Michigan.

These were people who worked hard at low-paying jobs and struggled to afford the rent, keep food on the table and shoes on their kids' feet. Their neighborhoods were run-down and riddled with crime, but the city didn't care because the poor had no political clout. On top of that, they had to deal with the daily abusive presence of the Chicago Police Department, as configured under the Honorable Mayor Richard J. Daley.

Nora understood completely and reinforced his decision: "Trust your gut," she'd said.

Stephen harbored no illusions about public defender work. It would often be fruitless and frustrating, both because he would be battling a well-oiled Chicago criminal-justice machine and because many, if not most, of his clients were actual criminals who were guilty of the things with which they'd been charged. He could hold his own, whether in the job or against the displeasure of his father, but it was nice knowing he had Nora in his corner.

"You'll be making a difference," she'd said. "Isn't that all any of us want to do?"

~

Arnie was jumping from lane to lane in the creeping Sprain Brook traffic, but the lane he chose inevitably came to a stop the instant he moved over. The frequent jolts from his impatient braking were beginning to hurt Stephen's neck.

Almost as if he'd been privy to Stephen's earlier thoughts, Arnie said, "Your father still pissed that you aren't going to join his law firm?"

"You heard about that?"

"My mother won't shut up about it. How upset your mother is that your job is in a dangerous neighborhood and you'll be working with 'those people.' And how pissed your father is." Arnie snuck a glance at him, then said, "What are they going to be paying you over there?"

Stephen could feel his cousin teeing up a guffaw, as though he knew in advance that the answer would be hilarious.

"About seven thousand a year, to start."

On cue, Arnie burst out laughing.

"Why is that funny?"

Arnie brought his chortling down to a snicker, then said, "I make more than that delivering cars! My cousin, the hotshot law school graduate."

"But you work for your father," Stephen countered. "And you can't be making that much more—I've seen that palace you live in."

"Hey, you don't know how I live," Arnie objected.

Now it was Stephen's turn to laugh. "What am I missing? Your father owns a Mercedes dealership, but you live in a cracker-box studio apartment and you're driving *this* gutbucket."

"OK, smart guy," Arnie objected, stung. "Lay off."

Stephen looked at his watch. He and his parents were staying at the Plaza Hotel in Manhattan, where Arnie's younger sister was getting married in the early evening, because of daylight saving time.

Once he knew his morning was clear, Stephen had called Arnie to see if he would drive him to North Tarrytown on Saturday. And Arnie said yes. *Unfortunately,* Stephen thought as they crawled through traffic.

Arnie had always loomed large in his life. Stephen only saw his New York cousin a couple of times a year, when Arnie and his family, who lived on the Sound Shore of Westchester County, would visit Chicago or Stephen's family would vacation in New York. The two cousins, the only boy in each family, inevitably would be left to play together.

The older Arnie was always the instigator, Stephen the unhappy accomplice, teased into complicity from a young age with Arnie's hiss of "What are you—a pussy?" Stephen had heard swear words at school, but Arnie used them in everyday conversation, though out of hearing of their parents and grandparents.

Arnie was his personal Mephistopheles, forever tempting him into hot water of one variety or another. When Arnie and his family visited

Chicago, they would stay at the home of their mutual grandparents, always in the summer when school was out. The large house, with its amply treed and fenced backyard, sat only a block or so from both Lincoln Park Zoo and Oz Park, just north of the Magnificent Mile. Stephen and his younger sisters would be dropped at their grandparents' house each summer morning that Arnie's family was in town, so the children could play together, while their parents entertained themselves elsewhere.

The older they got, the greater Arnie's ability to find new ways to get into trouble. The cousins' most notorious escapade was the time, in their mid-teens before either was old enough to drive, when they'd taken a bus to downtown Chicago. Stephen was focused on his hunt for a specific Gant shirt he'd seen an older kid wearing at a party earlier in the summer. He wanted that shirt to wear on the first day of high school that fall. When they couldn't find the shirt at Marshall Field's or a couple of other stores they tried, Arnie announced that they were changing their mission: He wanted to look for an address he'd gotten from a friend at home, where they were supposed to sell real switchblade knives.

In that pursuit, Arnie dragged him down a dark alley in a neighborhood Stephen was unfamiliar with. Arnie couldn't find the switchblade store—but he did find a game of three-card monte in progress.

There was a mixed-race crowd of men surrounding the gaming surface—in fact, a piece of a cardboard box laid across a milk crate, with three bent playing cards set in a row. The players and onlookers scared Stephen a little as they chattered at each other.

The men running the game all had a line of patter—"Where's the lady? Find the little lady, never know where she'll be. Put your money down"—and the players trash-talked each other incessantly over their cards as they played.

Without warning, Arnie confidently threw down a five-dollar bill, then turned grinning to Stephen and said, "I always win at this."

The dealer showed them the queen of hearts along with two black-suited number cards, then mixed up the cards, slowly at first, then with more speed, before throwing them all face down on the cardboard.

"Find the lady—where'd she go? Do you know?"

Arnie pointed to a card with a smirk, and the dealer flipped it: ten of clubs.

"You snooze, you lose, better luck next time. Find the lady, find the lady . . ."

Stephen was as startled as the dealer when Arnie snatched back the fiver from the board before the dealer could pick up the bill, then turned to Stephen, eyes wide, and said, "Run!"

They were chased for a block, with the dealer and his shills gaining on them, when a police car turned the corner on to their street. Stephen and Arnie ran into the road in front of the cops, waving their hands and yelling, "Help! Help!" Their pursuers skidded to a halt, then melted back into the alley.

After Stephen and Arnie explained to the police what happened, the pair got a severe talking-to by the officer who was driving the car about the dangers of gambling on the streets of Chicago. When he heard that Arnie had grabbed the money he'd bet, the officer angrily ordered them into the back of his cruiser.

"But that was bus fare—for both of us!" Arnie protested.

Shamefaced, Stephen had begun to comply when, as the cop helped him into the car, Arnie yanked loose from the cop's grip and bolted. Before the police officer could react, Arnie had sped across four lanes of traffic and disappeared into a department store.

The officer did not give chase. Instead, he closed the door on Stephen and got back behind the wheel, then looked into the rearview mirror. When he had Stephen's eye, he said, "Your pal just left you holding the bag."

Again, Stephen thought unhappily.

The officer drove Stephen to his grandparents' house, where he handed Stephen over to his stern grandfather, tarring Stephen with

Arnie's brush in telling the three-card monte story. After the cop left, his grandfather blistered Stephen's ears, and there was nothing Stephen could say in his own defense that didn't sound like a weak excuse. His grandfather ordered him to a sofa in the living room, minus TV or other distraction, to sit silently.

When Arnie strolled in the front door twenty minutes later, their grandfather seized him by one ear and sat him down next to Stephen. Well aware that this entire fiasco must have sprung from something Arnie had done, their grandfather verbally flayed Arnie, then left the two of them to wait to be collected by their respective mothers: "And no talking to each other! I don't want to hear a peep out of either of you."

On the car ride home, Stephen's mother gave him another earful, saying, "I expect shenanigans out of your cousin Arnold, but you I'm disappointed in."

"But I didn't do anything," the blameless Stephen protested.

"You were somewhere you knew you shouldn't be," she had replied. "I raised you better than that. You need to be a better influence on your cousin."

That was laughable. The raffish Arnold always had Stephen's number. Whenever Stephen balked at some questionable activity, Arnie would say, "C'mon, cousin—how often do we get to see each other? Let's have some fun." It always worked.

~

If Stephen had arisen at 7:30 a.m. Saturday morning and taken a cab to Grand Central, he could have caught a train that would get him to Tarrytown by ten at the latest, he later realized.

But, at the rehearsal dinner the night before, his mother had said, "You should spend a little time with your cousin Arnold. It looks like he's straightened out a little."

So he'd asked Arnie for a ride to Tarrytown on Saturday morning, unaware of what a production that would entail. Arnie was quick to agree but never mentioned that they would have to take the train to Larchmont to get his car at his parents' house.

By the time they reached Larchmont, the morning was half over. The drive to North Tarrytown was supposedly a half hour, but that was before they'd run into the jam on the Sprain Brook. Stephen could feel his time with Nora dwindling by the minute.

When the traffic on the Sprain cleared, Arnie sped up and switched lanes toward an exit to Greenburgh, saying, "Hey, I need to make a quick stop in Elmsford. A guy I know has something I need to pick up."

"Can't we do it on the way back?"

"No, he said he was going out in a little while. I need to catch him before he leaves."

"What's so important? You know I'm in a hurry."

"It's just a couple of bags of weed. I promised some of the car detailers at work that I'd get it for them."

"You deal drugs? At your father's garage?"

"It's just a little grass. You make it sound so sinister."

Stephen sighed. The clock in his imagination had hands that spun crazily forward, recording the time he was wasting. "OK, it's your car."

As they drove and Stephen sighed again, Arnie turned to him and said, "Hey, I've got a life too. And there's no way I'm putting on a tuxedo for my sister's wedding without getting stoned first."

"Yes, fine" was all Stephen could say.

"If you were in such a hurry, you should have just taken the train straight to Tarrytown and caught a taxi to her house," Arnie sniped.

"Next time," Stephen said as Arnie turned on to a street in what looked like an industrial neighborhood.

"This will just take a minute," Arnie said.

Of course, it didn't.

SATURDAY MORNING

A torn jacket is soon mended, but hard words bruise the heart of a child.

—Henry Wadsworth Longfellow

AMELIA

When her mother called to ask her to come over early to help Clara with Saturday brunch, Amelia said, "Yes, of course"—in part because she never wanted to disappoint her mother; in part because she needed some time alone with Clara. She had to ask her parents for something, and Clara always knew the best approach to take.

Amelia's son, David, who would be five in the fall, was a precocious child who was already starting to read. But New Castle, the suburban Westchester town where Amelia and her husband, Frank, lived, had a cutoff date of September 1 for kindergarten. Children whose fifth birthday fell after September 1 had to wait another year to begin school.

David's birthday wasn't until late October, but Amelia believed David was ready for school now and she didn't want him to waste a year. Then she discovered two separate facts that, together, seemed to offer her a solution.

The first was that while there was a cutoff date for kindergarten enrollment in New Castle, there was no such restriction for starting first grade. All you needed to enroll a new student in first grade was proof they'd completed kindergarten.

The second was that Hackley School, a private school in Tarrytown, had no kindergarten cutoff date, beyond a birth date within the appropriate calendar year. Attending kindergarten at Hackley in the fall would qualify David for first grade in New Castle the following year.

Hackley's only requirement was the parents' ability to pay its $2,500 annual tuition. But Amelia and her husband could not afford a sum like that—which meant Amelia would have to ask her parents for the money.

It was never easy to ask her mother for anything, whether it was new school shoes when she was a girl or help making a down payment on their house after she and Frank had gotten married. Amelia knew her father would always say yes. But she didn't want the kind of yes from her mother that meant a debt had been incurred. To avoid that took finesse.

Clara could always tell when her mother's mood was right for an approach, and the best approach to make. Amelia regretted how long it had taken her to recognize Clara for the resource she was.

Amelia arrived at the family home in North Tarrytown around 10:00 a.m., just as her mother was leaving for her weekly hair appointment. Her mother uttered a brief "Hello," then looked Amelia up and down, as though performing a military inspection.

"If you don't go on a diet, Amelia, you'll never lose that baby weight. It's been almost two years, dear."

All Amelia could say was "Yes, Mother."

"Now, go help Clara and Nora."

"Nora is here?"

It would be hard enough to ask her parents for money—again. She wasn't about to do it in front of her sister.

Amelia found Nora and Clara busy in the kitchen. "Hi, kids, what are we doing?" she said, assuming a cheer that mirrored her usual affect. But she thought, *I need to get Clara to myself.*

"Hi, Sis," Nora said, giving Amelia a hug while avoiding touching her clothes with wet hands. "Where are Frank and the kids?"

"They'll be here about twelve thirty, I think. That's when Mother said we were eating. I ran into her on her way out. Where's Daddy?"

"At his men's group meeting," Clara said, rising after extracting a heavy electric mixer from a lower cupboard.

"And what brings you home, Princess?" Amelia said, using a nickname she knew irritated Nora, though her sister didn't react.

"Nothing special—Daddy asked me to come down, so I did. We went to the Mets game last night." She turned to Clara. "Are we having bacon or sausage?"

"Davey, Sol, and Frank always want bacon—why fight city hall?" Clara said.

Amelia said, "Then why don't I get the bacon started?" She put on an apron she found in the broom closet, worried that she wouldn't get time with Clara alone. She took out a skillet and set it on the stove, turned on the heat underneath, and began laying strips of bacon in the center.

~

Like many only children unexpectedly presented with a sibling, Amelia had subconsciously resented Nora's existence from the moment she was born, though she would have denied that this was true and said she cared deeply for her sister.

Being an only child for her first five years hadn't been idyllic. Amelia spent her early childhood trying to meet an unspoken standard her mother set, which she seemed to learn only by trial and error. But at least she had her mother to herself and could remember moments of maternal approval.

Once Nora was born, those few happy intervals seemed to disappear. And when Amelia did get her mother's attention, it usually involved harsh words.

Amelia knew that at some point, Nora also became their mother's target. But Nora never seemed to care, and her ability to withstand their mother's critical appraisals angered Amelia, who worked so hard to pass her mother's unspoken tests.

Amelia sometimes worried that her mother didn't like her for a reason Amelia would never understand. Had she committed some sin she couldn't remember? She spent her life trying to atone for this imagined transgression, not understanding that this was a fruitless quest.

She remembered a day when her mother accompanied Clara and five-year-old Amelia to a nearby park. As she thought back, Amelia realized that her mother must have been pregnant with Nora.

"Don't get mud on your shoes": That was her mother's admonition as they approached a playground in the neighborhood. But as careful as Amelia was to avoid mud while still trying to enjoy the swings and other equipment, she walked through something that caused her shoes to make small gray footprints on the beige rug inside the front door when they got home.

"Look what you've done," her mother scolded her. "Take those shoes off right this instant."

Amelia stood precariously on one foot, tugging at the shoe on the other. When it didn't come off with the necessary speed, her mother reached down and pulled roughly at the shoe. Amelia lost her balance, sitting down hard on the floor. Amelia bit her tongue and opened her mouth to cry, until she saw her mother's face.

"Don't start," her mother said sharply.

"Um, Mrs. Levitsky," Clara said, "before you get too mad at Amelia . . ."

Her mother turned and said, "Yes, what is it?" with a glare that carried the message "This better be good." All Clara could do was point to her employer's shoes. They all looked at Amelia's mother's feet.

Next to the short row of Amelia's small faint footprints on the beige carpet, there was a trail of even darker footprints ending at her mother's shoes.

"I'll get some soap and water," Clara said, turning to little Amelia and taking her hand. "Why don't you leave your shoes here and come with me so I can get the rest of you cleaned up?"

But Clara realized that aside from the faint traces on her shoes, Amelia was otherwise unbesmirched, so she left her in her room before going back down to clean up. After waiting a moment, Amelia then crept to the stairs' landing, where she could observe the front hall, unseen.

Clara was on the floor with a bucket, sponge, and rag, rubbing and blotting at the footprints, while her mother, now in stockinged feet, watched with a sour expression. Then Clara stopped and looked up at her mother.

"Mrs. Levitsky," she said.

"What?" her mother said.

"You look angry at something. Are you mad at me for pointing out that you were making a mess?"

Amelia saw her mother stiffen. Her face took on an expression that reminded Amelia of a monster in a fairy-tale picture book.

Before her mother could speak, Clara continued, "Because you know Amelia didn't track dirt in here on purpose, any more than you did."

It looked to Amelia as though her mother was about to say something angry, when her face contorted, and one hand went to her pregnant midsection. "Ow! Stop *kicking* me!" she commanded, doubling over. When the pain subsided, Amelia saw her mother take a deep breath, as though testing for further twinges. Finding none, she straightened up carefully, then turned to Clara, who had jumped up to help her.

"When you're done with the carpet, you can start on dinner," she said, as though they hadn't just been at odds. "The meat loaf was too dry last time. You need to add an egg to the mix."

"Yes, ma'am" was all Clara said, before going back to work on the rug.

~

As Amelia tended the bacon, a bit of fat popped, sending hot droplets of grease flying from the pan. One landed on Amelia's wrist, and she yelped in pain.

"Ancient proverb: Never fry bacon with bare arms," Nora said with a smile.

"Very funny," Amelia said. She found a dishrag and dabbed at her burn. Then she looked at her sister. "So are you done yet with school? It feels like you've been in Syracuse forever."

"I'm all done," Nora said. "I finished a week or so ago."

"Amelia," Clara said, "does Davey like blueberries or strawberries on his waffles?"

"Definitely strawberries," Amelia said, then turned back to Nora. "So what are you going to do with that fancy degree? Daddy said you were moving back here to New York City to work."

"I'm considering a couple of things," Nora said vaguely. "Nothing's certain yet."

Amelia looked at her younger sister, wondering what she wasn't saying. Then the doorbell rang.

"You two keep working," Clara said, wiping her hands on her apron as she headed through the swinging door.

"How's David doing in school?" Nora asked as she washed some of the dirty dishes to make room for the rest of the breakfast preparation. "Is he in kindergarten yet?"

"We want him to go in the fall—he's already started reading," Amelia said. "But it will depend on a couple of things."

They heard voices from the front hall—male voices. Then Clara came back into the kitchen and said, "It's someone for Nora."

When Nora looked surprised and said, "Who?" Clara said, "Someone from school at Syracuse" and waggled her head, just enough to convey some secret bit of information.

The message landed, as Nora stiffened, then wiped her hands on a rag and hurried out of the kitchen without taking off her apron.

"Anyone I know?" Amelia asked Clara.

"I don't think so" was all Clara would say as she returned to preparing the meal. She disappeared for a minute to go to the pantry.

Through the kitchen door, Amelia heard Nora's voice—"What are you *doing* here?"—followed by a loudly hushed conversation. She heard Nora say "Keep your voice down" more than once.

Amelia took the last piece of bacon out of the pan and laid it on a plate. After turning off the burner and setting the skillet aside, she walked to the kitchen door and found she could hear the conversation in the front hall. So she listened.

A male voice said, "Is something wrong?"

Then Nora: "No. Just that my father has a problem, and I haven't figured out how to help him."

Problem? Amelia thought, then remembered what Frank had said about a lawsuit of some sort. She wondered why her father hadn't asked her for help, when she lived right there, and decided she'd ask him later, if she thought of it.

Then the male voice again: "I'm flying back to Syracuse on Sunday morning. When are you driving up?"

And Nora: "I should start back after breakfast. I'll definitely be up there by dinnertime."

"I'd offer to ride back with you, if my parents hadn't already paid for this plane ticket."

Amelia chose that moment to walk through the kitchen door. She adopted a chipper tone, as though she had something trivial to ask: "Nora?"

She found her sister standing by the open front door with two young men. There was a flash of something—guilt?—on Nora's face, and Amelia was almost positive she'd seen her drop the hand of the better-looking boy when Amelia came in.

Amelia widened her smile as she said, "Oh, hi. I didn't know we had company."

Nora gave her a blank look but said nothing, so Amelia stepped forward and extended her hand. "I'm Amelia, Nora's sister. Are you friends of hers from school?"

"School?" said one of the men, whose hair was unkempt and who wore a navy golf shirt, pink plaid madras shorts, and a pair of loafers without socks. "I haven't been to school in years."

He made no move to take Amelia's extended hand. The other one, the good-looking one in the white dress shirt and khaki pants, accepted her hand without missing a beat. "I am—a friend from school," he said. He smiled as he shook Amelia's hand, and she was struck by his warmth. "I'm Stephen Cantor. We were in the neighborhood and thought we'd stop in and say hi."

"Oh?" Amelia turned to the one in the shorts. "And this is . . . ?"

"My cousin Arnie Stulwitz, from Larchmont. Have some manners, man."

Arnie now stood straight, removing his sunglasses with one hand while extending the other hand to her to shake, saying, with a manufactured smile, "Nice to meet you."

"Stephen and I are friends from grad school," Nora said, adding, "Arnie is the one with the car."

"It was nice of you to drive him," Amelia told him.

"I'll say," Arnie agreed. "Particularly with the traffic on a Saturday."

"And you drove all the way here from Larchmont?"

"Yeah," Stephen said, "this joker's sister is getting married this afternoon at the Plaza, so we can't stay." Still smiling, he turned to Nora. "I'm sorry to drop in unannounced like this. I guess I'll have to meet your parents another time. C'mon, Arnie, let's head back. Our mothers will skin us if we're late for the wedding."

Stephen turned back to Amelia, shook her hand again, and smiled. "It was so nice to meet you," he said with a sincerity that made Amelia blush, though she didn't know why.

Then he turned again to Nora. Amelia saw Nora give an almost imperceptible shake of her head. Stephen's hand, which seemed en route to encircle her waist for an impromptu hug, recalibrated its trajectory, taking her hand instead, to shake it. "Good to see you," he said to her. "I hope we'll see each other again soon."

"OK" was all Nora said, as the two men headed out the screen door and down the front steps.

As they walked away, Nora returned to the kitchen, leaving Amelia to shut the front door. Instead of pushing it closed, she watched the two young men walk down the sidewalk and heard Arnie complain loudly, "We drove all this way for *that*? Five flippin' minutes? Steverino, cousin of mine, you must have it bad for this chick. That's all I can say."

Amelia saw Stephen turn back to look at the house. He said something to his cousin that she couldn't hear, then gave Amelia a little wave before he got in the car, and she closed the front door.

Clara and Nora were back in the kitchen finishing the brunch preparations, but Amelia stood in the front hall for a moment. She could still smell Arnie's cologne, which hung in the air. She recognized the scent: Canoe, for men who wanted to smell sweet but weren't quite brave enough to wear perfume.

This Stephen was obviously someone Nora was involved with in some way. But how seriously? Seriously enough, she decided, that Nora was trying to keep it a secret from her. And from their parents. Or, more specifically, their mother.

That made sense to Amelia. Nora had had a ringside seat while their mother tried to sabotage more than one of her older sister's romances.

~

Amelia's romantic life had been full of mild ups and downs, from the time she began drawing boys' interest with her ripening figure at twelve. Her parents wouldn't let her start dating until she was sixteen, by which time she had developed a lush, wholesome appeal. She dated several of the better-looking boys at her high school, most of whom were either obsessed with touching her breasts or talking about themselves, or both. Neither had interested Amelia.

While Amelia complained that men were only interested in the way a woman looked, she applied the same cosmetic standard to the bland, blond pretty boys she dated. Over the course of a couple of weeks or even months, each of these boys would catch, hold, and lose her interest, at which point she would move on (or, less often, he would).

There were enough boys at her high school that Amelia always had someone she was hoping to date, was currently dating, or had recently broken up with. This pattern held steady as she began her brief ramble through academia at City College.

But it all changed abruptly when, during her sophomore year there, she met Alan Gilbert, who was also a sophomore but was thirty years old. They met in a philosophy class in which Amelia was struggling. Noticing her confusion, Alan invited her to coffee after class one day and offered his help. Tutoring sessions turned into dates for movies and dinner.

Alan wasn't Amelia's usual type: swarthy and brutish looking but thoughtful, unassuming, patient—all the result of the decade of difference in their age and experience. Amelia fell hard, gushing to Clara about Alan and how he had been a construction contractor before the war. Now he had gone back to school to become a structural engineer.

Things were fine, as long as Alan flew under her mother's radar. That was easy to manage when the couple saw each other only at school in the city. But, hoping to push their relationship to a new level, she convinced Alan to drive up to her parents' house to take her out to dinner one weekend. Alan appeared at the Levitsky home, driving a car he'd borrowed from a friend, a fact he mentioned in front of her parents. Amelia saw her mother's mouth pucker at the revelation.

All Amelia had said prior to his arrival was that she was having dinner with a classmate from City College. When Alan came to the front door to pick Amelia up, it was obvious that this was meant as a romantic evening with a serious beau. She introduced him to both her parents without incident, but her mother was quick to express her disapproval at breakfast the next morning.

"How old is he?" her mother asked, then answered her own question: "Too old for you. That's how old."

"Mother, I'm twenty!"

"Which is not even old enough to vote. He's thirty? And he's still in college and doesn't even own his own car? Something's not right."

"He was in the war. He's a veteran!"

"I'm sorry," her mother said. "I just don't think he's appropriate for you to spend time with."

After that, Amelia made a point of seeing Alan only in the city, and she stopped mentioning these encounters to her mother. But she'd be exuberant with Clara every time she came home after a date with him.

She ascribed the fact that Alan never seemed passionate—or, at least, that he wasn't sexually aggressive—to his maturity. She had to push him at the end of each date to make plans for the next one, though he always did. And she had initiated their first kiss good night, though he'd taken the hint after that. But she mistook his restraint for chivalry and was still childish enough to spin a few dates with an older man into a budding romance that concluded in matrimony, at least in her imagination.

Amelia even said to Clara, with a shade too much eagerness, "Can you imagine the look on Mother's face if Alan and I went to city hall and eloped? Would that be a hoot?"

Yes, she had thought about the possibility—though when she brought it up to Alan, he said, "Don't you think you're a little young?" But she had made that same leap—in her imagination—with every boy she'd ever dated. Her remark to Clara was less about the actual possibility of running off than about her fantasies of scandalizing her mother, but it led Clara to slip and say something to her mother that she hadn't meant to.

"She caught me off guard when she asked why you've been in such a good mood," Clara told her when she apologized. "All I said to her was that you seemed to be getting serious with your new boyfriend."

That was all it took.

As she later learned, her mother got on the phone that night to Amelia's Aunt Lucille, who lived in Los Angeles. By the weekend, the unhappy but reflexively compliant Amelia was on an airplane to California, where she spent the summer living with Aunt Lucille and Uncle Ned while working as a receptionist at Uncle Ned's furniture store on Ventura Boulevard in the San Fernando Valley.

By the time Amelia returned in the fall, Alan had met someone else. Amelia, despondent, dropped out of City College midway through her third year, then realized she had condemned herself to spending her days at home with her mother.

So she asked Sol for a job at All-American Scrap. She began to work in the office answering phones, making coffee, filing—whatever Marlys, the head secretary, needed her to do. It wasn't particularly interesting work, but Amelia didn't have a lot of interests, so it was a good match. She'd gotten to spend time with her father and her Uncle Stan, both of whom enjoyed teasing and spoiling her.

~

Amelia returned to the kitchen from the front hall after seeing off the two young men. Finding only Clara there, she said, "What else can I do?"

"You can rinse and slice these strawberries for the waffles," Clara said, pointing her toward a quart basket next to the kitchen sink.

She'd just started on the berries when Nora, who had been putting the garbage out, came back in. "So," Amelia said, "is that Stephen in marketing also?"

"No, he just finished Syracuse Law School," Nora said, then turned to Clara: "What can I do?"

"Help your sister—no, wait, here—slice these up for the fruit salad." Clara handed Nora a bag of grapes, a bowl, and a paring knife. When Nora immediately started to slice grapes, Clara scolded her, "Well, wash them first, miss. What were you—brought up in a barn?"

Nora chuckled and joined Amelia at the sink.

"He's obviously not from New York," Amelia said. "Is he from upstate?"

"No, he's from Chicago."

"How'd you meet him?"

"We were in a literature class together."

"I assume you two are dating," Amelia said with a knowing smile, hoping to provoke a reaction, but all she got was Nora's nonchalance.

"Why do you say that?"

Amelia smiled at her, taking her time. She glanced at Clara, whose expression was as hard to read as ever. Amelia was sure Clara knew what was going on. Clara and Nora had always been close.

"Perhaps because he drove all the way up here from Larchmont to see you for five minutes. And why would he want to meet *our* parents? Who does he think they are? Liz and Dick? LBJ and Lady Bird?"

"He only wanted to meet Mother. He wanted to see if I was telling the truth about her having snakes for hair."

Clara, her back still to the girls as she worked at the counter, snorted. Amelia, however, hated it when Nora mocked their mother.

"Very funny," she said. "You always think you're smarter than everyone."

Clara said, "Nora, will you go look in the china cabinet and see if you can find eight of those blue napkins your mother likes?"

"Aye-aye, captain," Nora replied, clicking her heels and saluting, before leaving the kitchen.

Clara looked at Amelia and said, "You always let her get under your skin. But if you would just treat each other like sisters . . ."

"I guess" was all Amelia could manage. She indicated her empty hands and said, "What else can I do?"

"Start squeezing the oranges for the juice, if you don't mind," Clara said, without looking up from what she was doing.

Amelia grabbed a bag of oranges, found a cutting board, and began slicing them in half. At least now she had Clara to herself for a minute.

Amelia, in some ways, was her mother's daughter and, at adolescence, began to treat Clara the way her mother sometimes did: as the help, not as a potential ally who had been involved in her daily life almost since birth. She had shut out Clara for a while, after the business with Alan. But she knew it was a mistake not to use Clara as a resource, given the opportunity.

"Clara," she said, "let me ask you something quick before Nora comes back."

~

A month after she'd begun working at All-American, Amelia started spending her lunch hours at the soda fountain of Ring Pharmacy, around the corner from the All-American office. That was where she met her husband, Frank.

When she first started working for her father, Amelia tried to use her lunch hour to eat the sandwich she brought from home while reading at her desk. She usually had a mystery she had checked out of Warner Library in Tarrytown. She was slowly working her way through their collection of Agatha Christie novels. But, instead of reading, she inevitably wound up drawn into a conversation with the chatty Marlys, the head secretary, who had the desk next to hers and who insisted on eating her lunch (which she also brought from home) at her own desk at the same time as Amelia.

Marlys subscribed to *The National Enquirer* and brought copies with her to show Amelia almost every day. The flimsy newspaper was full of stories and pictures of human freaks of nature, aliens from outer space, and the bad behavior of movie stars. Marlys was always eager to show Amelia some salacious *Enquirer* tidbit. Their conversations lasted most of each noontime and always concluded when, fifty minutes into their lunch hour, Marlys headed for the bathroom and asked Amelia to cover the phones while she was gone ("Just for a sec—gotta run to the ladies', hon").

Marlys's bathroom trips lasted exactly the duration of a cigarette, eating up the lunch break's final ten minutes. The phones were always busy over lunch, so Amelia didn't have much chance to read when Marlys left her alone.

One day, Amelia picked up her book and left the office at noon, then walked around the block to have lunch at the corner drugstore. That became her new routine, and her father or her Uncle Stan began to slip her a couple of dollars to treat herself to a tuna on toast or a club sandwich, if they were around when she was leaving (and they usually were). Then she could eat and read the latest book she was involved in.

Her lunch hour solitude lasted about a week. Then the soda fountain's jack-of-all-trades, Frank Goldfarb, who had kept his distance but watched her from afar that first week, got up the courage to start talking to her while she ate and read by herself.

Though he was only a year or so older than Amelia, Frank was the pharmacy's assistant manager, qualified to do everything except dispense prescriptions. He made sodas and sandwiches behind the lunch counter, stocked shelves, ran the cash register, made deliveries, and did whatever else old Mr. Ringenberg needed him to do. Frank always had a good word for Amelia, and that daily good word soon expanded into brief conversations.

Before long, Amelia moved from a booth to a seat at the counter so she could more easily talk with Frank while he made her lunch. On days when Frank had deliveries to make, he would arrange them to accommodate Amelia's lunch hour so she could ride with him. She would bring her lunch to work in a bag, and she would eat while they talked and he made deliveries. If there was time and opportunity, Frank would pull over to the curb in a shady residential neighborhood in Queens and they would neck.

Frank told her he was the son of Latvian immigrants, who first had settled on the Lower East Side before moving a generation later to Yonkers. Frank, whose full name was Franklin, had been named after Benjamin Franklin, his mother's favorite founding father. Frank was tall, husky, and swarthy—like Alan Gilbert, he represented a marked change from the pale gentiles Amelia had dated in high school.

When Frank asked Amelia to marry him, Amelia remembered what had happened the first time she brought Alan home. So when she brought Frank to dinner at her parents' house for the first time, she introduced him by saying, "This is Frank. He's my fiancé. He asked me to marry him, and I said yes."

Amelia could still picture the expression of horror blooming on her mother's face. It was like a mushroom cloud, expanding in a terrible destructive storm of disapproval, remnants of which hung over her marriage to this day. From the distance of almost seven years, Amelia wondered if it had been worth it, just to see that one look. She wasn't sure.

In a similar way, she couldn't explain any of a dozen other things she'd done in her life simply to get her mother's attention for a few minutes. There always seemed to be a better way to handle any situation with her mother than the ones she tended to choose.

Amelia realized later that she had made a mistake in not enlisting her father in her cause by introducing him to Frank first. She knew if she'd taken her father to lunch at the pharmacy, he and Frank would have hit it off. Then Frank would have had Daddy in his corner from the start.

By springing it on her parents the way she had, she forced her father to side with her mother, to keep peace in his own house. Did Frank blame her for this? She didn't know, but she faulted herself.

Frank was bluff, friendly, and hardworking, though not nearly as sharp when it came to business as he thought, something Amelia didn't know how to tell him without hurting his feelings. Shortly before proposing to her, he'd landed a sales job in the Garment District. But he told her he had a plan to make the move from being a piece goods salesman, working on a commission for someone else, to fronting his own ready-to-wear line, with salesmen of his own working for him.

After Amelia and Frank were married, Frank suffered a series of business setbacks, and Amelia knew it confirmed her mother's already shoddy opinion of him.

Frank seemed to be making good on his plan to go out on his own when he found a connection to buy cheaply made piece goods ("But quality materials," he emphasized to Amelia) in China, through an import-export firm in Chinatown. He was able to round up enough cash to make the leap from salesman to entrepreneur—and made it work for the first two years of his marriage to Amelia.

Then, just as Frank made a deal with a cheaper Malaysian supplier for a new spring line after a particularly successful fall season, the US Senate roiled the waters with tariff talks. It happened at the same time that an upheaval in Malaysian politics caused a shutdown at Port Swettenham, one of the country's main shipping centers.

The ripple effects of the tariff news created a cash shortage for his business, even as the Port Swettenham problems caused a bottleneck of imports. Frank's costs soared, at a moment when he owed a balloon payment on the building he'd bought for the business. That break in the flow of goods lasted long enough that Frank was unable to deliver shipments that had already been paid for. He was forced to refund several large orders, with no way of recouping the loss. He had no choice but to dissolve his business and declare bankruptcy.

Her father hired Frank to work at the scrapyard—against her mother's wishes, Amelia knew. Her mother learned to disguise her distaste for him after an exchange with Amelia's then-three-year-old son, David, at a Hanukkah dinner.

During a quiet moment at the table, David piped up: "Grandma, why don't you like Daddy?"

Her mother calmly replied, "Of course I like your father, dear."

To which David had said, "Then why do you always look mad when you talk to him?"

~

Brunch was almost ready when Amelia's parents returned home. Her father gave Amelia a quick kiss, then went upstairs to change clothes before handling a couple of brief chores in the yard.

Her mother came into the kitchen, where Amelia and Clara were putting the final preparations in place. Once Frank and the kids arrived, Clara would crank up a finely tuned one-woman assembly line producing waffles, scrambled eggs, and more. This was the relative calm before the storm.

Her mother sat down in the breakfast nook to watch them finish their work and said, "I can't believe how slow they were at the beauty shop today."

"Oh, it didn't take that long," Amelia offered, looking at her watch. "And your hair looks nice, Mother."

"Amelia, you need to strain the orange juice before you put it in the pitcher," Lillian said as she watched her work. "You know the pulp makes my gums hurt."

"I was going to," Amelia said, trying not to sound defensive. "Um, Mother, after brunch, there's something I need to talk to you and Daddy about."

"What now?" her mother said, sounding exhausted.

Before Amelia could reply, the doorbell rang. Then it rang again and again and again, several times in rapid succession, before Clara could dry her hands and reach the front door. Seconds later, Amelia and her mother heard the voices of Frank Goldfarb and the Goldfarb children chattering to Clara in the front hall.

"I was ringing the bell!" they could hear David tell Clara from the front hall.

"I heard," came Clara's amused reply.

Her mother turned to Amelia, clearly annoyed. "It's only eleven forty-five," she said. "They always come early."

SATURDAY AFTERNOON

To him who is in fear, everything rustles.
—Sophocles

LILLIAN

Lillian Levitsky sat at the end of the large dining room table, surveying the family that surrounded her at brunch: her two daughters, her grandchildren, her son-in-law, her husband.

They were happily chattering and laughing, eating waffles, scrambled eggs, bagels and cream cheese with lox, and Clara's special hash browns, whose secret ingredient was minced onions caramelized to the brink of charring.

As she watched her family, Lillian wondered, *What are they hiding from me?* She knew there had to be something. She had lived with that feeling her entire life.

Her son-in-law, Frank, guffawed at a remark his son, David, made. *Frank is always laughing about something,* she thought.

With all the imminent upheaval in her life, Lillian felt a constant need to be on her guard. She lived with the sense that she could suffer a horrible betrayal at any moment.

Lillian had many fears, which she kept at bay by imposing as much control as she could over the other people in her life. When they had ideas of their own or simply went about their lives in a way she disapproved of, her tongue could be poisonous. In many ways, she spent her life operating from a defensive crouch, guarding against encroachment on the order she tried to impose.

The only person who was able to calm her fears—and then, only intermittently—was her husband, who now sat smiling at the head of the table, engaged in energetic conversation with their daughters. She knew she had no need to fear his betrayal yet was unable to appreciate the security he provided in her life.

Amelia and Frank and their children were regular visitors to the house. But this brunch was an occasion because Nora was in town for the first time since Christmas. Lillian knew her younger daughter had completed her PhD at Syracuse University. *In marketing,* Lillian sniffed to herself. She didn't know exactly when Nora would move back home, but Sol had said a couple of times that she'd be back by the beginning of July: ". . . and then, after Nora moves home this summer" was how he'd put it. So Lillian took it as a given.

Maybe now, a fresh start with her, she thought.

Brunch was set for 12:30 p.m., but Frank and the kids had turned up at 11:45. Lillian could hear them enter like a tornado of toys, diapers, and baby equipment, all concentrated in the front hall.

Lillian said, "They always come early."

"Grandma! Grandma!" David squealed, bursting through the swinging door to the kitchen and seizing Lillian around the knees.

"Yes, dear, not so loud," Lillian said, giving him a brief hug before sending him on to Amelia and Clara.

Lillian walked out to the front hall, where she found Frank, struggling with baby Judy, who was almost two and still in diapers.

"Clara in the kitchen?" he said, heading in that direction. "I need to put Judy's bottle and lunch in the refrigerator."

"They're all in there," Lillian said.

Frank said, "Thanks," then pushed through the swinging door to the kitchen. Lillian heard Clara greet the baby: "Well, hello, you little gumdrop. Come give Clara some sugar."

Lillian stood in the front hall, listening to David chatter to Clara and Amelia in the kitchen, until Clara came out to her and said, "I'm ready to set the table, Lillian." As they started for the dining room, Lillian heard Nora say to Amelia, "Meelie, come outside for a minute." Lillian's ears perked up. "Clara," she heard Amelia say, "would you mind keeping an eye on David for a sec?"

As Lillian entered the dining room, she found her daughters had already vacated it.

"Hey, Tiger," Clara called to little David, "come help Clara and your grandma set the table."

Then Lillian was distracted reminding David to pick up silverware by the handle, instead of the end that went into people's mouths. But she'd had time to wonder: *What are they talking about?*

~

Sol had mentioned earlier in the week that he'd asked Nora to come down for the weekend, though he hadn't said why. Since Nora arrived Thursday afternoon, Lillian and Nora had barely seen each other to speak. Which was, in its way, fine with Lillian.

Lillian had always been daunted by her younger daughter: by her quickness and intelligence, and by her sense of self-possession and confidence. Where had those come from? *Certainly not from me.* Nora had a self-assurance, almost since she was a toddler, that Lillian wondered at.

Lillian carried the year after Nora was born as a badge of shame, one that existed as a muzzy dream period with few sharp details, except for the anguish and fear. She had abandoned Nora as an infant, and Nora had bonded instead with Clara.

Lillian could remember the exhaustion and the need to place the blame for her problems somewhere—anywhere—except on herself. If the period was foggy, its central fact burned at her like a branding iron: She had ignored her baby for a year.

By the time she decided she'd made a mistake, it was too late. Unable to make up the ground she'd lost with Nora in the year she left her care to Clara, Lillian simply told herself that this was Nora's choice.

When she first became pregnant with Nora, Lillian thought she had some lingering gastrointestinal distress, which made her feel nauseated for two weeks. She was horrified at the doctor's diagnosis.

"You're not sick—you're pregnant," Dr. Stein, her internist, told her.

"Again?"

"Congratulations."

Lillian almost burst into tears.

She had figured out many years earlier that the world was divided into two types of people: those who take care of other people and those who are taken care of. From a young age, she was forced to be a caregiver. But, when she went to the movies, she saw a world where servants buzzed around you, doing your bidding, taking care of you. Lillian didn't know how she'd get it, but that was the life she wanted for herself.

When she married Sol, she thought she had moved from the ranks of those who did caregiving to the more exalted ranks of the cared for. That feeling was short lived because, after Amelia was born, Lillian felt the balance shift and realized that this set of scales would never again tip in her favor. Even after Clara arrived, Lillian knew the mother was always the caregiver, never the cared for.

Depressed and unhappy about the unexpected pregnancy with Nora, Lillian began to confide in Clara, in a particularly personal way. She would wander into the kitchen after Amelia went down for her afternoon nap and unburden herself to Clara, in stream of consciousness monologues:

"How am I going to take care of another baby? I feel some days like Amelia is trying to suck me dry—she needs so much all the time. Oh, Clara, how could I do any of this if you weren't here? Oh my God, I'm so nauseous."

Clara would calm Lillian, even when her fears turned her into a human snapping turtle. As Clara tended to her endless bouts of morning sickness, Lillian told her, "My sisters wouldn't do the things for me that you do."

In the months after Nora was born, Lillian had to fight feelings of repulsion at her own child. She could not bring herself to hold, feed, or otherwise physically interact with baby Nora, out of a fear that she might fling her away in a moment of acute despair.

The sense of shame encircled her, making it difficult to see anything clearly, other than her own failure: *I am a horrible mother.*

Lillian had received little affection growing up. Her parents treated her, at best, like an afterthought. She had difficulty accepting the warmth she received from Sol or learning how to reciprocate. The demands of motherhood had taken her by surprise and, she believed, found her wanting.

When Lillian came out of what she secretly referred to as "the fog," she started trying to insert herself into baby Nora's routine. But Nora was having none of it.

If Lillian offered her a bottle, she either refused and cried or, worse, she took it from Lillian and drank it herself, unassisted. If she sat on Lillian's lap, her attitude was one of pained tolerance. There was no snuggling in; from Nora's posture, she might as well have been perched on an uncomfortable bus bench. She would sit there a minute, then climb down from Lillian's lap and into Clara's, where she would cuddle like a kitten.

If Lillian tried to spoon-feed Nora, her daughter would bat the spoon away. If she tried to change her diaper, Nora would kick and buck on the changing table. If she tried to put Nora down for a nap, the baby would stand up in her crib and cry until Clara came to quiet her.

Lillian told herself that this was what Nora had decided their relationship was going to be. So she would simply honor her wishes going forward.

As Nora got older, Lillian focused on the role of responsible guardian and the authority it conferred. Even so, she found that Nora had a will that was equal to her own. Nora was never openly defiant, but Lillian felt her daughter always managed to do what she wanted, no matter what Lillian thought.

She remembered Nora's bat mitzvah—as glaring an example of Nora's strong will and sense of injustice as Lillian could recall.

The bat mitzvah—the female version of the Jewish coming-of-age ceremony—was not as common at that point in the 1950s as it later became. But when she was eight, Nora had come home from Sunday school and announced that she wanted one—and was willing to do the work necessary.

Nora made good on her promise. On her big morning, shortly after her thirteenth birthday, her voice was sure and clear in singing the prayers. But when her central moment arrived—her chanting of the haftarah—and Nora stepped to the pulpit to begin, the rabbi stayed there as well, standing next to her.

It was odd, Lillian thought, because the rabbi hadn't done that with any of the boys whose ceremonies Lillian had attended.

She watched Nora and could see her tense for a second, staring down at the pulpit without moving. Another couple of seconds passed, and Lillian felt the time pressing on her. She saw the rabbi give Nora a small nudge.

Nora then smiled broadly, turned to the rabbi, and said, "Thank you, Rabbi. You may be seated."

Lillian's gasp was echoed by people in the rows behind her. She saw the rabbi take a step backward, as though he'd been pushed. Then his face clouded, and he took his seat.

Before anyone could react further, Nora began chanting her haftarah, commanding the congregation's attention with her forceful performance.

The other worshippers may have been rapt, but Lillian felt as though her breakfast had turned on her. As Nora sang, Lillian fought the rising gorge, while her temper ran rampant, her mind afroth with what she was going to say to her daughter when she got her alone.

Then the service was over. The rabbi wished the congregation "Shabbat shalom," then started the final song, "Adon Olam," before leading a procession of Nora and the cantor off the bimah. They exited to the staging area behind the sanctuary, where the rabbi and the choir all hung their robes.

By the time Lillian reached Nora, her daughter was chin to chin with the burly rabbi, who towered over her diminutive daughter. When Lillian walked in, she heard him saying, "A shanda! I've never heard such a thing!"

Lillian whirled Nora around, pulling her away from the rabbi to bark at her daughter, "How could you embarrass us like that?" Then, downshifting her tone, Lillian turned to the rabbi to say, "Rabbi Singer, I am *sooo* sorry. I hope you'll be joining us for the reception."

"I'm afraid something has come up—I have another obligation," he said, hanging up his robe. He straightened his yarmulke, put on his overcoat, and walked out.

Sol had come backstage now, and Lillian turned to find him hugging Nora, saying, "You sang beautifully!"

Lillian pulled her away and said, "Do you know how this makes us look? In front of the whole congregation?"

But Nora stood her ground: "I worked just as hard as the boys who did this. None of them had to have him looking over their shoulder. Why should I have to? And I was better than any of them."

Lillian spent the reception and the dinner that evening accepting flattering assessments of Nora's poised performance. She was convinced every compliment masked a sentiment that echoed what Delia had said out loud after hugging Nora at the reception: "Quite the outspoken young lady." To Lillian, it had sounded like a smear.

Lillian wished she could talk to Nora about what was going on in her life at this moment. Her daughter had completed her PhD in less than three years, and even Lillian was impressed with her determination. But what was Nora going to do now?

As she waited for Nora's time in Syracuse to draw to a close, Lillian decided that Nora's return would be the moment to start anew with her daughter. Once she moved back to New York City, they would find things they had in common and spend time together—and they would do it because Nora wanted to, not because Lillian demanded it. With Clara leaving, having Nora close somehow seemed important to her.

When she tried to imagine the conversation that would bring about this rapprochement, she drew a blank. She had no idea how she would start—she only knew she would have to be the one who did.

Nor could she really envision the shape of this new relationship. Not friendship; Lillian believed that a parent gave up a crucial element of control once she traded authority for friendship. She wasn't ready for that. But she wanted something more than they had.

Lillian didn't know how they'd get there. Yet, once they did, she could picture it, like a scene on that TV show *That Girl*, which she'd watched by accident one night. Nora would be a carefree young career woman working in a Manhattan office with a desk and a window. Lillian and Amelia would go there to meet her for lunch. They'd dine at some smart bistro near Nora's office, which would be . . . where? Madison Avenue? Columbia University? Wall Street? And Nora would have an apartment somewhere safe and perhaps a fiancé Lillian approved of.

Things like that would require a serious shift in behavior. Lillian had convinced herself she could try, once Nora moved back, though the path forward remained unclear.

~

"Do you want napkin rings?" Clara asked Lillian as she finished redoing the place settings where David had "helped."

"Not for brunch, I think," Lillian said distractedly.

"C'mon, Champ, you can help me scramble the eggs," Clara said, taking David out to the kitchen with her. As she did, Amelia and Nora came back in the front door. Amelia was smiling, but Nora looked unhappy. Both their faces went blank when they saw their mother.

Just then, Frank came out of the kitchen carrying the baby, who was now wearing a different onesie.

"Can you take the baby, hon?" he said to Amelia, handing Judy to his wife. "I've got to toss this shirt in the laundry."

"What happened?" Amelia said.

"Exploding diaper," he said, raising his hands as if someone were pointing a gun at him. The front of his powder blue summer linen shirt resembled a Rorschach test of brownish splotches.

"If you go to the laundry room," Lillian said, "you can scrub it out in the laundry tub there, before you put it in the washing machine."

"Yes, ma'am," Frank said, stripping down. Lillian shuddered at the sight of her hirsute son-in-law, whose sleeveless undershirt highlighted the clumps of dark hair sprouting from his shoulders and back.

Sol came in from the garden, bearing a small cucumber: "First one of the year," he said proudly. After his men's group, he had changed into the short-sleeved seersucker jumpsuit he favored for summer weekend wear.

Lillian regarded Sol's garb with the same alarm as Frank's soiled shirt. "You're not coming to the table like that, are you?"

He laughed. "Why not? It's brunch with the girls, not Shabbas dinner at the rabbi's."

Lillian rolled her eyes and went out to the kitchen. Clara had put an apron on David before he started using a whisk on a large bowl of eggs. Nora stood nearby, cutting bagels in half, then putting them in a woven basket for toasting.

"Please cut those bagels away from your throat," Lillian cautioned. Nora snickered. "What's so funny?"

"I'm slicing bagels, Mother," Nora said, "not clearing brush with a chain saw."

Lillian "tsked" at her, then turned to Clara: "Did you put the cream cheese out yet?"

"Already done," Clara said over her shoulder, even as she used a hand to slow David's egg whisking. "Easy, Slugger—we don't want to make meringue out of the scrambled eggs."

David looked up and said, "Can I have some grape juice?"

"No, dear," Lillian said automatically. "Grape juice stains everything you spill it on. Clara will give you apple juice instead." She turned to Nora. "What were you and your sister discussing outside?"

Nora laughed. "We were plotting your overthrow, Mother. It's all set for this afternoon. When the firing squad arrives, we're having them set up in the backyard. But we told them not to trample Daddy's tomato plants. We have a guillotine on standby, in case all else fails."

Lillian shrugged. "Now you're just being idiotic."

"Honestly, Mother. We were just talking. We don't see each other that often."

"Some young women don't keep secrets from their mothers." Lillian sulked.

"Oh, please, Mother," Nora said, adding, "Not everything in my life concerns you."

"Excuse me for taking an interest."

"Why start now?" Nora said under her breath to Clara, then slipped through the swinging door to the dining room with an armload of food.

"What was that?" Lillian snapped, but Nora was already gone.

"Why don't you go tell your father brunch is almost ready?" Clara said to David. She lifted him down from his perch on a kitchen chair, pulled the apron off him, and sent him to the other room. Then she turned to Lillian. "Why are you picking at that girl? She's only here until tomorrow."

Lillian looked offended and said, "I was doing no such thing."

"Lillian," Clara said and gave her a look.

"You know how I hate secrets," Lillian said.

"Did you tell your mother every little thing you were doing when you were Nora's age?"

"I stopped speaking to my mother long before I *was* Nora's age."

Lillian felt herself getting angry and knew Clara was not the cause, though Clara was the one standing there disagreeing with her. Clara seldom gave her a reason to get mad, but Lillian sometimes couldn't stop herself.

Then Clara ended the discussion, saying, "I'm about to start scrambling the eggs. Call everyone to the table, please."

Lillian continued looking at her for a long moment, then left the kitchen for the dining room, where she found Amelia and Frank talking to Nora.

"Please, can everyone have a seat," Lillian said. "Time to eat."

"Daddy, brunch," Amelia called.

Frank, still in his undershirt, helped David climb atop a thick phone book on a chair next to him at the table as Amelia put Judy in a high chair.

"You're not going to sit down to brunch dressed like that, are you?" Lillian said to Frank, who looked as though he'd been caught stealing.

But Sol said, "You're fine, Frank."

Lillian harrumphed at being countermanded but left it there.

Sol slid into his seat at the end of the table, then turned to David and said, "Are you as hungry as I am? Because I could eat a horse." David giggled. Then Sol whinnied, and David laughed harder.

Lillian was still convinced something was going on, but as Clara brought out the eggs and waffles and the meal began, her mind was soon elsewhere.

While she wanted to know what Amelia and Nora had been talking about, she was also thinking about what Clara had said. She hated when Clara was right—and Clara was almost always right about these things.

But it had taken Lillian several years before she realized what she had in her housekeeper.

~

During brunch, Lillian's mind drifted as Nora and Amelia chattered to Sol. She wondered what Amelia needed to ask. They always needed something.

When she refocused on the table conversation, Frank was recounting a recent day when he'd gone to meet a potential client at a factory near Canal Street at the south end of Manhattan. Then he had walked up through Greenwich Village on the way to his next meeting.

"When I got to Washington Square, it was like the circus had come to town," he said.

Sol, between mouthfuls of eggs, said, "What do you mean?"

"These young people—teenagers, maybe a little older—it was like they were having a party in the middle of the week. In the middle of a workday!"

"What kind of party?" Amelia asked as she tried to police Judy's efforts to eat scrambled eggs with her fingers.

"Like, with people dancing and music. All dressed up, like for a costume party."

"Animals," Lillian pronounced.

"I saw someone smoking marijuana right out in the open in Washington Square Park. You could smell it. There was even a cop standing right there. Didn't do a fu—a damn thing about it."

Both Lillian and Amelia gave Frank sidelong looks at his near stumble into obscenity.

"I suppose you smoke grass at your fancy upstate university," Amelia said to Nora.

"That's none of your business," Nora said. "But no, I haven't. I *have* been at parties where it was offered to me."

"Oh my God," Lillian said.

"You went to a pot party?" Frank said, sounding impressed.

"It wasn't a pot party," Nora said. "A few grad students were passing around a joint on the patio at a faculty party. I didn't have any. But I'm interested in what it feels like."

"Nora Jane!" Lillian said.

"I'd like to try it. That's all I'm saying."

"You're too smart to get caught up in hard drugs," Sol said. "I worry about you, honey."

"You should," Lillian said flatly.

"What does that mean?" Nora said.

"Just what I said—a father should worry about his daughter."

"Especially the one spouting crazy ideas about taking drugs," Amelia said. She put her hands over David's ears, then said in a stage whisper, "You probably believe in that free love malarkey too."

"Amelia! Language!" Lillian said. Nora snickered. Lillian turned to her. "Did I say something amusing?"

"No," Nora said. "Sorry. But if that language shocks you, you must not get out much."

Lillian glared at her. "And since when is that a crime? Not to go where people use language from the gutter?"

Nora said, "It's not."

"Then I don't understand why I'm being held up to ridicule."

"Lillian—" Sol began.

"I learned a certain standard of behavior as a young woman. I have tried to instill it in you girls."

"Yes," Nora said, stopping to cough and clear her throat. "I think you forget sometimes that it's 1967, not 1927."

"Nora," Sol tried again, but this particular train had long since left the station and was now about to jump the tracks completely.

"OK, Thoroughly Modern Millie: So—do you take those birth control pills?" Amelia sniped as Clara walked in with the coffeepot.

Nora stared daggers at her sister even as she breathed deeply, then quietly said, "That is also none of your goddamn business."

"Girls!" Sol said.

Things were quiet for a moment, and Lillian glanced at Amelia. She had the look she got as a little girl, before tattling on her sister. Just then, Judy tossed a piece of bacon on the rug.

"Judy!" Amelia said, jumping up to snatch it before the grease could stain the carpet.

"Too bad you don't have a dog," Frank joked.

"That's the last thing anyone needs," Lillian said.

"Which explains why we never had pets," Nora cracked. Lillian rolled her eyes.

After returning to her seat, Amelia looked at her father and said, "That reminds me—Daddy, Frank said something about a lawsuit at your company. Is everything OK?"

Lillian's head jerked up. "Lawsuit? What about a lawsuit?"

Frank cut his eyes from Sol to Amelia. "No, I think you're mistaken, hon."

Lillian looked at Sol, who seemed about to growl at Frank and Amelia. But when he turned to her, his face shifted into a smile: "Amelia is confused, dear."

Amelia now turned toward Frank. "But you said everyone at work—"

"I was talking about my friend Jerry and his job. Remember?"

"There's no problem," Sol said to Lillian. "Nothing we can't sort out."

This only served to sharpen Lillian's focus: "What?"

At that moment, David knocked over a glass of milk, which ran off the table into his lap. He began to cry, saying, "My pants are wet!" Everyone then sprang into action, led by Lillian's cry of "Not the silk seat covers!"

Amelia and Frank jumped up, with Frank whisking David off the chair and down the hall to the bathroom. "We should probably go—we're done anyway," Amelia said.

They passed Clara, coming in with a pail of water and a sponge. "Davey has some dry clothes in Amelia's old room from his last sleepover," she said.

Lillian watched this activity with restless energy, pacing as Clara worked household magic. She knew she shouldn't be as upset as she was, but the fact that it was the silk seat cover grated on her nerves, which were already raw from . . . what?

Amelia had mentioned a lawsuit. While Sol had deflected, he hadn't denied it. "Nothing we can't sort out," he'd said.

Sol came in carrying a couple of old towels and offered them to Clara and Nora, who was helping her. "Maybe to absorb some of the dampness," he said.

He turned to Lillian as she paced at the end of the dining room table. Her eyes held his as she said, "You know I hate secrets."

As she uttered the word *secrets*, Amelia returned, carrying most of the toys and baby equipment they had come with. "Secrets?" she said. "Are we talking about that boy who stopped by to see Nora earlier?"

"What?" Lillian said, turning to Nora. "Boy? Who was here?"

"Nobody," Nora assured her. "A friend from Syracuse who happened to be in town."

Lillian, however, turned back to Amelia and bore down: "Now what's this lawsuit business about with your father?"

Amelia turned away to avoid her mother's gaze, then looked up and said, "I must have misspoken, Mother."

Before Lillian could interrogate her further, Frank came in, holding Judy in one arm, with David trailing behind. "I'm going to put the kids in the car," he said. "I'll come back for the rest of the stuff."

"I'll help you," Amelia said, grabbing their belongings to abruptly disengage from her mother. As she started to walk out, she bumped into her father, and Lillian saw them exchange a look.

Then there was the usual flurry of hugs and kisses as the grandchildren said their goodbyes. Lillian could feel the tension as Nora and Amelia exchanged a chilly embrace.

When she had Sol alone again, she picked up where she'd left off. "I want to know about this new lawsuit."

"There is no new lawsuit."

"Then what was Amelia talking about?"

"Just a little trouble at the office. Nothing for you to be concerned about."

Lillian could feel her pulse in her temples; she experienced a wave of nausea that made her shaky for a moment. She leaned against the table for support.

"Lil? Are you OK?"

She came back to herself, then fixed him with a disapproving look. As Nora came into the room, Lillian said, "I'm not feeling well. I'll be in my sewing room."

Lillian noted Sol's look of alarm. She knew he still associated the sewing room with that dark year after Nora was born, though that was a quarter century ago. Since then, though she referred to it as "the sewing room," it was mostly where Lillian went to read, nap, or just be alone. It was her refuge, her sanctuary. But its mention still appeared to give him pause, all these years later. They never talked about that time, but Lillian knew it haunted Sol almost as much as it haunted her.

In moments when she felt threatened, she used the sewing room as a control on Sol. She knew he feared that she might somehow return to the state she'd fallen into in that time, and that fear made him more pliable. The threat gave her a modicum of control, and control gave her life order.

Deep down, she knew his real concern was that she might try to kill herself. She knew this to be an unfounded fear; that was simply something she would never do, because it would be the ultimate surrender of control. But Sol believed it was possible, nonetheless, because of what she knew he thought of as her "overdose."

The real story was that she'd had the beginning of a migraine one afternoon a year or so after Amelia was born. The pain was such that twenty minutes after taking a strong prescription analgesic and getting insufficient relief, she had grown impatient and taken two more. Still in pain ten minutes later, she decided that sleeping pills might mask her pain with slumber. To be sure they worked, she took two. Then, after using the toilet, she felt an overwhelming urge to curl up on the cool bathroom tiles and go to sleep. That was where Clara found her, before she called a doctor.

Sol brought the subject up a couple of times, obliquely but portentously ("How are you . . . feeling?"), in the weeks afterward. In the end, she said, "I know what you really mean when you ask how I feel. Stop hounding me. I'm perfectly fine."

But she knew that had been his worry during the lost year after Nora was born. And she knew it still worried him after all these years.

~

Deciding she wanted to take a cup of tea upstairs, Lillian walked to the kitchen, where Clara was washing dishes. Clara's status as the family's longtime employee still served as the scaffolding of their relationship. But after three decades with Clara in her house, Lillian believed they had something deeper than that.

Again, not friendship; never friends, a status that conferred a sense of equality Lillian would never have been comfortable with. But something important that Lillian couldn't express.

Lillian had developed a large social circle through the synagogue in Tarrytown. She volunteered with the synagogue's women's group and regularly played bridge and mah-jongg with two different sets of women. She kept her sense of control over each collection of women by being the voice of authority everyone respected and no one was willing to clash with.

Was she "friends" with any of these women? She sometimes wondered. She certainly didn't know any of the dozens of women whom she saw regularly well enough to talk to the way she could talk to Clara.

Yet, as much as Lillian enjoyed having Clara as a female companion, she also valued the power structure that gave her the control in their relationship. At heart, she didn't trust that Clara would be her friend if she wasn't paid to be there.

When Lillian entered the kitchen, Clara looked up from doing the dishes and said, "Is there something you need, Lillian?"

"Just a cup of tea."

"The water in the teapot should still be hot enough without boiling it."

As Lillian got a cup and tea bag, her mind ping-ponged between two subjects, though she couldn't seem to focus on either of them. She turned to Clara and said, "I suppose you were in on this little secret."

"Secret?"

"About the young man who came to visit."

"I met him for a second when I answered the door," Clara said. "I didn't think anything of it until Amelia said something after brunch."

Lillian scowled for a second, then said, "Why would she come down this weekend when she'll be moving back home at the beginning of the month?"

"I thought Sol asked her to come down."

"But why?" Lillian's face clouded. "What do you know about this lawsuit business with Sol?"

"He hasn't said anything to me."

"But she's finished with her doctoral studies. I thought Sol told me that her thesis had been accepted."

"That's true. She's officially Dr. Nora Levitsky, PhD. You must be so proud of our girl."

At that, Lillian closed her eyes and held up a hand, as though warding off a blow. "Please," she said, almost as a warning.

Lillian knew she should be grateful for the way Clara had cared for Nora, as a baby and beyond. But it grated on Lillian on those rare occasions when Clara committed this minor act of verbal possessiveness.

Lillian didn't regard Nora as a possession (and it had stung when a teenage Nora once accused her of that). Yet her parental claim often felt tenuous, particularly when it came to Nora and Clara. She harbored too many memories of walking into a room where the two of them were laughing and talking, and feeling like an intruder.

Lillian found it impossible to be grateful to Clara without resenting it. Gratitude was a form of indebtedness, and to Lillian, owing a debt was cause for embarrassment. She blamed Clara when she felt like that.

What made it worse was that she did owe Clara a debt. Lillian would not have survived without Clara, and this weighed on her.

So the "our girl" slip tipped Lillian into a danger zone.

"Sometimes I wonder about your loyalties," Lillian sniffed.

Clara looked at her, long and hard, as though trying to decide whether to speak. Then she said, "Don't do this."

"Or what?"

"You don't want to find out."

"Or what?" Lillian said again, with more of an edge. "You'll leave? You're already leaving."

"Is that what you want, Lillian? Because I can pack tonight and be gone in the morning."

The coldness of Clara's tone stopped Lillian.

"Or I can pack right now and be gone before dinner," Clara said. "If that's what you want."

"No," Lillian said.

"Then I'm going to ask you to leave me alone to finish cleaning up brunch, before one of us says something we can't take back."

Lillian's heart was racing, as though she'd caught herself before taking a bad stumble. "I'll be in my sewing room," she said, clutching her teacup as she left the kitchen.

Lillian felt control slipping through her fingers like sand through a sieve. She could feel secrets swirling about her and wanted someone to blame, someone who could make it stop. She trudged up the stairs to the small room in the rear of the second floor. It had a wooden rocking chair with a small footstool and a good lamp. There was also a love seat, on which Lillian occasionally curled up and dozed.

She sat down in the rocking chair and pulled up a needlepoint hoop from a basket next to the chair: an autumn motif of rust- and yellow-colored leaves. She looked at it a second, then set it aside.

~

Self-pity was something Lillian abhorred in others: "Oh, stop feeling sorry for yourself," she would chide the girls, after almost any complaint when they were younger.

It may have been because Lillian had received no sympathy—or any expression of affection or concern—from her own parents growing up. From an early age, she was expected to pull her weight, whether by doing household chores and caring for younger siblings while her parents worked or by toiling in her parents' ever-struggling tailor shop. She felt less like a family member than an indentured serf working off an impossible debt.

That was why Sol had been such a revelation for her: someone who expected nothing from her but her company—someone who seemed to like her for herself and not for the labor she could render him. Someone who wanted to do and buy nice things for her just because he liked her and wanted to make her happy.

At times, she was able to luxuriate in the feeling, but not for long. Then the doubts and fears would return. She had no frame of reference for happiness that allowed her to trust that it would last.

She basked in the kindness of Sol's personality yet, at her deepest core, found it impossible to believe that someone—anyone—could care about her simply for who she was, with no other agenda. She was ever on the lookout for telltale signs that their courtship and marriage were all an elaborate hoax at her expense.

In time, the love Sol lavished on her allowed her to relax, at least for the first few years. Sol had an irreverent sense of humor that could surprise a laugh out of her more often than she expected, and she found she was able to join him in playful banter in the early years of their marriage.

Sol's work ethic had bought them a life she never could have imagined as an unhappy teen working in her father's tailor shop. Lillian spent her whole life in fear of being dragged back to the long-gone establishment.

Frank sprang to Lillian's mind, unbidden, and she remembered him sitting at the brunch table in his undershirt. She could never tell Sol that the reason she disdained her son-in-law was that he reminded her of her own father.

Isaac Pikorny had been a tailor of limited skill, whose talents were vastly exaggerated for advertising purposes. The comparison was unfair to Frank, Lillian knew, because, whatever else she felt about him, she knew Frank's business failure resulted from a run of bad luck, though she'd never admit it to her daughter. Her father, on the other hand, had simply been inept, an amiable nebbish whose business sense was even more limited than his dexterity with a sewing needle. He inevitably led his family business to the brink of disaster, pushed there by Lillian's harridan mother, Hannah.

Hannah insisted that Isaac produce more work in less time, to increase profits. Isaac's shortcuts led to shoddy craftsmanship and unhappy customers. Hannah always collected from their customers in advance, proclaiming all sales to be final as is, and refused to issue refunds.

With little repeat business, the shop's revenue dwindled to the point that the family struggled to pay rent. Still, Hannah was skilled at poaching customers from other tailors, promising quality at bargain rates, when she meant the opposite.

Lillian had been young, but she still had memories of the times when the family was forced to move. She remembered the moves with embarrassment: hushed, sneaky escapes under cover of darkness to avoid the landlord to whom rent was still owed.

Once Lillian left Williamsburg, she did not speak to her parents again. To her, it was as if they were characters in a book she'd started reading but never finished.

That was particularly true when she discussed them with her younger sisters. The parents they described might have been fictional creations, for all the resemblance they bore to the taskmasters from whom Lillian had fled to a boardinghouse in Manhattan when she was twenty.

Reading, learning, school—the order of that daily routine when she was a girl had given Lillian the smallest sense of control over her life. She had only just begun harboring adolescent career thoughts—*A teacher?*—when her mother announced one night when she was fourteen, "For you, school days are finished. Tomorrow, you start in the shop." That was the end of her formal education.

Lillian still felt anger at being made to quit school to work in the tailor shop. She had been both a bright student and an eager learner, who loved to lose herself in novels from the neighborhood lending library. Anytime her mother caught Lillian with her nose in a book, however, she'd thwack her in the back of the head, usually with a finger bearing a lead thimble. Lillian learned to do her reading in secret.

In the shop, Lillian was hopeless with thread and needle, so her mother put her to work managing the billing. Her mother had recently taken a used typewriter in payment for a suit and promptly declared that all prices in the shop would now go up because all bills would now be typed. Lillian, who read and did arithmetic better than either parent, taught herself the keyboard as she pecked out bills for money owed.

Once she was forced to leave school, she began studying shorthand surreptitiously, borrowing textbooks from local libraries. She would sit in cafés and eavesdrop on conversations, transcribing them to build up her dictation speed and fluency. She also squirreled away a portion of her meager earnings every week from the tailor shop, and after six years, she had saved enough to rent a room in Manhattan for a month.

The planning and execution of her escape took time and patience. On secretive weekend forays on the subway to Manhattan, she would visit neighborhoods with rooming houses for single women that advertised in the *Daily News*. She discovered a safe neighborhood not far from Union Square and, when she had sufficient funds, began to look at want ads until she found one she liked: the Pickwick Arms on East Twenty-Second Street. Lillian's plan was to move into the rooming house, then find work. The newspaper had columns of **Help Wanted** ads every day seeking stenographers who were proficient at dictation and shorthand. (She found a job on her second day.)

When all preparations for this escape had been put in place, Lillian feigned illness one afternoon at her parents' shop. A complaint about an unsettled stomach drew a rebuke from her mother ("Less complaining, more work"), so Lillian was forced to put a finger down her throat, causing her to vomit up her meager lunch. In disgust, her mother sent her home.

Once there, she packed her few clothes and other belongings into a travel satchel and waited for her parents to return from work. Her mother entered first, sniffing the air and making a face.

"Again, with the goyim downstairs and their corned beef and cabbage," she said, her regular complaint about food smells in the cramped tenement.

She looked at Lillian sitting quietly at the bare kitchen table, her hands folded on her lap, dressed to travel, her satchel at her side.

"And you, Queen Lillian, you're too sick to maybe think about making some dinner for those of us who still work for a living?"

Lillian's father, a defeated-looking man with arthritic fingers, came in, echoing Lillian's mother: "No dinner?"

"I'm leaving," Lillian said. "I'm done being your slave."

"What?" her father blurted out.

"Where do you think you're going?" her mother said angrily. "Who's going to feed you? Or give you a place to stay?"

"I've made arrangements" was all Lillian would say. "I'll let you know how to reach me."

She left and never came back.

Once settled in a new home and job, Lillian set out to catch up on the education she'd missed. She discovered the section of the main New York Public Library on Fifth Avenue where they shelved one copy of each textbook used in the New York public school system. For two years, she spent every possible minute in that room, learning about history, civics, literature, physical science, and the ascending levels of math, stopping when she got to algebra. She even found a way to take a test to receive her high school diploma.

But her finances were precarious on a stenographer's salary, even after several years in the job, and money remained tight. Her pride refused to allow her to let on to coworkers and acquaintances just how close to the margin her life was conducted and how many days she had to survive on one small meal.

Then, in 1934, along came Solomon Levitsky, a young Jewish prince of the Bronx, who saw in Lillian a woman in need of rescue by him. What more could Lillian Pikorny have asked for when she'd agreed to become Mrs. Sol Levitsky?

Yet, somehow, she still found ways to make herself unhappy.

~

Sitting in the sewing-room rocker, Lillian could see out the window to the backyard. A breeze was ruffling the leaves of the flowering crab apple tree and creating rippling shadows in the birdbath. The tree produced fruit that was particularly good in preserves or a cobbler Clara made every fall when the crab apples got ripe.

Then she remembered that they would have moved to the co-op by autumn. And Clara would be gone by then as well.

Lillian felt she might cry. She had never been given to displays of that sort, at least not since the year after Nora was born. She disgusted herself with her weakness when she gave in to emotion in that way. Nonetheless, the expanding web of events—selling the house, moving to an apartment, Sol's retirement, Clara's leaving, and, soon, Nora's return home—it was simply too much.

She felt her composure slipping, so she did the only thing she could: She slapped her own face, hard. Twice.

A few tears still came, but they were a physical response to the sting of the slaps. Lillian took a deep breath and let it out slowly.

~

Happiness had never been a topic of discussion in Lillian's father's house; it was like a word from a language for which Lillian had no translation.

Still, during her first years of marriage to Sol, Lillian learned to appreciate moments when she was happy. After her children were born, however, she was too fearful to recognize glimmers of happiness for what they were.

On the train ride back from their Niagara Falls honeymoon, Sol said, "No wife of mine will have to work outside the home. I want you to quit your job."

Perhaps if she could have detected any opportunity for advancement in the job she had in the steno pool, Lillian might have argued with him, but at the insurance firm where she worked, women never rose above the role of secretary. The salesmen, actuaries, bookkeepers, executives: all men. Lillian had no such ambitions in any case, so it was an easy world for her to leave behind. But, for a year or so after they married and moved to the Bronx, she felt isolated.

When Sol told her she should quit her job, Lillian envisioned a life of married leisure similar to what she'd seen in movies, with a housekeeper, at a minimum. She soon discovered that *she* was the housekeeper.

Her days, previously consumed by her job, now took on a different routine. Shopping one day, laundry the next, cleaning on yet another—as well as the daily tasks of dusting, making beds, doing dishes, cooking, and such other chores as became apparent.

Lillian mentioned at dinner one night how cut off she felt in the Bronx.

"What would make you happy?" Sol asked. "Do you want to go back to work at the insurance company?"

"No, of course not," she said. "Maybe it's just being stuck inside during the cold winter months."

That changed when her days began to include unannounced visits from Delia, Sol's sister. When Lillian married Sol, she had no clue that Stan and Delia's apartment was just around the corner from Sol's. Nor did she know that Delia would try to make Lillian part of her daily routine moving forward.

Not long after Lillian complained to Sol about being lonely, there was a knock at her apartment door one morning. Being alone, she answered the door cautiously, securing the chain before opening it a crack. She saw her sister-in-law standing in the hallway, purse in hand.

Without further greeting, Delia said, "Get your coat and handbag. Let's go."

"Where are we going?"

"C'mon, c'mon, we don't have all day," Delia clucked. "I'll tell you on the way."

Lillian was surprised into action. As the pair walked down the stairs from Lillian and Sol's third-floor apartment, Delia said, "What kind of bagels are you feeding my brother?"

"What kind?" Lillian said. "Plain, I guess."

"No—where are they from? Where do you buy them?"

"Oh. Katz's, on the corner."

"Oy, feh," Delia said as they reached the street. "Nobody with any sense buys the bagels at Katz's. I'll take you to Schweller's to buy bagels for Sol."

They had started up the street when something occurred to Lillian.

"Wait—did Sol say something to you about not liking the bagels?" Her sense of betrayal rose to the surface.

"To me? No. He was kvetching at work, and my Stan happened to mention it at dinner. I thought I'd help."

Delia's normal tone was brusque, as though her time was being wasted with Lillian's questions. For her, "helping" consisted of ordering Lillian around while circulating through the neighborhood, in and out of stores and shops.

A visit from Delia meant an errand to run, a task to complete—whatever it was, it always required Lillian's physical presence. The dress store, the butcher shop—how helpless was this woman? Delia always seemed to need an extra pair of eyes or an extra set of hands, and the ones she needed always seemed to belong to Lillian.

"I just have to run out for a minute—come with," she would say when she made what started to become daily visits to Lillian's apartment.

It was always stated as a question: "Come with?" But it always sounded like a command: "You will come with." It was delivered in a tone—superior, domineering—that struck a nerve in Lillian. She felt as though Delia had access to a hypnotic frequency that made her powerless to resist.

Once she had Lillian in her grasp, Delia never stopped talking. It didn't matter whether they were in Lillian's kitchen, in a store, on the sidewalk, or on the bus. Delia narrated and commented on everything that crossed her path. Her mouth never stopped as they would walk from Lillian's apartment on Decatur Avenue up Gun Hill Road. Her monologues seemed endless:

"There's Anderson from the liquor store. The man drinks, but what do you expect? Did you see what the *Daily News* said about Mrs. Roosevelt today? The no-good scheisskopfs. They call that a newspaper? Look at that—someone let their dog do that right on the sidewalk. Oy, the selection in this store is from hunger. We'll just pick up a few things so I can teach you how to make a brisket the right way."

"What do you mean, the right way?" Lillian said.

"The last time you made it for us, it was as tough as a boot," Delia said, then laughed at her surprised look.

Whenever Delia offered her help, she would follow the offer with an insulting joke about Lillian's abilities. Then she'd laugh at her own joke.

"You'd look stunning in that frock," Delia would say. "Let me buy it for you." When Lillian would thank her, Delia would add, "Just promise you'll never wear that dress you've got on ever again, at least when you're with me." And then she'd laugh again.

Lillian harbored a deep-seated fear that she and Sol were always on the brink of ruin. There had been an economic depression going on for close to a decade; every day, she read in the paper about the bank closures, the breadlines, the dust storms, and the wave of people from Oklahoma flooding into California, looking for work. Sol would remind her that his business was steady, but she was always imagining imminent disaster.

Delia would tease her for being cheap when Lillian balked at buying something for herself, telling her, "Go ahead. Our husbands make a good living. You can afford it." It didn't matter if it was a new pair of shoes or a lamp for the living room. Lillian always needed convincing to open her wallet and harbored the fear that Delia was trying to push her over the edge whenever she encouraged her to spend money.

Delia, on the other hand, seemed impervious to affront. She would casually say something cutting to Lillian ("Are you going to go out with your hair looking like that?"), and if Lillian managed to turn it around on her ("Why not? You are"), Delia would find that hilarious: "Yes, but I'm a witch, and everyone knows it. What's your excuse?"

Lillian got angry enough to snap at her one day: "Will you please, just for a minute—just shut up!"

Delia looked amused and said, "Gee, Lillian, I was only joking. You're a little touchy. Your monthly come early?" Which only made Lillian angrier.

Delia later mentioned Lillian's outburst to Stan, who said something to Sol, who then said to Lillian, "I wish you could get along better with my sister," as though Lillian were the one being so maddeningly condescending.

"But she won't leave me alone," she pleaded.

"She likes you. She wants to spend time with you. And they live so close. You were complaining that you didn't have friends."

Lillian had to endure Delia's regular visits for almost a year. In desperation, she accepted an invitation from Sol's mother, who wanted her to join the synagogue women's group. When she did, Lillian found herself making friends with a new group of older women who welcomed her as vital fresh blood, someone from a different generation. She discovered that the group was perpetually short of reliable volunteers for the most important—and least glamorous—tasks. She threw herself into the volunteer work and shortly made herself indispensable to the group.

Her work ethic made her popular, even if her haughty demeanor and her willingness to express blunt opinions kept some women at arm's length. Those qualities all helped her rise among a stratum of older women who'd been taught to defer and deflect. Even better, the volunteer work meant she had little free time for Delia, who had no interest in joining her mother's synagogue group.

Then the Levitskys left the Bronx for the suburban dream of North Tarrytown in Westchester County. Lillian's daily encounters with Delia became weekly, then monthly, before turning into family holiday gatherings a few times a year, after Stan and Delia moved to Port Washington on Long Island. Sol and Stan still saw each other every day at work, but Lillian thankfully had been pulled far from Delia's orbit.

~

It had taken longer for Lillian to become involved in the new synagogue after they moved to North Tarrytown. She knew how to go about it at that point but hadn't counted on being hobbled by the sheer exhaustion of motherhood. Indeed, she nearly foundered after they first moved, stuck with an empty house to unpack, alone and pregnant, each day after Sol left.

The houses in the new neighborhood were far enough apart that she rarely saw her neighbors after they first moved in. After Amelia was born, Lillian felt as if her life vanished into the vortex of bottles, diapers, and sleeplessness that came with a new baby.

Amelia was a sunny, even-tempered infant, much easier than Nora would be. But taking care of a newborn still overwhelmed Lillian. She felt like a failure when the baby would cry, but she also felt like she'd failed once Amelia was asleep—because then she was faced with her messy house, which remained untamed since she'd come home from the hospital with the baby. The laundry piled up, and the dirty dishes were stacked in the sink. There was still a pyramid of boxes in each room, waiting to be unpacked. The entire house seemed to call her name in an insidious voice that whispered, "You've failed yet again."

Amelia absorbed every spare spark of energy Lillian could generate. One evening, she broke down in tears at dinner with Sol—and by the end of the week, he had hired Clara.

Things improved once Clara arrived, though both Lillian and Clara went through a period of adjustment. In part, this was because of the decade-plus difference in their ages (Lillian was thirty-four when Clara arrived at nineteen). Lillian took time to warm to the gangly teen from Scranton as being anything more than her employee.

Here was Lillian's movie fantasy come to life: the kind of live-in help that waited on Myrna Loy or Jean Harlow in the pictures. Yet it was odd for her to have a stranger living in her home. Clara seemed to be everywhere in the house during her workday: making Sol breakfast before he left for work, cleaning and vacuuming, doing the laundry, taking one of the cars to do the grocery shopping. Most important, she spelled Lillian in caring for Amelia.

Lillian was glad for the relief yet felt a pang of resentment, the feeling of being supplanted in her roles as wife and mother. Despite everything that overwhelmed her, she was territorial about her house.

But she realized how ridiculous she was being the day Clara walked into the kitchen after putting Amelia down for a nap and said, "You look tired. Why don't you go take a nap now, too, and I'll call you when it's time to start dinner?"

Then, a month or so into Clara's tenure in the house, Lillian pushed through the swinging kitchen door one morning to discover Clara in the breakfast nook, head down on her arms on the table, sobbing.

"Clara?" Lillian said in alarm. "What's wrong?"

Taken by surprise, Clara jumped to her feet, wiping her face as she stood.

"I'm sorry, Mrs. Levitsky," she said. "I'll get back to work."

"You'll do no such thing," Lillian said. "Sit back down and tell me what's wrong. Here, let me make tea."

She put a kettle on and pulled two cups and some tea bags out of the cupboard. Clara sniffled out a final few tears and blew her nose as Lillian set the tea in front of them to steep and sat down.

"Now tell me why you're crying," Lillian said, putting a sugar cube into her cup before pouring her tea.

"I'm sorry. I'm just a little homesick, I guess," Clara said. "I've never been away from home this long before."

In fact, as she recounted, she had never been anywhere. But as Lillian listened to her story about growing up on a farm in Scranton, she thought, *Williamsburg was worse.*

Lillian had fled her family of birth and tried to create a more successful family of her own here in North Tarrytown. But she worried that she'd failed at this as well. So she moved forward as though nothing was wrong, hoping she could hide this shameful secret from the rest of the world, when she could never hide it from herself.

Clara's loneliness resonated with Lillian, whose early years in the Bronx had alternated between feeling lonely or being forced to spend time with Delia.

With Clara, Lillian could talk in a way she never could with other women—certainly not with Sol. The plain-spoken teen had no pretenses about her life: "I like to be useful," she told Lillian when Lillian asked if there was anything else she'd ever thought of doing with her life. Lillian took comfort in talking to her and assumed the reverse was true.

Clara had never presumed, as Lillian thought of it. After seven or eight years of calling them Mr. and Mrs. Levitsky, Sol said, "From now on, we want you to call us Sol and Lillian." But as close as Lillian let Clara get, she never let her lose sight of the power dynamic in their relationship.

Yet, Lillian found, Clara usually had a way to see through the anxiety, misapprehension, and unnecessary complication that engulfed her crises. "If it were me . . ." Clara would begin, casually taking a machete to the undergrowth blocking the path to Lillian's desired outcome.

~

Clara's homesickness had abated, but Lillian found they shared a sense of solitude that made Lillian think of them as being closer.

Lillian appreciated how easily Clara became her good right arm, irreplaceable, especially after Nora was born and Lillian's darkest year began.

In her secret heart, sometimes, Lillian would admit that in many ways, she felt closer to Clara than to Nora. She added it to the list of things that gave her a sense of shame.

She even confided her darkest secret to Clara: She was three years older than she'd told Sol. As a young woman, she'd looked mature for her age, but as she had aged, she had maintained a youthful appearance. While she looked thirty when she was eighteen, she also looked thirty when she was forty-five.

Why lie? she wondered as she gazed out the window of her sewing room and rocked slowly in her chair. *Why keep lying?* She hadn't thought of her secret in a while, even though it generated constant low-level tension.

The topic of her age arose when Sol and Stan hired a new female receptionist for their office in the late 1940s. Lillian had read too many women's magazine short stories not to take this as a warning sign of the imminent demise of her marriage.

"I think you're getting worked up over nothing," Clara told her. "Why would you even give this a second thought?"

"But, Clara, she's so young."

"The world is full of young women. Why would this one be different?"

Lillian paused, then reddened.

"What is it? What's wrong?" Clara said. By this point, Lillian was in tears.

"I lied to Sol about my age," she said.

"When?" Clara asked.

"Before we were married."

"Why would you do that?"

"Because I realized I was older than him. Only by a year or so, but no man wants an older woman."

"Why not?"

Lillian paused to consider this, then burst into tears again, saying, "I don't know. But I've always heard that."

"Old men marry young women all the time. Why not vice versa? Fair's fair."

Lillian just shook her head in misery, then said, "I'm sorry. It's just not done. I've lived in fear of him finding out ever since."

"I think if you were just honest with—"

"Never! I would be humiliated. He must never find out."

She gave Clara a portentous look. Clara got wide-eyed and said, "You know you don't have to worry about me."

Lillian knew she shouldn't pick fights with Clara. Clara never gave her reason to, and she tried not to. But occasionally, such as today, Lillian had managed to sting her, and invariably she regretted it.

And now she's leaving, Lillian thought.

~

"Lillian?"

She opened her eyes and realized she had dozed off in her rocking chair. Sol was standing over her, touching her arm.

"Dear, why don't you come downstairs? Nora and I have something we want to talk to you about."

Lillian roused herself from the chair and told Sol, "I'll be there in a minute."

What's going on? Lillian wondered. Did this have anything to do with the boy who'd come to see Nora? Or was this about the mysterious lawsuit? Were the lawsuit and the boy somehow connected?

She thought back to Amelia and the awkward exchange at brunch. Amelia was incapable of being deceptive because she was too easy to see through, Lillian knew.

So Lillian was convinced there was more than a grain of truth to Amelia's blurted revelation about the boy—and the lawsuit. What was Nora hiding?

She was convinced that Nora had always skated up to the edge of her rules. She found ways to violate them in spirit without technically crossing the line.

Lillian had grudging admiration for her daughter's rebellious spirit, though Nora's choices and actions seldom met with her approval. Nora had had a foul mouth from a young age; Lillian once walked in on a teenage conversation between Nora and her friend Gina, just as Nora said, "So I told him to go fuck himself."

"Oh my God," Lillian said, fanning herself in shock. "It's bad enough that *I* hear you use that kind of language—but the idea that you're using it in public is simply too much. Too much."

"I'm sorry, Mother. You weren't supposed to hear that."

"I should think not. What else are you saying in public that reflects so poorly on your parents?" Lillian demanded.

"Nothing," Nora said, then added, "Can we please finish doing our homework?"

"Oh, is that what you were doing?" Lillian said, not bothering to disguise her caustic tone. "I never want to hear that kind of language in this house again. Do you understand?"

"Yes, ma'am." Lillian was sure she'd seen Nora roll her eyes at her friend as she left the room.

What did Nora and Sol want now? Lillian often felt like a third wheel when the three of them were together. Sol had an easy, humorous give-and-take with Nora. The two of them shared any number of silly private jokes, none of which were at Lillian's expense.

But she didn't need to be the butt of a jest to feel excluded by it.

~

Lillian was on edge, but she could sense even greater tension between her husband and daughter, something she hadn't felt before, and wondered if they'd been arguing.

"So—what are you two cooking up now?" Lillian said.

Sol smiled. "Why are you always so suspicious?"

"Don't I have cause? Nora seems to be here for no reason, and Amelia was chattering about things going on behind my back."

"Nothing is going on behind your back, dear."

"Then explain to me what this business is with the lawsuit that no one wants to talk about."

Sol's smile held as he said, "We're fine, Lil."

"Then why is Nora here? Who was the boy who came to see her?"

"A friend from school," Nora said. "I told you." Lillian bristled at the impatience in her voice.

Then Sol said, "Lil, let's all sit down for a minute."

She hesitated, as though to say, "Don't tell me what to do." But then she sat down in her usual easy chair and put her feet up.

"Lillian, this is not a big deal, but there's been a hitch in the sale of the business. A lawsuit we won a few years ago after one of our trucks crashed was reversed on appeal. So the sale of the business has to be put on hold while we figure out what to do next."

"I knew you weren't telling me the truth!" she cried, then immediately spun her anger into anxiety. "But you're supposed to retire. We're selling the house and moving. Now what will we do?"

She felt her adrenaline surge when Sol said, "Yes, well, everything is a little up in the air at the moment. We'll move this fall, certainly—"

"Up in the air? What does that mean?"

"Calm down, Mother," Nora said.

Lillian turned to her. "I still don't understand why you are here now, when you'll be back home at the beginning of the month."

"I think Daddy thought you'd like to have me here for moral support when he explained this."

"Honestly, Lil, it is not that big a deal."

"Are we selling the house or aren't we?"

"We'll move, but we can't sell the house for the moment."

"But how can we afford to move? The rent, the maintenance fees . . ."

"We're fine. We have money put away, if it comes to that. Stop worrying about money."

"But if you can't sell the business, what will you do?"

"I'll work a little longer. The business is still the business."

Lillian grumbled to herself, unsettled, "I need a cup of tea." She strode to the kitchen, where Clara had just started dinner. "Can I have some tea, please, if you have a minute?"

"Of course," Clara said, and Lillian went back to the den.

She stopped at the doorway when she found Nora and Sol with their heads together, though they didn't notice her. Immediately, her temper surged: More secrets?

But even as the heat in her face began to rise, she felt something trying to pull her back from the brink of a tantrum: her plan to try to be on friendlier terms with Nora. She closed her eyes for a moment and tried to take a deep breath in and out, which made her shudder unexpectedly, though she felt her anger recede. Then she tried to soften her expression before she went in.

"I hope you'll be friendlier to me when you move back home. I'd like to think we could make a fresh start."

Lillian saw Nora freeze, then look at Sol. But all she said was "That would be nice."

Lillian looked at Sol, whose face seemed to be reddening but whose expression was unreadable.

"And when will that be, precisely?"

Nora was silent.

"You are moving back here, aren't you?"

After another hesitation, Nora said, "Actually, Mother . . ."

Sol, his face a deeper red, said, "Nora—"

"Actually, Mother—what?"

Nora closed her eyes a second and took a breath in and out. Then she opened her eyes again and looked directly at Lillian. "I'm not moving home. I've taken a job teaching at Northwestern University in the fall. Near Chicago. I'm moving there at the beginning of the month."

Lillian exploded: "What?! How dare you make plans like this without asking us? When were you going to get our approval for this little scheme?"

"I don't need your approval, Mother."

"No, you never have," Lillian said coldly.

"And what," Nora retorted, "have you ever approved of?"

"Nora—" Sol began, though he appeared to be struggling for breath.

Nora put up a hand to stop him and turned back to Lillian. "You *aren't* in charge of my life anymore. I make my own decisions, right or wrong. And I've already made this one, whether you approve or not."

"Well, I do not approve. In fact, I strongly disapprove."

"I'm sorry you feel that way," Nora said, "but that won't change anything."

Mother and daughter glared at each other for a moment. Then Nora turned to Sol and said, "Daddy, this is pointless. This is exactly what I expected. And what I wanted to avoid. There's just no talking to this woman."

"*This woman?* I am your mother! How dare you speak to me in this way."

"Because I'm an adult, Mother, not a child. You're the one who's raising her voice, not me."

"The ingratitude," Lillian said to Sol, who was perspiring freely, his worried eyes cutting back and forth between them. "After all we've done for you, this is what we get in return."

"All you've done? You were never my mother, not really. Not once that I can remember."

"What?" Lillian sputtered.

Nora had to pause to take a breath. Her breathing began to punctuate her speech, but she pushed forward. "You never wanted me. It took me years to figure that out." (Breath.) "For the longest time, I thought it was something I'd done; I couldn't figure out what it was." (Breath.) "And then it hit me one day—duh! *She didn't want you.*" (Breath.) "You weren't my mother—you were my keeper. My *boss.*" (Breath.) "I always wanted Clara to be my mother. And in so many of the important ways, she was. Not you." (Breath.)

"Nora—stop!" Sol said, his face now bathed in sweat.

"Daddy, you know it's true," Nora said. "I love you, but I've been trying to get away from Mother since I was old enough to figure out that she didn't care about me."

"Nora, no, that's not true," Sol said.

"I don't have to listen to this," Lillian said, starting to rise. Nora blocked her escape.

"Oh yes you do. Listen carefully because this might be the last time we ever speak."

Lillian dropped back into her chair, and Nora leaned in toward her. Lillian could hear the rasp of her breathing.

"Mother, I spent my life watching you browbeat Amelia, and I saw how that distorted her sense of who she is. And I vowed from a young age that you would never do that to me. I've consciously tried to be my father's daughter and not my mother's. I don't want to be bitter and suspicious my whole life. That's why I want to get away from you. Because I don't want to *be* you. Because that's the only thing that will ever please you—to let you mold me into the same kind of small-minded shrew you are. But I'm sure even that wouldn't be enough for you."

The air seemed to flutter and buzz before Lillian's eyes; it was as though Nora's words were a swarm of small biting insects. She tried to speak, but Nora was not allowing interruptions, even with her ragged respiration.

"So, yes, I'm leaving. I'm moving to Chicago at the beginning of July. Once I'm settled, the two of you are invited, of course, to come visit me, though, judging by the look on your face, Mother, I don't expect that to happen. If you decide to come anyway to punish me with silence and disapproval—well, save your money. I'm not going to put up with it. You won't be welcome in my house. Do you understand?"

She turned to Sol and, avoiding Lillian's eyes, said, "I'm sorry, Daddy. It's my life, not hers."

But Sol suddenly couldn't speak. His face was purple, and he was huffing and puffing, as though fighting to bring oxygen to his lungs.

"Daddy?"

"Sol?"

Sol, eyes wide now, said, "My chest—" before his eyes rolled up and he collapsed out of the chair onto the floor.

Lillian froze. She realized she must have screamed because, as Nora dove to the floor to help her father, Clara rushed in.

"Call an ambulance," Nora said as she began what looked like a series of hard blows with her fist to Sol's chest.

"What are you doing?" Lillian screamed at her. "You'll hurt him!"

"I think he's having a heart attack. I learned this when I was a lifeguard at camp. It could save him."

As she began compressions on his chest, Sol coughed and opened his eyes. When he tried to sit up, Nora said, "Lie still. The ambulance is coming."

Lillian sat watching Sol, who was now awake but confused. She was paralyzed by her fear of what was happening at that moment and what might happen next. Sol, his head resting on a cushion Nora had pulled down from the sofa, looked ghostly.

When the ambulance arrived and Sol was loaded on to a stretcher, Lillian remained motionless, frozen. Nora came over to her and said, "They're taking Daddy to Phelps Hospital. I'm going too. Do you want to come with?"

Lillian felt horror at the idea of a hospital. She instantly summoned the smells and sounds of the maternity ward and said, "I don't think so."

She heard Clara say, "I'll look after her. You go ahead," and then Nora was gone, trailing after the ambulance crew in her own car to the local hospital just a few blocks away.

Lillian sat for a moment, staring into space, not lost in thought but, for the moment, just lost. Clara caught her eye, put a bracing arm around her shoulder for a quick hug, and said, "He'll be fine. They'll have him at the hospital with doctors patching him up in no time."

"Do you think so?" was all Lillian could manage.

"Nora will call when they know something. The fact that he was awake when they took him is a good thing, I think."

"Do you think so?" Lillian repeated. She felt as though she'd been stunned into repeating the question but was unable to comprehend the answer it drew.

"You've had a shock. Why don't you go lie down? I'll get you up if Nora calls."

Clara walked Lillian upstairs and watched as she slipped off her shoes and lay on the bed.

"Would you like a comforter?"

"Please," Lillian said, desperately needing comfort. She lay back on her pillow, and Clara spread a quilt—colorful patchwork crocheted squares made from yarn of exquisite softness. It felt like an invitation to immediate slumber, and Lillian gladly accepted.

~

She awoke an hour later and was seized by panic: *Sol! What will happen if Sol dies?*

She sat up, noting the late-afternoon light in her room. When she stood, she felt unsteady for a moment, but the feeling passed.

The main floor of the house was quiet. Usually, she could hear Sol in the den watching a baseball game on TV at this time on a June Saturday. But the house was silent. Lillian finally found Clara on her knees in the kitchen in front of an empty cupboard, surrounded by several small appliances and mixing bowls.

Clara looked up and said, "I needed something to do, and it felt like I hadn't cleaned underneath here in a while. I'm sorry; I'll start dinner as soon as I put all this away."

Lillian sat down in the breakfast nook, then said, "Has there been any word from the hospital?"

Refilling the cupboard, Clara said, "Yes, Nora called a little while ago, but I thought you needed to sleep. All she knew was that they'd gotten him stabilized and admitted to a room. He hadn't seen the doctor yet."

"How long will he have to stay in the hospital?"

"I don't think we'll know that for a little while. Nora was going to wait and talk to Sol's doctor and the heart specialist who's seeing him, before she comes home. I wondered whether you might want to call Amelia."

"Oh no, not yet—I don't want her hovering around me, and there's nothing she can do here. Let's wait until we know more. It can wait until tomorrow."

Lillian stared blankly into the distance for a moment, until Clara said, "What can I get you? Do you want to eat something?"

"Maybe a little ginger ale. Do we have any crackers and cheese?"

"Why don't you go turn on the TV and let me see what I can rustle up. I think the news is on."

Lillian started to get up, then suddenly collapsed back into the breakfast nook, helpless to stop the wave of crying that overtook her. Her cheeks burned so red hot, she believed her tears might evaporate with a sizzle.

"Oh, Clara, what am I going to do if Sol dies?"

"Now stop talking like that. Sol isn't going to die, at least not today."

"But what if he does? What if this lawsuit is the thing that kills him? What if the lawsuit costs us everything?"

"What if what if what if what if!" Clara said, suddenly sounding angry. "Lillian, why don't you put 'what if' in one hand and shit in the other? Then tell me what you have."

Startled, Lillian said, "That's very crude." But she let slip a guilty smile. "But yes, I take your point."

"Now why don't you go watch the news? I'll bring you a bite to eat in a minute."

But, as Chet Huntley and David Brinkley commenced their recitation of the day's events, Lillian found herself thinking about what Nora said about Chicago. *A job?* Her temper sparked and crackled at her daughter's betrayal.

The very idea that a daughter of hers would make a decision as momentous as this without consulting her parents for advice or permission made her scalp feel tight. It represented a lack of respect that Lillian experienced physically. It stung because, while she never felt she had as much control over Nora as she would like, Nora also had never directly disobeyed her in a way that made her feel as betrayed as she was feeling at this moment.

She had exploded at Nora instead of trying to create a new connection, but the things that Nora had said: "Small-minded shrew"—was that how she saw her? She'd called her "this woman," as though she were a stranger. It was all fuel to the fire of Lillian's fear and anger.

But if she wanted to mend this, she would have to get control of those feelings. She couldn't let Nora leave; if she left now, Lillian sensed, she would never come back. It was something she should talk about with Clara; Clara always knew how to handle Nora. Perhaps she could help her figure out how to convince Nora to stay.

What if Sol dies?

She needed Nora to be here—not Chicago. But how could she change her mind? Lillian knew she had no real power over her. If she said, "I forbid this," Nora would ignore her.

But Nora wouldn't ignore her father's condition, Lillian realized, thinking that Sol's health now had to be her greatest concern. And, in that moment, she believed she had solved the puzzle.

~

Lillian had just started to watch a rerun of *The Rains of Ranchipur* on *NBC Saturday Night at the Movies* when she heard the sound of Nora's car in the driveway. A minute later, Nora walked into the den.

"Daddy's going to be OK," she said and, without restraint or second thought, hugged her mother.

Lillian couldn't remember the last time she'd received a spontaneous hug from Nora, and then she did: several years ago, at a family wedding at a Hartsdale country club, when she was still in high school.

Lillian had been talking to Delia when she felt herself taken in an embrace from behind and heard a girl's voice. She felt their cheeks touch and realized it was Nora behind her. Then Nora moved in front of her and squeezed her in a sloppy hug, before putting an arm around Lillian's waist and loudly proclaiming, "This is MY mom."

With the arm that wasn't holding Lillian, the clearly tipsy Nora now shook a finger in Delia's face, saying, "My mom. Not your mom—MY mom."

Delia laughed and said, "Who's arguing?"

Nora then swept Lillian into an impromptu waltz twirl before giving her a loud, wet kiss on the cheek. Lillian pulled back, holding Nora at arm's length, and said, "How much champagne have you had to drink?"

Nora laughed and said, "I love you too, Mother," then pulled away and disappeared into the gyrating mass on the dance floor.

Now here was Nora hugging her again. Lillian clung to her and thought, *Maybe we* can *start fresh.*

Nora told her that the cardiologist on call, Dr. Newton, had told Sol's physician, Dr. Bloom, that Sol had a myocardial infarction, a heart attack. Sol had a partial blockage in one of the arteries leading to his heart, which limited the heart's ability to pump blood. While there was no treatment for the condition, he would be all right if he could keep his blood pressure down, severely limit his intake of salt and sweets—and not exert himself to the point that it taxed his heart.

"But then what? What will he do when he gets home?"

"Mother, I wish I knew. This is all uncharted territory for me too."

"But you'll be here to help me. Won't you?"

She saw Nora's eyes widen, then just as quickly harden. She took a moment, then said, "You know what my plans are."

But Nora's look became more uncertain when Lillian said, "Who knows what kind of condition your father will be in when he comes home? But I'm positive he is going to need you. How can you even think about moving to Chicago now? When your ailing father will need your help?"

When she saw conscience flicker in Nora's eyes, Lillian felt a glimmer of hope.

"In his condition," she pressed, "do you think he'd be able to travel anywhere? Not for a long time, I think." She saw deeper conflict cross Nora's face. "He's going to be weak. He's going to need constant attention. He's going to want you here." She paused, then sank the hook: "Don't you think you owe him that?"

There it was: Nora seemed to have lost any resistance she might have offered. Then Lillian said, "So let's just forget this Chicago foolishness, shall we?"

Nora gave Lillian a look she couldn't interpret, then rose and said, "It's been a long day. I'm going to bed. Good night, Mother."

"We'll discuss this again in the morning," Lillian said, a note of optimism in her voice.

Nora disappeared up the stairs without a reply.

Lillian sat for a moment, wondering if she'd said enough, feeling as though she might need to talk to Nora once more, to get a real commitment to move back. She would ask Clara about it in the morning. At the moment, she was exhausted but could feel one of her nervous headaches coming on. So she headed for the kitchen, where she kept one of a couple of bottles of Miltown. They would help her get to sleep.

She was surprised to find Clara sitting in the kitchen, reading glasses on, perusing that day's newspaper.

"Oh, you're still up?"

"Yes, I wanted to hear what was going on with Sol."

"Nora just told me that he was OK for now."

"Yes, she told me as well."

"I need to talk to you about Nora in the morning. I think I've convinced her to stay."

"You have?" Clara said.

"Yes, but I'm obviously going to need your help. Let's discuss it in the morning. Right now, I need to take a couple of Miltowns and go to bed. My head is about to split open."

As she crawled into bed a little later, Lillian missed the sound of Sol's snoring in the next bed. She wondered whether he was thinking of her. Sleep came as she thought, *A new start with Nora. Tomorrow.*

SUNDAY

A mother is one to whom you hurry when you are troubled.
—Emily Dickinson

CLARA

As she lay in bed watching the dawn through the window in the bedroom she'd occupied for her entire adult life, Clara von Hollander wondered how this morning would end.

Nora was leaving early. Before Lillian got up.

Clara's heart would go with her, though Clara would stay. For now.

But Nora had to go. For good. Clara believed she'd gotten that point across.

Clara had stood in the kitchen the previous day, listening to Nora and Lillian's argument in the other room—until Sol's heart attack. The arrangement of heating ducts and vents carried the voices from the den as though by intercom.

It wasn't that Clara was an eavesdropper. But she knew how to listen. She found that the ductwork served as a conduit for voices from rooms in other parts of the house. While she worked in the kitchen, she would tune in to conversations the way she would a radio show:

as background noise and, when something interesting was said, as a method of keeping up with the family news.

She also discovered early in her tenure that Sol and Lillian carried on all kinds of conversations while Clara was working in the room with them, as though she weren't there. That was when she realized that invisibility could work to her advantage. In this way, she unobtrusively kept tabs on all the household affairs.

As she listened to the conflict between Nora and Lillian—a clash that never seemed to change from year to year—Clara could tell that Nora's asthma had been bothering her.

She missed Nora's presence deeply—her smile, her humor, her affection, her voice, her touch—since she'd left for college. Clara wondered how she would make it through the day in front of her. Nora was leaving for good, and Clara could feel the pain of her absence already, in every fiber.

Yet, as much as her departure would hurt, she had engineered this moment. She had spent years helping Nora build toward it. This was as it should be—this was what she had raised her for.

Nora needed to spread her wings in a life far from this house in North Tarrytown. Nora wanted a life of the mind, and Clara understood why she would never find it here.

~

Clara remembered arriving at the Levitsky house and meeting Lillian for the first time. The house itself, lovely from the outside when she drove up the driveway with Sol, turned out to be a childcare disaster zone on the inside.

Lillian, dark circles around her eyes, was in the kitchen, which was decorated with stacks of dirty dishes. There was a large pot of water boiling on the stove, full of rubber nipples and glass baby bottles. Lillian's hair flew about her head in frizzy wisps. In a powder room off the kitchen, Clara could see a pail that threatened to overflow with dirty diapers awaiting the laundry.

A baby was crying in a high chair in the corner of the kitchen. Without hesitation, Clara doffed her coat and lifted the wailing child out of the chair. Holding her to her shoulder, she cooed to her and rocked her, until the baby quieted.

"You must be Amelia," Clara said to the baby, then turned to see the frazzled Lillian, mouth agape at the baby's sudden calm.

"How did you do that?" Lillian said.

Before Clara could answer, Sol entered the kitchen carrying Clara's suitcase.

"Oh, I see you've met," he said. "Lillian, this is Clara von Hollander. She's going to be helping you. This is my wife, Lillian."

"Pleased to meet you, Mrs. Levinsky."

"It's Le-VIT-sky," Lillian corrected her in a way that warned Clara against making the same mistake twice.

"Sorry," Clara said, dipping her head.

"You seem to have a way with my daughter," Lillian said, softening, as though she hadn't just reprimanded this stranger in her house who had come to help. When Amelia began to fuss in her arms, Clara casually held the baby up in front of her and sniffed at her diaper.

"No, not that," Clara said. "Is it time for her bottle?"

"There's one in the refrigerator, but it needs to be warmed," Lillian said, and Clara sprang into action.

She had only just walked into the Levitsky kitchen and was still holding a fussy baby in her arms. Yet Clara's instincts led her to the cupboard with the saucepans on her first try. She plucked a pan from the cupboard, slid it under the kitchen faucet, and ran water. At almost the same time, she opened the refrigerator and pulled out the premade bottle, set it in the saucepan, then placed it on the stove, lit a burner beneath it, and turned it to low.

Directing her attention back to the still-whiny Amelia, Clara helped the baby guide her own thumb into her mouth. Amelia smiled while sucking furiously. Within a couple of minutes, the thumb had been replaced by the warmed bottle, as Amelia nestled in Clara's lap, drinking contentedly.

Lillian watched this bit of domestic prestidigitation with exhausted fascination, then said again, "How did you do that?"

~

At that point, at the age of nineteen, Clara had already been taking care of babies for almost ten years, in aid of her shockingly fertile mother.

Clara, the oldest of six children, was tasked with the care and feeding of her younger siblings after her mother died of influenza, in an epidemic that also took Clara's six-year-old brother. After her mother died and the rural Scranton area endured spring flooding that washed out planting season, their father was forced to sell the farm and move the family into Scranton proper, where he bought a small house and found work at a textile factory.

Clara's unmarried aunt, her father's eldest sister, took care of the nine-month-old baby and the two- and four-year-olds while ten-year-old Clara and her eight-year-old sister, Margie, went to school during the day. But after school, care of the three younger children reverted to the older girls.

By the time Clara finished high school, she was almost nineteen, after being forced to drop out for an extended period. At that point, her siblings were old enough to be self-sufficient. But when their father was injured in a factory accident and could no longer work, Clara had to find a job so the family wouldn't lose their house.

Clara answered Sol's ad, "Immediately seeking a housekeeper with childcare responsibilities," which had been placed in small newspapers all over the area by a New York agency Sol employed. The pay, which included room and board, was greater than she'd make at any job in Scranton. She'd be able to send most of it home, until it was no longer needed.

Having managed her whole family after her mother's death, Clara found taking care of Amelia, Lillian, and Sol comparatively easy. The care and feeding of one baby? And a couple of adults who could and would do for themselves? To the nineteen-year-old Clara, that seemed like light duty: cooking, cleaning, childcare. There were routines she mastered and improved, and others that she created, to Lillian's growing, if grudging, admiration.

Amelia was a happy baby who thrived on the attention Clara gave her. But Clara had no one to talk to other than Amelia, an infant, and Lillian, her boss. She was unprepared for the loneliness, which seemed to crush her at times.

She tried to strike up conversations with other nannies at the park near the Levitsky house, where she took Amelia in a stroller. But Amelia needed her full attention, and most of the other women were part of a clique of older Irish immigrants who all went to the same Catholic church—except for one Jamaican woman, who didn't speak to anyone.

Growing up, Clara had shared a bedroom with at least one and as many as three other siblings. Having an entire apartment to herself at the Levitskys' should have felt liberating. Her quarters above the garage were cozy, including living room, kitchenette, bedroom, and bathroom, though it was much larger than any room in the house back home. Yet she felt only the solitude of the spacious accommodations, which emphasized how alone she felt.

It didn't help that the Levitsky house sat on a quiet residential street, too far from Tarrytown's hilly central commercial district for an easy walk into town. Clara wrote letters regularly to her family, but only her sister Margie ever responded, and she didn't write often enough to boost Clara's spirits.

When she first arrived in North Tarrytown, Lillian made her so nervous that Clara spent her initial month waiting tensely to be told to pack her bags and leave. Clara could not escape the feeling—whether dusting the valuables on display or chopping vegetables for dinner—that Lillian was watching her.

There was also, at first, the feeling of being an intruder in someone else's home. It took her several weeks to break herself of the habit of walking on tiptoe or of peeking into a room before she entered.

For a long time, anytime she had to share a room with Lillian or Sol while going about her work, she felt self-conscious. Then she figured out that Sol and Lillian rarely registered her presence in a room unless they needed something from her.

Get over yourself, Clara thought.

Before long, she made the kitchen her own; she rearranged the drawers and cupboards to meet her needs. The rest of the house was Lillian's, and Clara was the unofficial caretaker who maintained it.

For hours at a time, Clara could lose herself in her chores. She had been taught from a young age about the necessity and value of work. Her education began the one and only time seven-year-old Clara whined to her mother, "I am so bored."

Before she knew it, the young Clara was seated at the kitchen table in their farmhouse, a huge pile of freshly picked peapods and two empty bowls sitting in front of her. Her task was to separate peas from pods, putting the shelled peas in one bowl and the empty peapods in the other.

"Tell me when you're done with these," her mother said. "There's more."

For the next hour, Clara shelled peas, while making a mental list of all the other things she would rather have been doing. When she finished the chore and presented the bowls of peas and pods for inspection, she said to her mother, "Can I go play now?"

"Not bored anymore?"

"No, ma'am."

"Never mistake not having something to do with boredom," her mother told her. "Boredom is for lazy people, and lazy people aren't much use to anyone. Next time, instead of saying, 'I'm bored,' start by thinking of all the things you'd rather be doing than shucking peas. Then stop thinking about yourself and ask me, 'What can I do that would be helpful?' Because the answer to that question is that there's always something you can do. If you can teach yourself to ask that question, you'll never be bored. And you will always be welcome because you'll always be useful."

That proved true through the rest of Clara's life at home and made her perfect for her job in the Levitsky household. Cleaning, cooking, shopping, laundry, childcare: Clara was the master of the family schedule in all the important ways, the engine who drove the household. She had always deferred to Lillian's authority when Lillian asserted her status as employer in one of her dark moments—but in most ways, Clara ran the house.

~

Lying in bed as the sun rose on the day Nora would leave, Clara knew that Sunday breakfast was not going to make itself. She wanted to cook one last meal for Nora before she left, and she wanted to make it a good one. She sat up and stretched, then went into her bathroom to get ready for the day.

She looked at herself in the mirror as she brushed her teeth and noticed how much the gray was beginning to dominate her hair.

Beauty fades, she thought, then chuckled to herself. She had always thought herself plain. Now, examining her reflection, she updated her assessment: *Plain, with wrinkles.*

She thought about moving back to Scranton. She remembered the homesickness that first gripped her, how hard it was to leave Scranton to go back to North Tarrytown after each visit when she was younger. Now she wondered if any part of Scranton would feel like home after all this time.

The family house had long since been sold. Of Clara's siblings, only Margie still lived in Scranton. Widowed, her children living in other states, Margie was the sole occupant of a house that had become too big for her by herself after her Parkinson's disease diagnosis.

As Clara finished dressing, she remembered enduring Amelia's departure, when she married Frank and moved out. It was also easy to summon the separation pain she felt when Nora left for Syracuse. Still, Amelia lived nearby and visited regularly. Nora came home on school breaks, if only briefly, and wrote to Clara regularly.

But the combination of Nora's imminent departure for Chicago, coupled with her own impending return to Scranton, threatened to upend her emotional equilibrium.

When she'd heard Lillian pressure Nora to stay to help care for Sol, Clara understood why Lillian always won at bridge. She kept her cards close to the vest, understood how to execute a sneak attack, and saved a trump card until it would absolutely devastate her opponent.

Nora would never stay simply because her mother wanted it; if anything, Clara knew the opposite was true. But Sol's sudden health crisis and uncertain future—medically and legally—tugged at Nora. She had said as much when she came to Clara's room, after Lillian had gone to bed the night before.

Clara thought about the French Resistance in those World War II movies, people going about their daily lives while secretly working against the Nazis and the Vichy collaborators who were their neighbors and employers. Somedays, she felt like a spy in the House of Levitsky.

She treated both girls as her "secret daughters," a phrase Nora first had uttered when she was eight, while tearfully complaining to Clara about her mother's refusal to allow Nora to attend a friend's sleepover. Out of nowhere, Nora said, "I wish you were my mother instead of her."

"Oh, honey, no, don't ever say that," Clara replied, even as she inwardly rejoiced. Nora didn't voice the sentiment often, but when she did, it gave an added sense of meaning and purpose to Clara's life. But she had never put it in such naked terms before.

That time, Nora had gone on to say, "Sometimes I pretend that I'm your secret daughter."

"And don't say that either," Clara said, pausing before adding, "Yes, I feel that too. But it's our secret, all right? We can't say it out loud."

"But I *do* wish that. Mother doesn't care about me, not the way you do."

"Now that's not true," Clara lied, glad she wasn't hooked to a polygraph machine.

In all the important ways, the girls had grown up as Clara's children. She dressed both girls for school each morning, made their breakfasts, and made sure they had lunch money or a lunch she'd packed. She had a snack waiting for them when they got home but insisted they first changed out of their school clothes and into play clothes. Then she checked their homework before they were allowed to watch TV or play outdoors.

She prepared the family's dinner each night, though she didn't eat in the dining room with them. But, most weeks, there were two or three evenings when Sol's late work and Lillian's social groups meant the girls and Clara would eat together in the kitchen, meals that all three of them looked forward to.

She also oversaw their preparations at bedtime: bath, pajamas, toothbrushing, tucking into bed. If they were home, Lillian or Sol would usually appear at the end, issuing good night kisses and proclaiming, "Lights out." Neither Sol nor Lillian were there every night for this ritual; with the exception of her days off, Clara always was.

Clara knew what a miserable time Lillian had during the final months before Nora's birth and the dark year that followed it. At that point, Clara's relationship with Lillian had grown to include elements of friendship, though those seemed to flow mostly in one direction. Yet Clara had sympathy for this vain, imperious woman because she had seen her at her lowest moments and understood how shameful they were for Lillian.

"Don't worry—I'll be here to help you," Clara had reassured her when Lillian learned she was pregnant with Nora. "You won't have to do it alone." That appeared to be Lillian's big fear: being left alone with two babies. *I should have been a psychiatrist,* Clara thought one day, after an hour spent listening to Lillian's fears and trying with limited success to parry them with common sense.

~

Clara remembered the year after Nora's birth as the turning point. While Lillian had disappeared for hours at a time into her sewing room, Clara had taken command of the household and the childcare, before Sol took Lillian to a doctor for "vitamin shots." Those brought her out of the sewing room, but she remained in a fog for the rest of the year.

Lillian would ignore both Nora and Amelia for long stretches, abandoning their care and feeding to Clara, who quietly reveled in her time with the two little girls. She couldn't reciprocate their physical affection in Lillian's presence, but that wasn't often a problem. A shadow existence as parent was better than no existence at all.

She felt bad when Lillian tried to reengage with Nora and the baby would have none of it. It appeared to Clara that at some point, Lillian had simply given up.

Clara decided that Lillian could never have a real maternal connection to Nora. In Clara's mind, Lillian treated her daughters as unruly extensions of herself, rather than as the flesh of her flesh. They were to be kept in line, occasionally brought out for inspection, display, and admiration.

At almost every birthday party for the girls, Clara was the one who managed the children and helped Sol cut the birthday cake. She was the one who tended to the birthday girl while Lillian held court with the mothers in another room. Clara baked the girls' cakes, accompanied Amelia and Nora to other children's parties, wrapped their gifts from Sol and Lillian—and picked up the discarded paper after the presents were torn open.

Having raised Nora and Amelia almost since birth, Clara disapproved of how cavalier Lillian was about motherhood in general and her children in particular. Yet Lillian's missing maternal impulse was the thing that gave Clara the chance to be a mother, which she would otherwise have been denied.

Only her sister knew of Clara's loss, and she was the only one who understood why Clara felt entitled to steal Lillian's daughters from her, without Lillian realizing it.

Clara's girl was named Lynette, after Clara's grandmother. The child had been stillborn, but Clara insisted on a christening and burial, though her family was against it, for fear of calling attention to their shame.

The baby's father was a young man named Theodore. Clara had known him since they were toddlers and believed she was in love with him. Theodore confessed to Clara that he didn't like working on his father's dairy farm, that he wanted to be an auto mechanic, and that he had applied for work with the Tennessee Valley Authority, helping to build dams to generate electricity for rural areas. After he'd signed a six-month contract with the TVA, he told Clara that when the contract was up, he would have enough money to come back, marry her, and go into business for himself fixing cars.

They both got caught up in the passion of their farewell, though the inexperienced Clara didn't realize just how far she'd been carried away. Then, three months after Theodore had left, a doctor confirmed what fifteen-year-old Clara had suspected after waking up nauseated several mornings in a row.

Clara said nothing to her father. She secretly imagined a future in which Theodore returned from the TVA before she gave birth. He would sweep her off her feet with a wedding and a home with a yard in a nice neighborhood of Scranton, where they would raise several children and live happily ever after.

The next week, Theodore's family received a telegram from Chattanooga, telling them Theodore had died after being buried alive in a construction-site accident.

It wasn't long before Clara's father figured out that his daughter was pregnant and not just gaining weight. Clara was shuffled off to the same elderly aunt who had cared for her siblings as tots, who now lived in a distant corner of Scranton. The aged relative agreed to take Clara in until her baby was born, when the baby would be given up for adoption and Clara could go back to finish high school. Clara was expected to do a little light housework and cooking. But she was mostly there to hide her pregnancy from the neighbors at home, as well as to be a companion to the old woman, who'd grown increasingly feeble.

Midway through her sixth month, Clara felt something was wrong: cramping and sudden bouts of intense nausea far beyond what her morning sickness had produced. But Clara simply lived with it for a week, gritting her teeth at the pain.

Then, one morning a week or so later, she began to hemorrhage and was rushed to the hospital. An emergency caesarean removed the blue, unbreathing baby. When Clara didn't stop bleeding, the doctor went back in and performed a hysterectomy. Clara was not yet sixteen.

It wasn't until a subsequent doctor's visit that she learned the extreme measure taken to save her life after her stillbirth. It was explained that her uterus had been removed (in an effort to keep her from bleeding to death). She would never be able to have children.

It wasn't as if Clara had spent her adolescence craving children of her own, because she had reared four siblings, including babies. She had no romantic illusions about the demands of being a mother.

Yet, when she learned that children of her own were no longer a possibility, Clara felt a bottomless sense of loss. Theodore had been her first and only boyfriend. Who would want her, now that she was damaged goods? And barren, to boot?

She spent the first year after her stillbirth mourning her baby's loss. She kept her grief to herself because her family treated her loss as a scandal, never to be spoken of. When she returned to school, the note explaining her monthslong absence attributed it to scarlet fever.

But she'd privately marked Lynette's existence on the same day each year. She would try to imagine what her little girl would have been like had she lived, at each anniversary of her birth and death.

~

It wasn't until Clara had grown comfortable as part of the Levitsky household that she realized that Lillian was paying her to be mother to her children.

It began innocently, with the kind of singsong patter that Clara mindlessly sang as she would bathe or dress Amelia. One day, as she swaddled the toddler in a new diaper, she listened to her own words and realized she was singing the phrase "You're my little girl," over and over as she fastened a safety pin and put rubber pants in place.

Clara stopped and looked around the baby's room, then peeked out into the hall, to be safe. But there was no sign of Lillian. She smiled at Amelia, who reached to be picked up, and Clara obliged.

"Best keep that little ditty to ourselves," Clara told Amelia as she carried her downstairs to her playpen.

After that, Clara took every opportunity to quietly act as mother to Amelia and Nora. She had to hide those feelings from Lillian, but Lillian was not paying close enough attention to notice.

Yet it was a narrow line for all of them to walk with Lillian. She may not have been concerned about her daughters, but she could be jealous of perceived incursions into her domain. Clara remembered Amelia's tenth birthday party, when Nora was almost five. The day had included a party with Amelia's friends and ended with a family dinner. There, Sol and Lillian gave Amelia her big gift: a new two-wheel bicycle.

After dinner, Clara called Amelia into the kitchen, then pulled out a package wrapped in plain brown paper, with a red ribbon tied around it.

"Happy birthday, honey," Clara said. "I know you'll be starting home economics in school in the fall and thought you might need this."

Amelia tore open the paper to find an apron in a shade of blue-gray. Red and yellow tulips were embroidered in a row across the front, next to a hand-stitched image of a small pond. It was identical to the apron Clara had worn every day since Amelia was a little girl. Amelia's face lit up.

"Your apron." She beamed.

"Not exactly, but close as I could copy, sewing it myself."

"Oh, Clara, I love you!" Amelia cried, throwing her arms around her in a warm hug, just as Lillian came through the swinging door to the kitchen.

Lillian, a scowl on her face, had Nora by the wrist to keep her from touching anything with a hand smeared with chocolate frosting. When she heard what Amelia said to Clara, Lillian stopped in her tracks.

"Oh no you don't," Lillian exploded at Amelia.

She dropped Nora's arm, momentarily forgetting Nora's dirty fingers. Clara saw Nora wipe her hand on the seat of her pink shorts, leaving chocolaty streaks.

"You don't say 'I love you' to Clara," Lillian said heatedly to Amelia, shaking a finger at her. "That is something you only say to members of your own family."

Clara learned something about Lillian's anger and insecurity that day, something she had suspected but hoped she'd never encounter. After almost ten years in the house, Clara understood she'd mistaken familiarity for friendship, something she vowed she wouldn't do again.

~

Yet she'd made the same mistake a few years later. Clara had been in her early thirties when she attracted a beau who wasn't put off by her work schedule or her living situation.

His name was Sam Klay, and he was a conductor on the Hudson River Railroad Line, which she rode from Tarrytown to the city and back on her Wednesdays off. She'd noticed him on her train, taking tickets and announcing stops every week for a year. Then he paused one day to talk.

After punching her round-trip ticket, he said, "Do you mind if I ask you something?"

"Try me," Clara said with a smile. She'd already decided she liked his friendly manner.

"I see you on this train most Wednesdays, going in or coming out. Sometimes you have those little girls with you. Do you mind me asking what you do while you're there?"

"In the city, you mean? What does anyone do? There's so much to choose from. What do you like to do when you're there?"

He gave her a sheepish smile and said, "I've never been more than a block from Grand Central."

"How is that possible? You ride the train into New York City every single day."

"Sure—and then I ride it back out again. Over and over." He paused, adding, "So? What do you do there?"

Clara told him that when she visited Manhattan on one of her days off, she would see a movie in Times Square, visit a museum, or, once every month or so, splurge for a balcony seat to a Broadway show. "I like musicals," she told him.

Sam had a wolfish smile but kind eyes that softened it. His conductor's uniform seemed a little snug, as though he was well fed.

"How long have you worked for the railroad?" she asked him.

"Since the war. I moved down from Albany to take this route a year and a half ago."

"You could go in on the weekend, when you're not working. I'll bet they let you ride for free," Clara joked.

"They do," Sam replied. "But I spend weekends helping my mom. She lives in Yonkers."

The train was nearing the next station, and the conductor, who wore a name tag that said **Samuel K.**, started to leave to attend to his duties. But he turned back and said, "I'm Sam, by the way. Maybe I'll see you again."

"I'm Clara," she responded. "Nice meeting you."

She ran into him again a couple of weeks later, on a late train out of the city. She'd been to see *Guys and Dolls*, which she'd heard Lillian talking about, and which she'd enjoyed. She wound up in a deserted car near the rear of the train. When Sam Klay came through to collect tickets and saw her, he lit up.

"Hey, Clara, right? What'd you see tonight?"

Before she could say anything, he said, "Wait—let me take care of something quick. Then you'll tell me all about it."

He was gone less than five minutes, and when he returned, he said, "There—the cars in the back are closed. And there's hardly anyone on the rest of the train. So the assistant conductor will cover for me until you get off in Tarrytown."

"How did you know Tarrytown is my stop?" she said with a sly smile.

"Because I just took your ticket. I'm trained to notice those things."

That made her laugh. She told him about the show she'd seen, and they wound up talking for the next forty minutes, until Sam said, "Your stop is next."

As Clara put her coat on at the approach of her station, Sam followed her to the door, then worked the mechanism to open all the doors on the train once it stopped. He stepped out onto the platform first, then extended a hand to help Clara off. As he did, he said, "Would you like to go out to dinner sometime?"

Clara said, "Yes, I'd like that."

He pulled a small pad and pencil out of a pocket and said, "Write down your phone number, and I'll call you."

As he handed it to her, the train whistle blew a long blast, then another one. Clara wrote the number, saying, "Aren't you afraid the train will leave without you?"

Sam laughed as he retrieved his pad and pencil, saying, "The train can't move when the doors are open. That's why they're blowing the whistle at me."

He stepped back on to the train. As he released the door, he said, "I'll talk to you soon."

~

Before long, dinner and an evening out with Sam Klay on Saturday night became a regular thing for Clara. Amelia and Nora began referring to Saturdays as "Sammy-day." After meeting him, Sol later told her, "I wish I had a couple of Sams at work to help us out."

Clara liked Sam because he knew what he wanted, but he wasn't pushy about it. She enjoyed talking to him because, like her, he read the *New York Post* and kept up with current events.

Sam was a year or so older than she was. He had an apartment in Yonkers, near the house where he grew up, where his mother still lived. "But I'm over there so often helping her that I might as well still live there," he told Clara.

Sam had completed a year at City College when he was drafted at the beginning of World War II. Aptitude tests landed him in officer training, but instead of combat, he wound up in the military police, spending the war at Fort Bragg, in North Carolina, maintaining order among the one hundred thousand or so young soldiers training there before shipping out to the war in the Pacific and the European Theater.

After the war, when Sam mustered out, he tagged along with an MP buddy who was driving to Albany, New York, to apply for a job with the police department there. At that point, Sam had no interest in a law enforcement career, but while scanning a newspaper as he waited for his friend to undergo a job interview, he spotted an ad for conductor trainees at the Hudson River Railroad. By the end of the day, both he and his buddy had landed new jobs: his friend as a patrolman with

Albany PD, Sam as a would-be conductor on the run between Albany and Poughkeepsie.

By the beginning of the 1950s, Sam had seniority as a full conductor. When his mother's health became a concern, he requested a transfer to the Manhattan end of the line and moved back to Westchester County to work.

Clara enjoyed Sam's company; they shared a sense of humor that could be silly. But she'd always taken a practical approach to men, figuring that they were interested in the kind of women she saw on TV and in movies, not someone who looked as ordinary as her.

Since she'd gone to work in North Tarrytown, she had learned to enjoy what could be a hermit-like existence. The men she met in the course of her day were deliverymen, the butcher at the supermarket, the plumber, and the electrician. Some of them expressed tentative interest in seeing her socially, but her work schedule tended to discourage more than a movie date or so. But that was before Sam.

She wasn't surprised when he kissed her one night at the end of their fourth date, deciding she liked it. But as they began necking regularly at the end of their evenings together, Clara felt herself holding back. She feared going further and the discussion about her past that might ensue. She couldn't imagine sharing the story of Lynette and Theodore, no matter how close they became.

Then one Saturday after they'd been dating for a while, after the waitress had taken their dinner order and brought their drinks, Sam said without any preamble, "Hey, I was wondering. What would you think about us getting married?"

Clara had been a dreamy-eyed teen when she and Theodore spun their simple idea of a house and family in Scranton. She remembered the heady feeling—like champagne bubbles bursting in her heart—when she kissed Theodore. Kissing Sam felt familiar, even comforting, but she was sorry to realize it would never thrill her.

When he finished asking, Clara kissed him, then gave him a hug. Sam pulled back, smiled, and said, "Is that a yes?"

"A tentative yes. How would you feel if I kept working at the Levitskys' after we got married?"

"But you wouldn't still live there?"

"No, of course not."

"What will happen when we have kids?"

Clara hoped he didn't notice her hesitation, before she said, "One step at a time." They left it at that.

The next night, as she served dinner to the family, she asked Sol and Lillian if she could talk to them after the meal. She went to see them in the den after she and Nora, her self-appointed helper, had finished the dishes.

"I wanted to tell you that Sam asked me to marry him, and I think I'm going to say yes."

Sol jumped up to take Clara in a fatherly hug, saying, "That's wonderful, dear. I'm so happy for you."

"Yes, I'm glad for you," Lillian added. "And where will you live?"

"He has an apartment in Yonkers because he needs to be close to his mother. But his place is small, so we'll look for something a little bigger, hopefully closer to here, so I can get here easily in the morning."

Something changed in Lillian's face as she said, "What do you mean?"

"Well, just because I'm married with a husband doesn't mean I can't keep taking care of your family, Lillian. And I told Sam that. He's fine with it."

"But I'm not," Lillian said, and Sol's head spun toward her as Clara's heart sank.

"Why not?" Sol asked.

"Clara is going to want a family of her own. It's only a matter of time before she has one."

Clara started to say, "We aren't—" But Lillian cut her off.

"Let me finish, please. When she does, then where will we be?" She turned from Sol to Clara. "I'm going to need someone ready to step in on the same full-time basis as you, once you get married. Because, at that point, you'll want to focus on your own family."

Clara was having trouble forming words, even as Sol said, "Now, Lil, I don't see why she can't stay on after she's married."

"So she gets married and stays on. And a year from now, she has a baby and goes off to be a mother. Where does that leave us? Right back where we are now, looking for someone to replace her."

"I guess I need to think about it a little" was all Clara could come up with, then turned to go to her room. As she left, she heard Sol say, "I think you're wrong, Lil," and Lillian's reply: "Fine. *You* find her replacement." And, faintly, Sol's rejoinder: "I did pretty good when I hired *her*, didn't I?"

Back in her room, Clara felt angry tears streaming.

She couldn't leave Nora behind, and Lillian knew it.

Nora was almost ten, and Clara had long seen the girl's special quality; it had been there from birth. Nora was perceptive and quick-witted in ways that unnerved Lillian, something Clara saw every day.

Nora had always been a "Why not?" child, where Lillian was a "Because I said so" disciplinarian. Clara spent hours each day with the little girl in the years before she started school, and from the time she learned to talk, Nora had questions about everything. Clara loved the quirky jumps their conversations took as Nora grew up.

But she'd also heard how Lillian responded to Nora's incessant curiosity.

"Why do you read that newspaper to her?" Lillian said to Clara in frustration one morning after Nora had asked her, "Who are the Rosenbergs, and why are people mad at them?"

More than once, Clara heard Lillian tell Nora, "Little girls should not ask so many questions." Clara would always find a moment to get Nora alone and tell her, "Don't ever be afraid to ask a question. Asking questions is how you learn."

The idea of leaving Nora—*my girl,* Clara thought—to Lillian was more than she could bear. Her vision for Nora's future had Nora fleeing Tarrytown for a life of—what? Learning. Achieving. Accomplishing. None of that would happen if Nora's future was dictated by Lillian.

For a moment, Clara couldn't decide if Lillian was purposely pitting Sam against Nora but then realized she was overcomplicating things. While Lillian could be jealous of her hold on Nora and Amelia, she didn't appreciate the depth of Clara's connection with the girls or feel threatened by it. In forcing Clara to make a choice, Lillian was focused on her own selfish interest and nothing more.

Bitterly, Clara came to the conclusion that it was also about control. If Clara wanted to stay as part of the Levitsky household, she had to forsake that other part of her life.

And if she had to do that, then she would make Lillian pay. Eventually.

A day or so later, Clara quietly told Sol that she and Sam were going to talk about holding off on a wedding for the time being.

The following Saturday at dinner, she said to Sam, "I don't think now is the right time to get married. Can we wait a bit?"

Clara saw the light dim in his eyes. His smile remained steady as he said, "Can I ask why?"

She found herself fumbling for a good reason, but all she could come up with was "I just need a little more time to think about it."

She couldn't tell him the truth: This girl is my daughter. I can't leave her. I can't abandon her to the care of a woman who will stifle and diminish her. I am the only one who can make sure she escapes into the future she deserves.

Her meaning—that marriage was not in their future—was apparent, and Sam's calls quickly dwindled until he stopped calling altogether. And then she noticed she stopped seeing him on the Wednesday train.

For months afterward, Clara worked to bank the anger that flared at Lillian. She made a point from then on of relishing every second she had with Nora, to cement their connection even further. She never tried to alienate Nora from her mother, as she easily could have, because she didn't need to. Lillian did an adequate job of that by herself.

Her anger subsided, but she never found forgiveness for Lillian. The business with Sam had been a constant reminder that as much as Clara tried to treat Lillian as a friend, she knew Lillian would never see her as an equal. That would never change.

~

Now, contemplating Nora's imminent departure, Clara wondered why she had ever wanted this haughty woman's approval. Proximity was part of it; you didn't want to spend time with people who didn't like you.

As she went into the quiet kitchen to start making Sunday breakfast, Clara recalled the numerous occasions when she'd seen how scared and insecure Lillian was, and she'd felt for the older woman. It was one of the principal differences between them: Clara had a well of sympathy for other people. Lillian only pitied herself.

There would be long stretches when she would be lulled into thinking that Lillian had come to appreciate the multiple roles she filled in her life. Then she'd encounter the Lillian who insisted on thinking of Clara as "the help."

She was often the rod for Lillian's emotional lightning bolts. She saw her role as conveying those flashes safely to ground before they could strike the girls. Loyalty to the girls, and her feelings for Nora, had kept her in place for years.

Finding this job—this life with the Levitskys—had been a tremendous gift. Losing Lynette and being denied the chance to ever be a mother herself, Clara found two other babies to rear as her own—and was paid a salary for the privilege. In private, that was how she always thought of Nora: *my girl.* And that was the reason she stayed.

~

Clara had visited Nora in Syracuse annually while she was in college and graduate school, though Sol and Lillian knew nothing about it. Each winter, starting when Amelia was in high school, Sol would drive Lillian to Palm Beach, Florida, at the beginning of February. He would stay the rest of the week, then fly back, leaving her the car. Lillian would spend the rest of the month under Florida sunshine, playing bridge and mah-jongg with the same women she played with all year in Tarrytown. Sol reversed the process at the end of the month, flying to Florida to drive Lillian back to New York.

Clara's duties while Lillian was gone consisted of filling in as parent, which she would have done for free. Once the girls moved out of the house, her brief during the month amounted to cooking for Sol and otherwise maintaining the status quo on cleaning, laundry, and the like. But each year, starting when Nora left for college, Clara was given the first week that Sol and Lillian were gone as time off with pay.

A couple of weeks before Sol and Lillian were to leave during Nora's freshman year of college, Clara received a letter from Nora in Syracuse. She found it when she brought in the day's mail and immediately put it in her apron pocket, before setting the rest of the mail on the front hall table where it usually went. She read the letter when she was alone in the kitchen.

> If you have the time off the weekend after the folks leave, why don't you take a bus up and visit? My roommate is going home that weekend, so you could stay in the dorm with me. It will be fun!
>
> Love, Nora

Clara knew better than to mention this to Lillian. At the end of August before Nora's freshman year, when Sol and Lillian had been making plans to drive her to school, Nora said, "Can Clara come too?"

To which Lillian responded, "Why would Clara want to visit Syracuse? *I* don't even want to go—but I'm coming anyway."

When Clara heard about the conversation from Lillian, Lillian acted as though she'd done Clara a favor.

"What a ridiculous idea," Lillian said. "Why would *you* want to go all the way to Syracuse and back, when you don't have to?"

To which Clara answered, silently, *To be with the person I love the most dearly in the world.*

To Lillian, she said, "I'm sure you'll have more fun without me."

"Oh, I doubt we'll have fun," Lillian predicted.

She was prescient: The ride was too long. The road was too bumpy. The diner they stopped at on the way up wasn't clean enough. Syracuse was a dingy city. The campus looked ugly. Lillian was sure she saw cockroaches in Nora's dorm.

Clara heard it all when Sol and Lillian returned. It tempered her resentment at being summarily excluded to learn what a hellish trip Lillian had made it.

Nora was witty about their visit in a subsequent letter to Clara. She described Lillian wearing one of her most disapproving facial expressions (Nora called it "the Fishface") all weekend long. Clara knew exactly the look she meant.

Clara didn't mention her approaching Syracuse trip to Sol or Lillian, even as she found the bus schedule and secured a round-trip ticket out of White Plains. Lillian would never think to ask how she planned to spend her time off, so Clara didn't need to worry about having to lie.

She caught an early-morning bus on the Thursday after Sol and Lillian drove off for Florida. The ride to Syracuse took roughly six hours, stopping in towns along the way like Binghamton and Cortland. It had been a snowy winter already, and while the roads were clear, Clara marveled at the size of the snowbanks thrown up by plows in the center of New York state.

Nora was waiting at the Syracuse bus station in her beat-up '55 Plymouth. Nora drove it with the abandon of a cabbie, grinding gears to shift up and down on hills and flit in and out of openings in traffic.

"Slow down, Parnelli," Clara said, clutching the door as Nora took a sharp corner, acing out a station wagon.

Nora's dorm room did, indeed, have an extra bed—a bunk bed. Seeing the look on Clara's face when she saw the accommodations, Nora laughed and said, "I probably should have warned you. You can have the bottom if you want."

"I suppose because I'm over forty, you think I'm too old to climb up there," Clara said. Then she chuckled and said, "Well, you're right. I am."

They ate dinner in the dorm, where Nora introduced Clara to everyone as "my secret mother," which made Clara blush. Clara also felt a flush of pride that Nora knew all the women serving food on the cafeteria line by name and greeted them as friends.

"This meat loaf isn't as good as what you make at home," Nora confided as they ate.

"Yes, but I don't have to cook for two hundred people at a time."

As they got ready for bed that night, Nora offered to skip all her Friday classes to spend the time with her.

"Nora Jane, don't even dream of missing class," she said. "How else will I see what your life is like up here?"

Nora had a full load of required courses, four in all, each of which met every day.

"Four classes every day? Isn't that a lot?" Clara worried.

"I scheduled my free periods between classes so I can do the homework for the class I just took," Nora explained. "So I may leave you to your own devices for a couple of hours here and there."

"I can keep myself amused," Clara said.

After breakfast in the cafeteria, where Nora introduced her to the morning serving crew, they walked the several blocks to Nora's first class, English Composition for Freshmen. The instructor preached the evil of adverbs, as it pertained to a recent writing assignment.

Gazing around the college classroom as the professor spoke, she felt awe at the formality of the lecture hall amphitheater, with its rows of wooden desks aimed in the direction of the speaker. Clara had labored to finish high school but had been determined to do so, after missing time for her pregnancy and Lynette's stillbirth. College never seemed like an option, given her family's need for her to work and make money.

Like Lillian, Clara was an autodidact, though in a different way, in that she read voraciously but with catholic taste. She thoroughly read a daily newspaper and all the magazines that came into the Levitsky house, from *Time* to *Redbook*. She was a regular at the Warner Library in Tarrytown, checking out everything from books of popular history to biographies of the famous to the latest potboiler.

Sitting in the back of the class and watching the other freshmen, called to order so early on a Friday morning, Clara decided that she'd feel lucky to be a teenager in a place like this. But most of the teens surrounding her were slouched over inattentively, paper cups of coffee perched on their desks, cigarettes burning between their fingers, not concentrating on what was being said.

But a few, like Nora, weren't afraid to question the professor's assertions about an essay that had been assigned reading. In Clara's view, they battled him to a draw—pretty good for freshmen.

Then Nora was off to the campus library, parking herself in a carrel to write the one-hundred-word essay that was the weekend assignment. Clara tagged along and was delighted to find a library rack containing that day's edition of twenty different newspapers from around the country. She selected the *San Francisco Chronicle* and was absorbed in a story about how long it took to paint the Golden Gate Bridge, when Nora tapped her shoulder and said, "Time for my next class."

The rest of the day followed the same pattern: class, library, class, library, class, with a lunch break sandwiched in. By the end of the afternoon, Clara had the chance to wander through most of the Syracuse campus, while Nora finished three of her four weekend assignments.

"Now let's go have a beer," Nora said as she and Clara came out of a History of Journalism lecture. They walked across University Hill to the Crouse–Marshall business district, where Nora led them into a place called Cosmo's.

"Best pizza on campus," Nora said as they tucked into a booth in the crowded bar. "A couple of my friends from the dorm are going to join us."

Clara spent the next several hours happily eating pizza while helping the girls drain several pitchers of watery beer. Nora's friends all treated Clara as an instant pal of long standing, roaring when she told stories from Nora's youth.

"Like that time you put chocolate-covered ants in a Fanny Farmer box, then left it backstage in the boys' dressing room of that play you were in."

To which Nora said, with exaggerated disbelief, "*Moi?*" which was met with gales of laughter from her friends.

Clara wasn't exactly drunk when they got back to the dorm, but she was definitely hungover the next morning.

"Well, let's go eat something," Nora said, then proceeded to devour a huge plate of scrambled eggs, bacon, and toast in the cafeteria. Clara picked at a bowl of oatmeal.

They spent Saturday driving around Syracuse and the surrounding area. Nora showed Clara her favorite restaurants and some of the quirky stores she'd found while exploring different parts of the city. They drove the circumference of Lake Onondaga, then drove the forty miles to Oswego. There, they stood on a snowy beach, watching ice floes wash ashore along the banks of Lake Ontario, the first of the Great Lakes that Clara had ever visited.

It was a perfect weekend, Clara thought on the bus back to White Plains Sunday morning. They had spent the kind of time together many mothers took for granted. In her ex officio role, Clara never seemed to get enough of that.

She never told Sol and Lillian about that or subsequent trips. It was yet another of their secrets—hers and Nora's—part of their history of hidden moments that bound them more tightly than Lillian could ever imagine.

After each trip, Clara would mentally catalog—so she could later summon—every detail of every moment of the weekend. The smell of Nora's dorm and, later, her apartment. Nora laughing at her friends' teasing. Riding in the car with the smart, capable girl, who had learned her way around a whole new city in a few short months—and then the whole Finger Lakes region.

Everything about those weekends had bonded her to Nora. They'd fortified and invigorated Clara in the weeks and months between Nora's visits home. In low moments, those memories could instantly lift her spirits.

~

Seeing eggs and milk in the refrigerator and knowing she had an ample supply of Bisquick, Clara decided she would make pancakes, one of Nora's favorites. She was on her knees, digging in the back of a cupboard for the griddle, when Nora came through the swinging door, carrying her suitcase.

"I'm making pancakes," Clara said. "You need to eat something before you get on the road."

"Oh, I don't know."

"Now, don't argue. You need something in your stomach. I'll have these ready in a jiffy."

Nora sighed and set her suitcase down. She settled in the breakfast nook, where Clara saw her looking out the window with a troubled expression. Reading her thoughts, Clara spoke first.

"Your mother is wrong, and you know it. Your father's care is not your responsibility. You need to put her out of your mind so you can do all the things you planned to do. Starting with leaving here this morning and moving to Chicago next month."

Nora looked as though she'd been caught in a lie. "I was thinking of postponing Chicago for a year. Just until Daddy is better."

Clara came over and sat next to her in the breakfast nook. She put an arm around the tearful young woman's shoulders, enjoying the physical closeness of the moment. Then she said, "But what if he doesn't get better in a year? What if you pass up this opportunity and move back here instead—just for a year, like you say—and then he gets worse? Then what?"

Nora's disconsolate expression deepened.

"If that happens, do you think your mother will say, 'Oh, that's all right, you can go ahead and move to Chicago now'? Because you know she will never say that. Even if he gets better tomorrow—or, by some miracle, they find a way to magically give him a healthy heart—she will never agree to you moving to Chicago, no matter what happens to your father, because it wasn't her idea." Then Clara faced her, holding her by the shoulders. "Go to Chicago. Stick to your plan. I'll be here to make sure your father is taken care of. Don't worry about that."

Nora was quiet a moment. "I know you're right." She sat still another minute, then looked at the kitchen clock and said, "Seven fifteen. I don't want to see Mother this morning."

"You won't. She took two Miltowns last night, so she won't be up until at least ten. I'll have you out of here by eight at the latest. Now help me with the raspberries for the pancakes."

Clara started to measure milk and Bisquick, while Nora rinsed the berries in a strainer. As she did, she turned to Clara and said, "Think my mother will be any nicer to my father, now that he's had a heart attack?"

"Hard to say," Clara said. "I used to think she'd work him to death. I wonder if she even knows how to baby him."

"I've always wondered what he saw in her."

Whisking milk and pancake mix, Clara said, "Maybe she was a different person before Amelia was born. That's the only thing I can think, because I didn't get here until after that and she's pretty much the same person she's always been since then. Sometimes better, sometimes worse." She backhanded a lock of hair out of her eyes and kept at the pancake batter. "Your father is a loyal man."

~

But that was something Clara wondered about as well. What had Sol seen in Lillian? Not just why had he married her—but why had he stayed with a woman around whom he seemed to spend his life walking on eggshells?

Early on, Clara noticed that Sol didn't often speak up when Lillian browbeat Amelia. She seldom heard Sol say more than "Now, Lil . . ."

While Sol always greeted the various young men who dated Amelia with warmth, Clara knew that the only thing Amelia heard was Lillian's postmortem: "His sport coat certainly didn't fit very well, did it?" Nor had Clara seen Sol do more than protest impotently when Lillian sent Amelia to California to break her up with Alan Gilbert.

She knew the girls lived for Sol's attention and affection, which Clara saw him reciprocate. He was an exemplary father on his own with the girls, helping with homework, playing Mr. Fix-It to broken toys, generally being the girls' daddy in a way Lillian never would be their mommy.

The question Clara wrestled with was why Sol didn't do more to protect his own daughters when their mother lashed out.

Clara endured bolts of pain when Lillian would lay into Amelia verbally over some infraction. Her breastbone ached when Nora was Lillian's target. Yet it was rare for Sol to utter as much as a gravelly "Lillian!" at those moments.

She remembered a night, after a stormy dinner that saw Amelia leave the table in tears, when Sol came to see Clara later in the kitchen. She was doing dishes when Sol walked in and happened to be washing crystal, so she didn't dare look up, for fear of letting pieces collide and chip.

"I know my wife can be a difficult woman," he said. "I find it best to maintain peace in the household." Then he walked out, before she could look up. She never knew if he was talking to her or to himself.

Was Sol as guilty of letting Lillian browbeat the girls as Lillian was of doing it? Could she have done that without his tacit approval?

Clara came to the unhappy conclusion that Sol was a nice man but a weak one, willing to sacrifice his daughters to his wife's outbursts to maintain harmony.

As she parsed the equation further, she saw a deeper, still darker truth: Sol had been willing to sacrifice the girls to keep Lillian from training her anger on him. He played the supportive spouse to Lillian, then would turn around and be the sympathetic dad to the girls, salving their hurt feelings with largesse and affection as an apology for his failures as their protector against their mother.

~

She had expressed that thought a month earlier, in her weekly Sunday-night phone call with her sister Margie, in Scranton. But Margie, who had listened to years of Clara's stories about Sol, Lillian, and the girls, knew there were other things on her sister's mind. Just as she was the only one who still remembered Clara's girl, Lynette, Margie was the only one who understood Clara's relationship to Nora.

Now, after a quiet moment, Margie said, "How are *you* doing, with Nora moving to Chicago?"

Clara felt the sudden lump in her throat and the tears rolling down her cheeks. "I'll be fine," she said, voice thick with emotion.

"I can hear how fine you are. I know what she means to you after—am I allowed to say her name after all these years?—after your little Lynette. But Clara—you are not that girl's mother."

"The hell I'm not," Clara said, flashing anger. "I am Nora's mother, in every way that matters except one. Lillian doesn't love her or worry about her the way I do. Lillian doesn't know her like I do. She never will."

"What difference will all that make once Nora goes to Chicago?"

There was quiet for a moment on the line. Clara heard the click-snap of a cigarette lighter and said, "Margie, are you smoking a cigarette? In your condition?"

"The doctor made me cut back on the champagne and caviar and my many Continental lovers. What vices do I have left?"

"I'll bet Nora could get you some marijuana at her school."

"Thanks, but I'll stick with coffin nails. And the occasional old-fashioned—or as much of one as I can drink before it spills out of my glass."

Then Clara said, "Did I ever tell you that Nora has written me a letter every week she's been at Syracuse? I've got a shoebox full. They're right here in front of me. She never wrote letters to Lillian. She sent her birthday cards and valentines and Mother's Day cards, but she wrote her letters to me. *Me.* So when she leaves for Chicago, I know *I'll* be the person she misses, not Lillian. She's my girl in every way that's important. And that will always be true."

Clara paused to dry her eyes and loudly blow her nose into a tissue.

"That one had the timbre of a Canadian goose," Margie said with a laugh. The two sisters had a habit of comparing each other's embarrassing bodily noises to animal calls.

"More bull moose, I think," Clara had said. "Did I tell you Nora got a grant to lead her own research study?"

"You mean the one from the Ford Foundation? Only once, so far, but I'm sure you'll find a way to work it into the conversation a couple more times. Like any proud parent."

~

Nora helped Clara wash and dry the breakfast dishes.

"My old helper," Clara said, "moving on to greener pastures."

Then she walked with Nora out to her car and watched her put her suitcase in the trunk. They hugged for a long time, Clara savoring the seconds. With arms around each other's waists, they pulled back to look at each other, eyes glistening.

"I'm so proud of you, honey," Clara said. "I miss you already. But you have to go because the world needs you to do great things, and you won't do them here."

Nora tried to smile through her tears. After a moment, she gathered herself, then said, "Do you think they'll let me in to see Daddy at the hospital this early? I wanted to stop on my way out of town."

"I think if anyone can get them to bend the rules, it's you."

Then she took Nora in her arms, squeezing her tight—a final hug that would have to last her for who knew how long. Clara found it difficult to let go but made herself release this precious young woman who meant everything to her.

"I love you, Clara," Nora said.

"I love you too, Nora Jane," Clara replied as both wiped at tears. "My secret daughter."

Nora held Clara at arm's length and said, "And I expect you to come visit me in Chicago. I want Stephen to meet you. Bring your sister too. I've been hearing about hilarious Margie my whole life. It's about time I met her." She turned serious. "I mean it. While she still can."

"You bet—she's always wanted to visit Chicago," Clara said. Then she took Nora's face in her hands and smiled as she said, "You will never let anything stand in your way. Be smart, be strong, be kind—what else is there?"

They hugged one last time. Then both put on brave faces as Nora got in the car.

As she sat behind the wheel, Nora glanced up at Clara and put two fingers to her heart, then to her mouth, then blew a kiss up to Clara. Clara put her fingers to her lips, then to her heart. Nora drove away with one last wave.

Once she was gone, Clara let her tears come, and she was racked with sobs. Her little girl was gone. She couldn't have loved Nora more if she were blood. She'd raised her to be loving, curious, and funny—*she* had, not Lillian.

"Our girl." She'd occasionally made the mistake of referring to Nora that way to Lillian.

My girl, she thought when she was alone. In a few more months, Lillian and Sol would no longer be part of Clara's life. But Nora always would.

She thought of Lillian, asleep upstairs, and of Sol, lying in a nearby hospital bed. While she had conflicting feelings about both of them, she was no longer confused by the clash between being a family member and an employee. She had always known where she stood with Lillian. And even then, she had stolen Lillian's daughter right out from under her, like a sleight of hand trick.

She understood the buffer she played between Nora and Lillian. She played the same role between Sol and Lillian, and viewed it as part of her job. But soon her job would be ending—and Lillian and Sol would have to learn to live with each other. They would no longer be Clara's responsibility.

Before she left, Nora had said, "Tell Mother I'll call when I get home."

Clara knew how much her daughter's abrupt exit would anger Lillian. But then, what could she do about it? At that point, Sol would still be in the hospital, so Lillian couldn't take her frustration out on him. Amelia wasn't there, and now Nora was gone.

Clara knew that, finding herself alone in the house, Lillian would turn to her, as she so often did, as an ally—a subordinate ally—rather than as a target.

Because without me, she's alone, Clara thought. She knew that frightened Lillian. When she got that way, she was so focused on her own fears that she failed to realize that the person she relied on was someone who was stealing her daughter.

Not her daughter. Mine.

My girl, she thought.

Always was.

Always will be.

My girl.

Clara looked at her watch and dried her tears. There was time to start a load of laundry before she began making lunch. She dabbed one final tear, got up, and went back to work.

ACKNOWLEDGMENTS

There are a number of people I need to thank, starting with my family—my sons, Jacob and Caleb; their mates, Angie and Erin; and, of course, my beautiful wife, Kim Jacobs, my lifelong reminder to be a little bit better than I am.

There were several people who were kind enough to read this book in its early stages and offer their thoughts, all of which were invaluable and greatly appreciated: Linda Lombroso, Georgette Gouveia, Evelyn McCormack, Larry Sutin, Melissa Hield, and Robert Klein. My wife and my cousin, Jennifer Abrams, offered particular insight into the subject matter.

This novel began its life at the Sandy Haven Resort, nestled into Seven Mile Beach near Negril, Westmoreland, Jamaica, in March 2023. The Sandy Haven was also the site of this book's major overhaul and reconstruction in December 2024. If I could stay in that little bit of paradise and write every day for the rest of my life, I would. Special thanks to Chantol Hines and Leonesha Nelson, angels of mercy who delivered hot Blue Mountain coffee and cold Ting (the Jamaican soft drink: "It's da Ting!") to my beachside "office."

As always, I want to acknowledge the efforts of my agent, Murray Weiss. I also want to thank the entire team at Amazon and Lake Union Publishing, including Jen Bentham and the estimable Alicia Lea. I want to offer particular gratitude to my editors, Selena James and David Downing. Their belief in what this novel could be spurred me to dig even deeper into the material, at a point when I didn't think I could.

DISCUSSION QUESTIONS FOR *Hemlock Lane*

1. Whose story is this?
2. Who is the hero of this story? Is there one?
3. Is Nora justified in her need to flee her mother's control? Or is she overreacting to normal parental concern?
4. What does Sol see in Lillian at this point in their life?
5. Who is happier: Nora or Amelia?
6. Is there anything that would make Lillian less critical of everyone around her?
7. Does Lillian's early life in Williamsburg excuse or explain her fearfulness at this stage of life?
8. Do all families have to make accommodations for strong personalities among them?
9. Do Clara's history and her motives justify her actions regarding Nora and Lillian?
10. Is Sol a good or bad father?
11. Is Clara an admirable character?
12. What does the future hold for Nora and Stephen?
13. What will life be like in Sol and Lillian's new apartment?
14. Did you enjoy the way the author used the narrative structure to reveal new facts that made you reassess a previous part of the story?

ABOUT THE AUTHOR

Photo © 2023 Marshall Fine

Minneapolis native Marshall Fine's career as an award-winning journalist, critic, and filmmaker spanned fifty years. Before his bestselling fiction debut, *The Autumn of Ruth Winters*, he wrote biographies of filmmakers John Cassavetes and Sam Peckinpah, directed documentaries about film critic Rex Reed and comedian Robert Klein, conducted the *Playboy* interview with Howard Stern, and chaired the New York Film Critics Circle four times. The author currently lives in Ossining, New York. Find him at www.marshallfine.com.